W9-AJO-976

Better Than the Best Plan

LAUREN MORRILL

Better Than the Best Plan

FARRAR STRAUS GIROUX · NEW YORK

Farrar Straus Giroux Books for Young Readers
An imprint of Macmillan Publishing Group, LLC
175 Fifth Avenue, New York, NY 10010

Copyright © 2019 by Lauren Morrill
All rights reserved
Printed in the United States of America
Designed by Aimee Fleck

First edition, 2019

1   3   5   7   9   10   8   6   4   2

www.fiercereads.com

Library of Congress Cataloging-in-Publication Data

Names: Morrill, Lauren, author.
Title: Better than the best plan / Lauren Morrill.
Description: First edition. | New York : Farrar Straus Giroux, 2019. |
   Summary: Seventeen-year-old Ritzy's carefully made summer plans are ruined
   when she is sent to a foster home with a cute boy next door, but when her
   old life catches up with her, plans and hopes collide.
Identifiers: LCCN 2018035462 | ISBN 9780374306199 (hardcover)
Subjects: | CYAC: Foster children—Fiction. | Mothers and daughters—Fiction. |
   Family life—Florida—Fiction. | Dating (Social customs)—Fiction. |
   Florida—Fiction.
Classification: LCC PZ7.M82718 Bet 2019 | DDC [Fic]—dc23
LC record available at https://lccn.loc.gov/2018035462

Our books may be purchased in bulk for promotional, educational, or
business use. Please contact your local bookseller or the Macmillan Corporate
and Premium Sales Department at (800) 221-7945 ext. 5442 or by email
at MacmillanSpecialMarkets@macmillan.com.

For Adam, who never stopped believing in me

Better
Than the
Best Plan

PROLOGUE

THE DAY MY MOTHER LEFT, I WAS MOSTLY thinking about a chemistry test. Mr. Hearn's most fearsome exam wasn't his final, but the exercise in torture he inflicted on us two weeks before. Armed with nothing but a pencil, a ruler, and a blank legal-sized piece of white paper, we were supposed to draw the periodic table from memory. Elements, atomic weights, and all.

So when I woke up that morning and stumbled into the kitchen of our tiny apartment, I barely paid any attention to the note scrawled on a personalized notepad from a bank my mom must have wandered into once. I was too busy trying to burn the various metals and nonmetals into my brain. I blame that stupid test for my not reading that note and not realizing for nearly a day that it said my mom had gone to Mexico. It didn't say when she'd return, or *if* she'd return.

I bombed that test, by the way. It's like my brain rejected the information, because who is ever going to use that knowledge? Even chemists have big posters of the periodic table on the walls of their labs, and you know, iPhones. And since I had no interest in being a chemist, it felt doubly ridiculous.

When I did finally read that note, sitting alone at the wobbly wooden table shoved next to the stove, eating ice cream to soothe the sting of my shellacking in chemistry, I wasn't even sure I believed it.

My mom has always marched to the beat of her own drummer, and that drummer is a white guy with dreads playing bongos in a public park. For my whole life, or as long as I've had memories of my life, my mom has been searching for her place. She's limited her search mostly to a specific corner of the world, the corner populated by handicrafts and people who earnestly discuss karma. She's never afraid to try on a new kind of enlightenment, even if that enlightenment lives on a commune in Oregon or at a yoga center in Arizona or requires her to eliminate gluten and sugar and happiness. And she's never had a problem shaking that enlightenment right off when it starts to feel like a wool sweater shrunk in the wash.

Because of this, she's never been the kind of mom who will proofread your papers or make dinner and ask you about your day. But it's never bothered me much. My mother's free spirit means plenty of freedom for me, too. *Curfew* is a word that's never been in my vocabulary, and I've never had to answer for any failing test grades (of which there have only been two) or questionable boyfriends (of which there have been zero). She's one of those moms who I'm always surprised doesn't insist I call her by her first name, because "Mom" always feels like a dress that doesn't fit her quite right.

Which is why when she first told me about the Bodhi Foundation, it wasn't a shock. It was early May, the cool spring just starting to turn warm. It was my favorite time of year in Florida, when it was warm enough to be outside without sweating to death, and we had the doors to the deck open to let in the cool night air and the sound of traffic from the interstate. I was at the stove making a pot of store-brand macaroni and cheese while Mom paged through a yoga magazine she found in the recycling bin, dog-earing an article about newer, better sun salutations.

"I've been thinking it's time for me to set some intentions," she said, and my stomach flipped. *Here we go*, I thought. We'd been living in Jacksonville since just before the start of my freshman year. We'd come so Mom could apprentice with a friend who did massage therapy, but nearly three years later, she'd yet to enroll in any kind of certification program. Instead, she'd been working with her friend Rose, otherwise known as Rose Renee, roadside psychic and purveyor of the finest goods to help predict your future (activate eye-roll sequence *now*). We usually would have moved on by this point, but after I started high school, I begged her to let me stay put for a while. I'd jumped schools every six months to a year for most of my entire life, doing brief chunks of "unschooling," which is what my mother called her brand of homeschooling when her newest vision quest didn't leave room for a formal education for me. But to my surprise, she'd managed to keep her restlessness at bay these last three years, letting me make my way through Southwest High, build up a pretty good transcript, and actually have a shot at getting into college. She'd bopped around in a few different jobs (receptionist at a yoga studio, cashier at a craft store, and a brief stint selling mead at a Renaissance Faire), but hadn't said anything about leaving the city.

I should have known it was too good to be true.

"I've been turned on to this new program through an organization called the Bodhi Foundation," she said, as if I hadn't heard some version of this monologue a thousand times before. Somehow, she managed to be giddy and full of excitement each and every time. Her belief that *this* might finally be the *thing* never ceased to amaze me. "It's all about working toward your own personal level of enlightenment and not conforming to anyone else's standards. It's about knowing *yourself*. The program itself is a path, and each level of the path is a stone. So at the retreat center, I'll study and devote myself to working through each stone."

"This sounds like Scientology," I replied, stirring the neon-orange powder into my pasta.

She scoffed. "No! This is nothing like that. Once I've reached the tenth stone, I can go and run Bodhi workshops anywhere in the world, teaching new followers the method so *they* can go teach the method, and onward it ripples like a pebble in a pond."

And apparently, she's swallowed the brochure.

"So it's a pyramid scheme. It's basically spiritual Tupperware."

Mom sighed, then crossed the kitchen in this very deliberate way, like she was walking on water. She had this calmness to her that was unnerving. She took my chin gently in her hand.

"Oh, Maritza, I've tried so hard to raise you to be a person with an open mind and an open heart."

Now it's my turn to sigh, because what she'd really done was raise me to be a person skeptical of the open mind and open heart, because it was usually followed by a request for an open wallet.

"Where did you hear about this place?" I asked instead.

She dropped my chin and returned to the table, where she continued flipping through her magazine as if it were an act of meditation.

"I attended an info session," she replied.

"Where?"

"The Hilton by the airport."

I had to stop myself from snorting. Of course.

"The workshops are at the Bodhi Foundation's retreat center in Mexico. It's a lovely place, truly, right on the water," she said. "The program begins in June, though they like you to arrive early to really *connect* with your surroundings, and the

5

program can take anywhere from four months to a year, depending on your dedication to the path."

It took me just a moment to calculate that math. "Mom, we can't go to this Bodhi place for four months!" I said. "I have senior year, and you promised we would stay here long enough for me to graduate!"

"And you will, Ritzy," she said, but then she was noticeably silent. I felt that little itch in the back of my brain, something telling me that there was more.

"So you're starting next summer?" I asked, even though I think I already knew the answer.

Once again, she was out of her chair, crossing the floor in a deliberate choreography. This time, she came and gripped my shoulders like she was trying to prove the connection between us.

"You're on your own path, Ritzy," she said, her voice low and breathy. "And I honor that."

I wrinkled my nose. "What does that mean?"

"It means you can stay here for your senior year if you want, and then when you graduate, if you'd like to join me on my path, the Bodhi Foundation will be there for you, too. By then I'll be qualified to be your sponsor!"

I shook her hands from my shoulders. "Gross, Mom. Don't try to recruit me to your multilevel marketing scheme masking itself as religion."

That was exactly the wrong thing to say. She shook her head, clearly disappointed in my lack of vision. I was losing her. "I wish you'd join me now," she said. "I've always felt it was important to reject the traditional schooling model in favor of a more self-directed brand of education."

Only my mother would encourage me to drop out of school the summer before my senior year and ascribe it to virtue.

"Okay, well, we both know that's not going to happen, so what then?" I asked. "Are you saying I'm going to stay here . . . by myself?"

"Why not?" she said. "I've been on my own since I was seventeen . . ."

"Oh, so I'm supposed to go bang a tambourine at an airport, that's what you're saying?" I asked, referring to Mom's favorite story about her first foray into spirituality as a teenager. I was going for a joke, but it seemed to miss the mark, because she looked wounded. Again, I redirected. "How am I supposed to pay for stuff?"

"The universe provides, Ritzy," she said. "So does your job."

I knew the fact that I handled all the bills was going to come back to bite me eventually. She had absolutely no idea how our finances work if she thought twenty hours a week making tuna melts at Roasted is going to come close to covering the rent. This whole thing was sounding more nuts by the second.

When she got like this, with one of her new schemes gripped tightly in her psyche, there was no talking her out of it. Not right away, anyway. Sometimes I could wait her out and hope she came to her senses before she dove in. It worked when she decided we were going to go live in a "silent community" for six months. I knew my mother wouldn't last six minutes in a place like that. Talking is definitely her favorite pastime, after searching for higher power. I'd simply said, "Let's talk about this tomorrow" for several days until she let the idea go completely.

"Can we talk about this more tomorrow?" I said. "I really need to study for my chemistry exam."

The smile on her face told me I'd made the right move. "Ritzy, you know I love you, even when I don't understand you."

"Ditto, Mom."

She leaned in and touched her forehead to mine, reaching her hand behind my neck to hold me close. It was a gesture she'd picked up at some Zen retreat somewhere, and even though she ditched *that* particular path a long time ago, I'm glad she hung on to this. It made me forget, for a moment, that my mom was a hippie flake who was proposing abandonment. It was a gesture that felt full of love and connection and protection, which was ironic, truly.

"I trust you and I believe in you," she said finally.

She smiled and kissed me on the forehead. A bowl of macaroni and cheese in my hand, I shuffled out of the kitchen and back to my room, where I spent the next several hours flipping flashcards and trying to make my brain hold on to the atomic weight for antimony. The next day I went to school, where I flailed my way through my exam, and when I got home, she was just gone. She'd left a note, a brochure on the Bodhi Foundation, and her house key. When I checked her room, I found her suitcase gone, along with a good portion of her wardrobe and toiletries.

Ritzy,

I've gone to journey down my path. I wish you well on yours, and will see you soon. I love you. Stay true.

Love,
Mom

There was four hundred dollars cash in tens and twenties in an envelope, which would *almost* cover a month of rent. Did that mean she'd be back by then? I reread the note several times a day for the next several days, looking for clues, still not quite believing she'd actually gone to Mexico. Sure, the Bodhi Foundation sounded exactly like the kind of nonsense my mother would be into. But she'd never undertaken a path or a vision quest or any other quirky scheme without bringing me along. Even though I had no interest in organic farming or sheep shearing or goat yoga or freecycling, I'd still been happy to be included. Our *Odd Couple* dynamic had been honed through each of her wild journeys, and even when I was eating bean sprouts while sitting cross-legged by a bonfire, I found comfort in it. I maybe even liked following my mother down her own path.

But now, for the first time, my path was the only path, and I had no light to see where I was going.

CHAPTER ONE

"OH MY GOD, OH MY GOD, *OH MY GOD*, IS this really happening?"

Every part of me feels warm and clammy, and it's only partly because I'm standing on blacktop in 90-degree weather with 100 percent humidity. If I stand here much longer, my shoes are going to melt into the pavement.

"Josh told me during third period that Ali told *him* during homeroom that he was going to ask you out after school." Lainey scans the parking lot and spots Ali coming out of the main entrance of the school. "There he is. Okay, are you ready?"

"For my eternal crush of forever to finally ask me out? I don't know, how do you get ready for that?" I have to will myself not to look at him, just in case he sees me and we have one of those awkward staring moments. I want to turn around and be all fresh-faced and *Hi!* about this, like I'm in a face wash commercial or something. I want *awkward* to have no part of this, which, let's be real, is going to be an uphill battle.

Lainey's eyes dance from me to somewhere over my shoulder. She looks as giddy as I feel, but she's got the freedom to let it out. "I could slap you in the face. Do you want me to slap you in the face?"

"Why would I want that?"

"I don't know, it's a thing people do on television. Maybe it calms you down?" She shrugs.

I casually turn and bump her hip, like maybe she just said something funny or we're having a moment of solidarity or something. It brings me around to her side so that I can see Ali across the parking lot without staring over my shoulder, you know, like a weirdo.

"Smooth," Lainey whispers.

"I try," I reply.

She returns the hip bump. "I'll meet you at the car," she says, then trots off.

I see the exact moment when he spots me. He gets a wide grin on his face and gives this adorable little half wave, two of his fingers up in a lazy peace sign. His pace picks up to a trot as he heads for me. Ugh, he's so pretty. Tall and lanky from year-round soccer, with deep tan skin and dark wavy hair. He's got this great smile that uses his whole face in a way that you can't help but smile back. It's the most contagious grin I've ever seen.

"'Sup, Ritzy? Happy summer!" His eyes drop to his shoes,

those black flat sneakers that all the soccer players wear, before flicking back up to me. It's the only indication that he, too, might be a little bit nervous.

"Thanks," I reply. "Back atcha. Big plans?"

He cocks his head and shrugs. "The usual. Beach. Soccer. Working at the restaurant." His parents own this amazing Indian takeout place near the mall. His mom is super nice and always gives us discounts or free samosas. Ali has worked there since he was old enough to make correct change. "Probably doing college stuff. You know the drill."

"Totally," I say, though I won't be going on any college visits or taking SAT prep like Ali or some of my other classmates who just finished junior year. Even though we had to endure endless lectures from our teachers and an hour-long assembly in the gym where the guidance counselors acted like if we didn't tour *at least* five schools before the fall we might as well give up and join the circus, I have no plans to go anywhere. My future is a little up in the air right now, and all I know is that I need to spend the summer working as many hours at Roasted as Mr. Reynolds will give me. And I may even try to score a second gig, though the only places still hiring are probably the string of fast-food restaurants that line the road up from our apartment complex, and I really don't want to go there. The thought of spending the hot Florida summer smelling like a deep fat fryer kills a little bit of my soul. And I'm not totally convinced it won't clog my arteries by osmosis.

Still, rent is due at the end of the month, the electric bill a week after that, and I have no idea how long paying those will be my responsibility. But that's a lot of backstory that I definitely don't want to get into with Ali, especially if he's about to ask me out.

"Hey, I was wondering if you had plans for tonight?" The words come out in a rush of a single breath.

This is it! Okay, be cool, Ritzy. Be. Cool.

The mental reminder keeps me from barking out, *Yes, I'll go out with you anytime anywhere AWESOME!* Instead, I manage an only slightly cooler, "Um, no, I don't think so. Why?"

"I was thinking maybe we could hang out. Grab food at the Mexican place on Division? Their queso rocks." He pauses, kicking at a pebble on the blacktop between us. He bites his lip, a tiny smile tugging at the corner of his mouth. When he glances up at me with those deep brown eyes, I nearly melt into a puddle right at his feet. "Just us?"

And there it is. Ali Anikhindi, my crush since freshman year, who has been solidly in my friend zone since we were first paired up for a group project on *To Kill a Mockingbird* in ninth grade, is asking me out on a date. An actual date. Just. Us.

Every cell in my body is vibrating, just begging me to explode with a *Hell YES!* And maybe even a fist pump for good measure. But I manage to wrestle the energy into a confident, yet still somehow cool, "That sounds great." Though I'm pretty sure I've got a manic smile on my face to give me away. Which is fine, because Ali's giving me one of his trade-mark giant smiles. I swear, even his *ears* look happy.

"Awesome. Pick you up around six?"

"Perfect," I say, already mentally scanning the meager contents of my closet for the perfect, not-trying-too-hard outfit.

"Well, I guess I'll see you tonight," Ali says. He gives me one parting smile, then heads off to his car, his keys swinging around his index finger. I wait until he's backed out and his taillights are disappearing out of the parking lot before I race off toward Lainey's usual spot at the back of the lot. By the time I get to her, all of the excited energy is bursting out of me like a faulty water fountain. When I skid to a stop at her rear bumper, where she's leaning against Barney looking smug, I'm actually squealing.

"Dinner tonight at Margaritas!"

"The one on Division?"

"Yep."

"Good, because the one on Third is ass." Lainey grins and heads for the driver-side door. I take my spot at the passenger side, waiting for her to get in and lean over the center console to unlock my door. When she does, I pull it open, my shiver at the usual creak of metal coming a beat early. Barney, short for Barnacle, is what we call Lainey's ancient Volvo, so named for the ring of brown rust that clings to the lower half of the car. She inherited it from her grandmother who moved into a nursing home sophomore year. I climb in and adjust the frayed beach towel on my seat so the old, cracked leather, which has been cooking in the parking lot all day, won't scorch my thighs. It's only May, but May in Florida is like late July anywhere else, hot and thick with humidity.

"Cherry limeades?" Lainey asks as she shifts the car into reverse. "My treat."

"Yes, please."

We roll down the windows, since the air conditioner in Lainey's car is barely a suggestion of cold air. I turn on the radio, tuned to STAR 102.1, the oldies station, and before we're even out of the parking lot, we're singing along at the top of our lungs to a Motown hit, attempting harmonies only dogs can hear.

There's usually a long wait to get out of the student parking lot after school, as people linger, rolling down their windows to chat with friends or make weekend plans. But today everyone puts the pedal to the metal, off to the beach or the pool or somewhere else to celebrate our three months of freedom. Some more free than others, of course.

"Did you hear Vera Braxton talking about going on a cruise?" I ask when we stop at a red light. "Apparently, her dad won it from his company."

"You couldn't *pay* me to go on a cruise," Lainey replies. She reaches into the center console and digs out a pair of sunglasses. "People are always getting norovirus on those boats. I can't imagine anything worse than crapping your pants on the high seas."

"Okay, but not *everyone* gets norovirus. And wouldn't it be nice to take a trip?"

"Sure, a trip would be nice. But when Mommy and Daddy aren't paying for it, the costs add up. And seriously, do you really want to spend every penny of your sandwich-making money on five days at the beach?" Lainey squints into the bright sun, her sunglasses no match. "When, by the way, there's a perfectly good beach twenty minutes away."

I sigh and prop my feet up on the dashboard, a move I've done so much there's practically an outline of my flip-flops there.

"Buck up, Reed," Lainey says, flipping her signal as she turns into the Sonic parking lot. "Soon enough we'll graduate and leave here. And then you'll be glad you saved all that money."

I wince at her reference to my savings account, because it's not exactly what it used to be. But even though I usually tell Lainey everything, I haven't been able to bring myself to tell her *that* yet. I think I'm hoping the situation will resolve itself, but it's been two weeks now with no end in sight.

Lainey's been saving every penny she can from her paycheck at the library (minus the occasional Sonic splurge), which she took because it was the only job where she could both study and earn minimum wage. For Lainey, it's all about leaving not just Jacksonville, or even Florida, but the south entirely. I don't blame her. Lainey is one of the few black kids in our school. She tries to downplay all the ways that she feels like an outsider at Southwest, but I've known her long enough that I see how much the lazy, offensive jokes of our classmates and casual bias of our teachers gets to her. I know her well enough to know that even as her best friend, I still can't grasp even a tenth of her experience here.

Lainey and I met freshman year in detention, which is notable because it's the only detention Lainey and I have ever had. Lainey was there because she poured her soda on Nate Blackburn after he pulled one of her braids in the cafeteria. I was there because my mother had embarked on a spiritual quest (her words) to live a simpler life, so she unplugged every electronic device in our apartment. This included my alarm clock. And Mr. Hardiman, my homeroom teacher, was a stickler about tardies.

I was halfway through writing an essay on punctuality (like I said, Mr. Hardiman equals stickler), when I heard a whisper coming from the table behind me. "You got a pencil?"

I turned to Lainey. "Just pens. You want one?"

"Nah. Doing math. Pencil's a must," she said with a shrug. "I like your sweater."

I was wearing my favorite cardigan, which I'd found at Darcy's Closet, a thrift store near my house. Not a trendy thrift store, with actual vintage clothes the girls in my school might think were stylish or cool. Darcy's Closet was a thrift store for people who actually needed to be thrifty. And since I was too young to have a job, I was still at the mercy of my mother's clothing budget. On top of her spiritual quest, she was also deep in her "make, do, mend" phase and had convinced herself that with just a little more practice she could knit all the clothes we'd ever need. Thus far, she'd only succeeded in crafting a series of wonky dishcloths, so I needed to buy my clothes on the cheap.

Darcy's Closet had a back room with a dollar-a-pound pile, which was an enormous mountain of fabric. You pulled out what you wanted, the cashier weighed it on an old-fashioned produce scale like they have hanging in the grocery store, and you paid based on weight. It sounded like a great deal until you realized that 99.9 percent of the clothes in the pile were utter garbage. Stained, moth-eaten, smelling vaguely like attics and cigarettes and one time, in the case of a particularly putrid-looking puffer vest, tuna fish. Most of the stuff was decades old and not even in fashion when it was new. There were a lot of clothes that looked like they were once part of someone's work uniform, a lot of khaki and button-up shirts and mom jeans. I almost never bought anything from the pile, but that didn't stop me from digging.

Which was how I came to find my cardigan, my one and only big score. It had arms that were just a little too long, which was perfect for pulling my hands inside when the air-conditioning in school got too frigid (which was often). It was long enough to cover my bum, which meant every once in a while I could get away with wearing leggings to school, in direct defiance of the sexist dress code. It had two big pockets on the front, perfect for holding a phone or some cash or a plastic baggie full of tortilla chips that I sometimes had to sneak during third period when we had last lunch. The best part? The cardigan was tie-dyed. *Rainbow* tie-dyed, and the colors were still completely vivid. My mother called it the fashion equivalent of a bad acid trip, but I loved it.

I told Lainey the whole story, and as soon as she nodded, familiar with Darcy's Closet and their dollar-a-pound policy (she'd scored a yellow rain slicker from the pile, which she said made her look like the Morton Salt Girl), I knew we could be friends.

We order our cherry limeades and bop along to the piped-in oldies, stumbling through the words to "Leader of the Pack," a song that is 100 percent ridiculous and fun to sing. When our drinks arrive, we hand over our cash and an extra dollar for the carhop. Lainey takes a long sip, the only source of cool in the stagnant humidity. I pry off the lid to fish out the maraschino cherry. Lainey always saves hers for the end, but I can never wait. I love the sweet crunch of the fruit, which has been processed to the point that it barely resembles something that grew out of the ground. As soon as I pop the lid off, I grin. Sometimes I have to dig for the cherry, performing delicate surgery with the red straw to bring it to the surface amid the lime wedges and crushed ice, but today, floating right on top, is not one but *two* cherries.

"Score!" I pop one off the stem, then fish out the other, letting the cold sweetness linger on my tongue. I throw my feet up on the dashboard and lean back into my seat, breathing out a satisfied sigh. "Best day ever."

CHAPTER TWO

THE APARTMENT IS EMPTY WHEN WE GET there, just as it's been every day since my mom left. At first it was unnerving, being there alone. You never realize how much noise another person's mere existence makes until they're gone. Footsteps, sniffles, banging around the kitchen, even the occasional sleep talking all serve to fill up a space. The silence felt oppressive in the days after she left. I took to leaving the TV on all the time, until all my dreams started to involve home renovations and the words *stainless steel appliances*, and I had to stop.

But over the last two weeks I'd gotten used to my mother's absence. I became accustomed to living alone. I threw out the disgusting hemp milk she insisted upon and replaced it with a half gallon of skim. I moved my speakers into the living room and started to listen to music that wasn't chant based when I ate. I stopped closing the bathroom door. There was no one to see me pee anymore.

I'd managed to find more than a few upsides to abandonment.

Lainey and I drop our bags by the door, though since we turned in our textbooks today, they don't make much of a thud (which is good, because Mrs. Sazonov one floor down doesn't like it when we're loud, a fact she makes known by thumping her cane on her ceiling). Lainey heads for the bathroom while I make a beeline for the thermostat, cranking up the AC. According to the digital display, it's 84 degrees in the apartment. After the shock of the electric bill that arrived last week, I've been making an effort to cut costs by turning the AC off while I'm at school so I won't waste the electricity when I'm not home. But I've only been in here a few minutes and already I can feel my shirt starting to stick to my back, so I drop it down to a chill 68 and hope it won't take long to work its magic.

I wander into the living room and collapse onto the sofa, digging the remote out from between the cushions. I begin flipping through the channels, wondering how much longer I'll be able to afford the bill. If Mom doesn't come back soon, I'm going to have to cancel the cable.

"Looks like the options are the last half of a Lifetime movie, the last half of a James Bond movie, or a *Brady Bunch* marathon."

"Definitely the Bradys," Lainey says, plopping down next to me.

"But it's one of the Lifetime movies with Tori Spelling!"

I say, less out of enthusiasm for Tori and more out of apathy for the Bradys.

"Unless it's the one where she's the cheerleader who gets knifed, I'm not interested."

"I think it's the one where she's the girlfriend who gets knifed. Or the sister. I can't tell yet."

Lainey rolls her eyes. "White girls screaming is not really my genre. *Brady Bunch*, please."

Lainey is obsessed with retro TV. I can't tell if it's part of her love of history or if she just really enjoys a good laugh track. I find anything made before I was born to be 90 percent boring, but since she spotted me the money for the limeade, I go with it. But not happily.

"Ugh, fine," I mumble, and flip to Marcia carefully brushing her hair a bazillion times. The episode bops along, hitting the familiar beats before each commercial break, cruising toward a lesson learned and a happily-ever-after, all in the span of twenty-eight minutes. We zone out in front of it as we let the end of the school year and the beginning of summer wash over us. On-screen, the *Brady Bunch*'s maid is wagging her finger and rolling her eyes at the boys as she wipes her hands on that blue dress she's always wearing. When I was younger, I was sort of obsessed with the idea that maybe, if my mom met some nice architect or someone else who wore a tie to work, our family could double in size overnight like the Bradys' did. I could go from lonely latchkey kid moving every couple of years (sometimes more, if my mother's schemes came fast and frequent) to being a sister with matching comforters and dinner at home every night. I liked imagining us moving from any of our string of crappy apartments to one of the Spanish-inspired subdivisions across town, where all the houses have tile roofs and stucco exteriors with elaborate palms as land-scaping. Maybe we'd even have a pool, one that's just for us and not to share with the six million little kids in the complex and the creepy guy who likes to sit on a lounge chair and chain-smoke over his lunch break.

But it only took a few of my mom's boyfriends for me to realize that the *Brady Bunch* was not in my future. I mean, Hunter, the freegan lumberjack she dated when we lived in Oregon, was never going to move us into a subdivision (his screeds on the American suburb could have you trapped in a conversation against your will for hours). And Haven (whose real name was Bill, but his face got incredibly red if you pointed that out) was too busy rehearsing with his steel drum band (which I quickly learned was code for getting stoned with three guys named Jared) to attempt a home-cooked meal. No, my mother had a yen for guys whose futures involved a beanbag chair and long lectures on the evils of factory farming. I don't think a single one of them even owned a necktie, unless it was iron-ically.

And besides, even if Mom had stumbled into a relation-ship with some upwardly mobile, upstanding citizen with a job and a suit, she had no desire to get married. She never made any noise about shopping around for a dad for me. Mom loved that it was *just us girls*, a sparkle in her eye always accompanying the phrase. Maybe it was left over from the semester she spent as a women's studies major, or maybe it was the womynist colony we lived in when I was five. Whatever it was, none of those dudes was ever going to put a ring on it, and after meeting a few of them, that was just fine with me.

"So what are you going to wear tonight?" Lainey asks when the show goes to a commercial break on a cliff-hanger over who Marcia is going to take to some dance.

"I hadn't thought about it," I say. I suck the last of my limeade through the straw until the ice rattles in the cup.

"Liar," Lainey replies. "You've been planning this date for forever."

I grin and spin on the couch, crossing my legs so I can face her. "Okay, true. I was thinking maybe that white eyelet lace skirt, the one that's short but not like 'come and get it'? And then just a tank. I'm not sure what's clean."

"You've got to wear the green one. It brings out your eyes," Lainey says. "There's probably time to run it to the laundry room if you need. I've got quarters in Barney."

I glance at the clock and start doing the math (twenty-three minutes on the short cycle, then probably thirty in the dryer if it's a small load), but my calculations are interrupted by a knock at the door. The sound nearly makes me drop my empty cup. The only people who knock on our apartment door are people who are going to cause a problem: our landlord, looking for the late check again, or a guy from the power company, threatening to turn off our electricity. Sometimes it's Mrs. Sazonov, waving her cane and threatening to call the cops if we don't "walk nice."

Lainey is focused on the TV, where the Bradys are resolving their conflict right on schedule, so she doesn't see me get tense. I've never liked when people come to the door, but it's worse now that I live alone. If Lainey weren't here, I'd probably go grab one of the sharp knives out of the kitchen before checking the door.

The blinds are closed already, but the TV volume is up high enough that whoever it is might wait us out if properly motivated, so I decide I better face the music. I tiptoe over to the door and peer out the peephole. The view is blurry and more distorted than normal thanks to some condensation trapped inside. Despite that, I'm pretty sure I can see a woman standing there. I don't recognize her, and her clothes, polished and professional, are too nice for her to be from the electric company or the city water department. She's clutching what looks like one of those thick leather pad folios that lawyers have.

"Shit," I mutter, then take a few steps backward. A lawyer? What could a lawyer want with me? Sure, last month's rent came in a few days late, but I still paid it. And this month's isn't due for another couple of weeks. I know, because the date is circled on my calendar several times in red pen. I don't know what will happen if I get evicted from this apartment, but it won't be good.

"What is it?" Lainey asks, and I wave my arms wildly to shush her.

There's another hard knock on the door, this one louder than the first, and after a beat of silence, a voice calls out, "Maritza? Maritza Reed?"

Okay, this is bad. Usually, people who come to the door are looking for my mom, and I can smile and put on my youngest-sounding girl voice and weasel out of whatever it is. But getting out of someone looking for *me*? That's not a strategy I have in my arsenal.

"Maritza, I heard the TV. I know you're in there," the female voice says. It has a touch of a southern twang that she's trying to mask with sounding official. "I promise you're not in trouble. I just need to talk to you."

I tiptoe back across the living room toward Lainey. "You should go out the back," I say. I try to make it sound like I'm trying to protect her, but really I'm just protecting myself. At this moment, I wish I'd told Lainey right away, even called her the moment I realized Mom had actually gone. Why didn't I? Maybe because I didn't really believe she'd actually left, and by the time I did, it felt too weird to admit that my mom had abandoned me. And it definitely wasn't as tragic as all that. So I was living alone. So what? Other than the need for money, which I was handling, it wasn't that bad. Besides, Lainey has her own problems. I didn't want to burden her with mine.

And to spill it all now would be a much bigger conversation than I have time for, especially with that business lady outside my door calling my name.

"You sure you don't want me to stay?" she asks.

"Positive," I say. "I'll text you when I know what's what."

Her face tells me that she's going to expect an explanation later, but she reaches for her bag and heads for the sliding door that leads to the deck and down the back stairs.

I take a deep breath and make my way back to the front door. I look through the peephole one more time to see if she's given up and left, which would mean it probably wasn't all that important. Maybe a surveyor or a solicitor. But no, she's still there, her shoulders squared, her gaze leveled straight at the peephole, like she knows I'm standing here, looking out at her.

I'm going to have to deal with this one way or another, so I take a deep breath, open the door, and plaster on my best teacher-pleasing smile.

"Hi," I say, trying to sound like she's any other visitor. Now that the woman standing there isn't magnified through a fuzzy lens, I can get a good look at her. She's wearing a pair of black dress pants, cropped and cuffed, with a white button-down shirt with the sleeves rolled up and black patent leather ballet flats. She has a leather bag slung over her shoulder that looks stuffed just a little too full with papers and folders, her blond hair pulled back from her face. Despite the heat, she doesn't seem to be sweating off any of her perfectly applied makeup.

She's definitely not a cop, and that somehow makes me feel more nervous.

"Maritza?" the woman asks.

I try to answer, but my voice feels trapped in my throat, so instead I nod.

She sticks her arm out, and her manicured hand reaches across the threshold of the front door. "Hi, I'm Tess Lloyd. I'm with the Florida Department of Children and Families. Do you mind if I come in?"

There's a brief moment where I consider slamming the door shut and cranking the dead bolt, then maybe running back to my room and burrowing under the covers. As if that will make whatever's coming next stop. But the door is open, and as soon as she introduces herself, passing a crisp white business card to me, I know that I'm in trouble.

Still, I try to salvage what I can. It takes everything I have, but I manage to open the door wider and step aside, ushering her into the living room like *hey, I've got nothing to hide.* I see Tess glance around, and I imagine her sweeping the room for drugs or weapons or other signs that I'm in trouble. Or that I *am* trouble. But of course, she doesn't find anything. I may be alone, but everything is fine. It's all under control. I'm handling it all better than my mother would, if she were here. I'm not starving. I'm healthy and my grades are fine. Hell, I'm seventeen, just a couple months away from being eighteen. Old enough to vote and buy lottery tickets and serve my country.

Certainly, I can be trusted to stay in a furnished, air-conditioned apartment with a decently stocked fridge all by myself.

But if I'm going to convince this very well-dressed social worker of that, I'm going to have to start doing the work, and fast.

"Can I get you anything?" I want to ask her what's going on, but I find it best in situations like this to make the other person say it first, in hopes that maybe they'll chicken out. We had a landlord once who did that when I was ten. We were living in Maryland, where we'd moved after my mother decided "professional political activist" was the nonpaying job she wanted next. That had meant a lot of days spent either making signs or holding them at some protest or another. I was never totally clear on the issues we were protesting, and sometimes I got the impression that my mom wasn't either. Our landlord at the time was this little old lady who wore velour tracksuits and visited the beauty parlor once a week. We were renting the mother-in-law cottage behind her house. She'd come over to inquire about the rent check, and my mother would simply act like it was a social call, offering her sweaty glasses of iced tea and packages of off-brand Fig Newtons, diving into the neighborhood gossip and treatises on the weather. It took poor Mrs. Healey four months before she could work herself up to asking my mother to actually pay her, at which point we packed up and moved out.

"No, I'm fine," Tess says, and I hear the southern come out in the *fiiiiine*, a word she flattens and stretches just a little too long. "But that's sweet of you to offer. Why don't we take a seat?"

And in that moment, I know I'm not dealing with a Mrs. Healey. Tess doesn't seem nervous. She seems in charge, offering me a seat in my own house. And that makes me nervous, because if she's in charge, then I'm not.

She reaches into her bag and pulls out a file folder, but I can't read the label printed on it without making a spectacle of my attempt. She flips it open.

"Is your mother home, Maritza?"

I shake my head. "No, she's not here right now." A reply that has the virtue of being 100 percent true.

"When will she be home?"

"I'm not sure exactly." *Still true.*

Tess flips the folder shut again, squares it on her knees, then folds her hands in her lap. She looks up at me with a smile that seems kind and sympathetic. "Okay, well, I really need to speak with her, so would it be okay if I wait?"

Crap. This lady clearly has my number already. Who ratted me out? Definitely not Mrs. Sazonov. If anything, she's happy my mom is gone, because it means she's no longer burning incense in the apartment. Mrs. Sazonov always claimed the smell drifted down through the ventilation system and aggravated her allergies. And I'd mailed in the rent check on time, so it wasn't our landlord.

"Maritza, let me be honest with you," Tess says, as if she can hear the thoughts running through my head. "We've received a report from your school that you're living alone."

Ah, Ms. Silverstein, my guidance counselor. When my mom didn't show up to the end-of-the-year college-counseling session she hosted for all juniors and their parents, she started asking me a lot of questions. It was only two days after Mom had left, and I wasn't prepared with answers. I fumbled, and she got curious. She made a few calls home that I'd tried to deflect by saying my mom was at work. But there was nothing I could do about the emails I'm sure she also sent, emails that I'm sure went unanswered. She may have even called my mom's work number. Who knows how much her friend Rose, the psychic who paid Mom to run her little crystal shop part-time, knew or told. Ms. Silverstein had to have been the one.

Tess leaves a good, long silence for me to say something, but I'm out of somethings to say. So Tess continues. "In the state of Florida, a minor cannot live independently unless they've been emancipated."

"I'm hardly a minor," I say before I can think better of it. At this point, I'm just operating in damage-control mode. I need to reassure this woman that everything is fine so I can get her out of my living room. "I'll be eighteen in September."

She nods. "But you're seventeen now."

Now it's my turn to nod.

"And your mother isn't here."

I leave my own good, long silence, but Tess is ready to wait me out. Finally, I nod again.

"See, that's where we have a problem. I suspect your mother has been gone"—she glances down at her notes—"at least two weeks. And you have no idea when she'll be back." She looks up at me for confirmation, but all I can do is stare down at my lap. "You cannot continue on in this living situation."

What does she mean "this living situation"? It's not like I'm living in a tent. I look around the apartment, which I'd vacuumed a few days ago and which I tidied every night before going to bed. It honestly looked better than it did when my mom lived here with me. In the two weeks since Mom left, I hadn't missed a single day of school. I'd eaten three decent meals every day, some of which included fruits and vegetables. I'd done laundry and washed my sheets and cleaned the apartment. How would adult supervision improve my living situation? I open my mouth to tell Tess all this, but she's already shuffling papers, moving on to the next step.

"We have a few options. The first would be a kinship placement. Do you have any family in the area you could stay with? Maybe your dad?"

Her voice is tentative, like she knows it's a long shot, and boy is it. I almost laugh out loud at the question. Family in the area? I don't have family *anywhere* other than my mother. The only evidence of my father is my mere existence; otherwise, he's just a passing thought to me, a fact of biology and nothing more. I stopped asking my mother about him long ago, as soon as I was old enough to realize that her evasive responses were less about her sparing my feelings and more about sparing her own. Because it isn't just that he doesn't know about me, it's that she's not entirely sure who he is. And who wants to spend too much time thinking about *that*?

"No," I reply. "He's not . . . I mean, I don't even know . . ." I trail off, because I can tell from her face that I don't need to say more.

"That's fine," Tess says. She nods, ticking off a mental box in her head before moving on to the next item. "No grandparents? Aunts or uncles?"

I shake my head. My mom's an only child, and all I know about my grandparents is that they're dead, and before they died they definitely didn't approve of my mother's "journey."

Tess nods, taking it in, the fact that with my mother out of the picture, I'm as good as an orphan.

"Well, do you have a friend you could stay with? We could do a quick visit and background check to make sure everything's in order, and then we could pack up some of your things."

My mind flashes to Lainey, who is probably halfway to the little shotgun house she lives in with her mom. I've stayed over at her house plenty of times; I know it wouldn't be a problem with her mom, except for the whole social-worker thing. Lainey's mom has been working two full-time jobs for the last few months to pay off some car repairs after an accident. Days at a factory that makes organic soap in neon colors (as if highlighter yellow is a color that occurs in nature), nights at the Salt and Pepper Diner near the airport, and doubles at the diner on the weekends. She's been working so hard Lainey has barely seen her lately. I have a feeling that if DCF knew that Lainey spends every night at home alone, cycling through a selection of the finest frozen dinners the 7-Eleven around the corner has to offer, Lainey would have her own social worker to deal with. I won't do that to her.

"I don't really, no," I reply. Part of me is hoping that with my options dwindling, Tess will decide that I'm really already in the best possible situation.

"Okay, well, in that case, we're going to need to head over to my office to make some arrangements," she says, confirming my very worst fears.

"This seems silly," I say, attempting one last-ditch effort at making this all go away. "I mean, I'm almost eighteen, and everything is fine here. Seriously, look around. You can make surprise visits whenever you want. I promise, I'll get to my eighteenth birthday unscathed and in one piece. And besides, my mom could come back anytime!"

But none of it penetrates. Tess keeps that kind, sympathetic smile on her face as she seals my fate. "And when she does, we can reassess. But for right now, you're a minor with no adult supervision, which is a problem we need to solve.

Luckily, you have me here to help you solve it. So let's head on over to the office, okay?"

I have this moment where I think of that old saying about kidnapping: Never let them take you to a second location, because the second location is where things go bad.

I think the saying applies to social workers, too.

CHAPTER THREE

MY PATH HAS LED ME DIRECTLY TO A vinyl-covered chair, where I'm trying to keep the peeling piece of duct tape that's covering a crack from poking into the back of my thigh, while a social worker tries to find a place for me to stay.

"Okay, Maritza Reed," Tess says as she squints at her computer screen. I'm not sure if she's asking me or just saying it out loud to fill the silence. Either way, it feels weird to hear it. *Maritza*. Mom always told me she picked the name up from a waitress at the Mexican restaurant she went to all the time when she was living in Taos and pregnant with me. "You were very nearly named Guacamole, but Maritza won out in the end," she liked to say, which is why I liked that she called me Ritzy. It seemed like something she came up with for *me*, something that grew out of her actually paying attention to who I was.

"Middle name?" Tess asks, as she squints at the computer screen.

"September," I reply.

"Date of birth?"

"September fifteenth." Again, my mom with the careful name selection. You wouldn't think she'd had nine months to decide. I shouldn't complain, though. I'm just lucky my name isn't Harvest Moon or Karma Sunshine or something equally ridiculous.

I give Tess my address and my Social Security number, which I've had memorized since second grade (this was about the time when I realized my mom was never going to be very good with filling out forms for school).

Amid the *clackety-clack* of the keyboard, I hear my phone buzz in my back pocket. I pull it out to see a text from Lainey.

Lainey: Everything ok?

My thumbs are poised over the screen, but I have no idea what to type. And I'm so busy trying to come up with an answer that I don't notice at first that Tess's brow is furrowed as she clicks through something on her computer screen. It's not until she leans into the screen and mutters, "This is interesting," that I'm finally pulled back into reality.

I drop my phone into my lap. "What?" I ask.

"You already have a file." She holds up a manicured finger. "Just give me a minute. I need to check a few things."

And then she's gone, leaving me with a thousand questions. Or maybe just a few questions repeating over and over again in my mind. *I already have a file? With DCF? How can that be?*

After what feels like an eternity, Tess returns. She sits down in her chair, then turns to face me. She leans forward, her elbows resting on her knees. And that's how I know something is coming. Something big. Because no one makes that kind of full-body eye contact with you unless they're about to turn your world upside down.

"Maritza, did you know that you've been in foster care before?"

This is *not* what I was expecting.

"What are you talking about?" I feel tears prick my eyes. "Are you sure?"

She nods. "You have a file. It indicates that you were in foster care when you were very young. Shortly after you were born, in fact. You wouldn't remember it, but I didn't know if anyone had told you." The *anyone* hangs between us full of things literally unsaid.

"Wait, this was in Taos?"

Now it's Tess's turn to look confused. "No, here. In Jacksonville."

"But that can't be right," I say. "I was born in Taos, New Mexico. I only moved here three years ago."

Tess glances at her computer screen, looking slightly pained. "Not according to our system. You were about six months old when you entered foster care here in Jacksonville, and you remained there for almost eighteen months."

"This has to be a mistake," I say.

"It's your name and Social Security number," she says gently. I know what she's saying has to be true, but it still doesn't feel right. Tess gives it time to sink in.

I try to think back. My mom has always been a bad keeper of our history. She'd mix up our stint in Oregon with our time in Maryland. She'd think it was San Diego where we tried our hand at freeganism, when really it was Portland. She misremembered dates all the time. But I would have thought at some point she would have mentioned that we lived in Jacksonville before. That was a hard thing to forget. So was me being in foster care. So if I didn't know, it was on purpose.

"This is a lot of information, I know," Tess says. She looks like she wants to reach out and pat my knee, but she stays in her own space. I immediately wonder if it's part of some kind of protocol, if she's not supposed to touch me. But I wish she would. I wish she'd reach out and put a hand on each of my shoulders and hold me down, because I feel like I'm going to float away if someone doesn't grab hold of me right now. I need someone to do my mom's hippie Zen forehead trick.

I need my mom.

After a moment of waiting, of letting this all wash over me, Tess gets back to business. "I actually spoke to the woman who you stayed with when you were in foster care the first time. Her name is Kristin. There's a note in your file saying that should you ever end up back in foster care, she wanted to be notified. She had said back then that she was open to you returning to her if necessary. And while it's been a lot longer than she maybe thought, when I called, she said she was more than happy to have you come to stay. But if you'd rather I find another placement, I can do that."

A choice. The first one I've had since Tess showed up at my door and shook up my life like a snow globe. The fact that my mom's parting words to me were about following my own path seems so completely laughable right now. I'm not on a path, I'm on a loop, and apparently, it's leading me right back to where I started. I stand up from the chair so fast that it rocks backward, echoing on the linoleum floor. A look of concern flashes across Tess's face, so I gasp, "I have to go to the bathroom" before bolting out of the office and toward the door in the corner of the main room.

I shut myself in the bathroom, clicking the lock before anyone can follow me, then fumble along the wall for the light switch. The cold, buzzing glow of the fluorescent bulb fills the room, and immediately I catch sight of myself in the mirror on the opposite wall. My usually tanned skin looks pasty, and I can't tell if that's from the light or the shock of the day. My long, almost-black hair that I braided down my left shoulder this morning before school is now limp, and strands are falling out and curling all around my face.

I stare hard into the mirror, looking at my own reflection. Only this time I'm not looking for recognition, I'm searching for a memory. *Did I know this woman? Did Mom ever tell me about her? Was I just not listening? Did I just not care?* I can't recall anything, and for the first time since she left, I feel really and truly angry at my mother. How could she leave me? How could she leave out this giant piece of our—of *my*—history? What else did she omit? What else don't I know?

And then, like the last anchor on a hot-air balloon has snapped, I feel completely untethered, floating away, aimless and lost. It's just me. Alone.

CHAPTER FOUR

OUR APARTMENT IS IN A COMPLEX CALLED
Windridge Estates, which makes it sound way more fancy
than it is. When it was built, about twenty years ago, it was
probably considered if not luxurious, then at least *nice*. But it
had been built fast and cheap, and the years have not been
kind to it. The pastel Easter egg paint jobs on the different
buildings are weathered and chipping, and dark mildew blos-
soms out from all the rain gutters. Our apartment is on the
top floor of Complex C, near the back of the development,
cheaper because it's far from the pool that's always full of
leaves and is a chemically unnatural neon-blue color. Our
building backs up to the interstate. At night, I usually lie in
bed falling asleep to the sounds of cars and trucks whizzing
down I-95.

Tess waits in the living room, perched on the fake leather
couch that came standard in our furnished apartment, while

I attempt to gather anything I think I might need, or anything I don't want to see wind up in a landfill. There isn't much. After all the moves, I've learned to travel light. Most of my possessions fit in either my one battered suitcase or my backpack. Still, the apartment is full of the detritus that accumulates when you live somewhere for more than six months. Somewhere along the way, we'd become the kind of people who keep a vase on the dining room table, a garlic press in the drawer by the stove. There are books on the shelf in the living room, mostly cheap paperbacks from used bookstores and a few manuals from my mother's various hobbies (yoga, massage, general karmic self-help). Two blankets are thrown over the arm of the couch, and more than a few candles in jars and on pedestals are scattered around the apartment. None of it is important or meaningful. But realizing it will probably soon all be gone makes me feel very, very alone.

I throw all my clothes into one half of a suitcase, thankful that I'd been to the laundry room over the weekend. Showing up at my foster home with a suitcase full of dirty laundry would have felt even more pathetic somehow. I empty my top desk drawer into the other half of the suitcase, placing a small photo album in there, along with my phone charger and a couple of the fifty-cent paperbacks I'd picked up at the library sale and had been planning to read over the summer.

I'm just closing the suitcase when my phone buzzes with a text from Ali.

Ali: Here. Parked by the pool. Come down when
you're ready.

For one passing moment, I wonder if I can ask Tess to come back and pick me up later. But as quickly as the thought comes, I let it go. I'm not having queso at Margaritas with Ali tonight. Even if Tess would agree, which I doubt, I'm too much of a mess in the head to be good company. My long-awaited first date will have to be a little more long awaited.

I slam the suitcase shut and yank the zipper so hard I end up losing my grip and falling back on my butt. Mom thought she was setting me free? What a bunch of bullshit. She's off milking goats or practicing her asanas or lord knows what else while I'm being yanked out of my life, away from my friends and my crush and my last summer with all of them.

I go to the window and see his car parked nearby, an old Jeep Cherokee with the Taste of India magnet still affixed to the side. Ali uses the car to make deliveries sometimes, and he often forgets to remove it, bringing the Taste of India with him wherever he goes.

I can just make out his figure in the driver's seat. He's staring down at his phone, the glow of the screen illuminating his face. I think about the other version of me, the one who didn't have Tess show up at her door. The one with the mom who's flighty and a little odd, sure, but who at least managed to stick around until her daughter graduated from high school. That version of me is racing out of the apartment right now and climbing into the front seat of Ali's car. Instead, I'm a new version of myself, one who's packing all her stuff into a broken suitcase to go live with a woman she doesn't remember, with no idea what's going to happen tomorrow, much less what the summer holds.

That doesn't feel a damn bit like freedom.

And so, after a little fine-tuning on the message, I finally fire off a reply.

Ritzy: Disaster at home. So sorry!
Have to reschedule. :(
Soon, ok?

I read it back one last time before I hit send, hoping it's enough to keep Ali from asking questions, while also letting him know that what's keeping me from our date is a big damn deal and that I really, *really* want to go.

His reply comes almost instantaneously.

Ali: Bummer. Hope it's ok.
Can I help?

My heart swells, my eyes itching with the threat of tears. I don't know what my mother had in mind when she left with instructions to follow my own path, but in my opinion, my path should be leading, at least in the short term, to Ali. Instead, I'm heading to a foster home.

Ritzy: Nah, it's all good

But thanks

Talk soon?

Ali: Definitely.

And then I watch as he pulls out of the parking space, his taillights disappearing out of the lot.

I don't say a word to Tess as I trudge past her, dragging my wheeled suitcase over the carpet, where it wobbles thanks to one cracked wheel. I stride straight out the door, no last look over my shoulder, which is how I imagine my mom departed. I wasn't there to see it. She left for the airport while I was at school, and I never imagined her being even a little bit sentimental about our apartment. She probably didn't give a single thought to the garlic press or the patchouli candle on the coffee table. It was nothing more than a way station before her next great adventure. I can be charitable and imagine that she saw me going off on a great adventure, too, but the truth is, I don't think she was really thinking much about me when she left. She meant what she said. It's my turn now, and I have my own journey to take. Unfortunately, since she decided to leave four months shy of my eighteenth birthday, my journey is being charted by the Florida Department of Children and Families.

I heave the suitcase into the back of Tess's car, a

nondescript sedan the color of wet sand, then climb into the passenger seat, buckle my seat belt, and stare straight ahead into the fading sunlight. Soon it'll be dark. Soon this day will be over. Soon everything will be different. This is the last day of the before. Soon everything else will be after.

"What's going to happen to the rest of our stuff?" I ask.

"It can stay here through the end of the month," Tess says, "but once you're settled, we'll probably have to make some decisions. Potentially storage?" She doesn't tell me what the other potential outcomes are, but a dumpster is probably one of them. Storage will be cheaper than rent, but I'm guessing my job at the sandwich shop is on hold, which means no income. Which means we, or more accurately our stuff, will definitely be evicted. It'll be boxed up, and with no one here to claim it, will it just wind up on the curb with the trash? I'm positive Mr. Benson, the property manager who wears his polo shirt tucked into his jeans and the kind of glasses that make you look like a serial killer from the 1970s, won't be holding it for us beyond that.

Tess and I zoom up the interstate toward this new/old home of mine. She fiddles with the radio, but turning the dial seems to yield alternately Christian, rock, Christian rock, or about forty-seven different country stations. She finally stops on public radio, where a reporter with an authoritative voice smooth as butter spends the next few minutes talking about the unrest in the Middle East. I try to focus on what she's saying so I won't have to think about my own reality, but after several minutes, I'm still not sure if she's talking about one war or several.

The segment ends, and a man's voice comes on with a news report.

"According to a recent study, at-risk teens are six times more likely to be arrested, nine times more likely to visit rehab, and . . ." He continues in that semi-robotic but somehow still soothing voice everyone on public radio seems to have. I remain stone-still, though out of the corner of my eye, I can see Tess shifting slightly in her seat, her hands tightening on the steering wheel. I can practically hear her wondering if she should change the station, but she doesn't, and the newscast continues on. I want to laugh or point out that despite all indications to the contrary (Mom gone, me sent off to a foster home), I'm not at risk for *anything*. My grades this semester are fine, mostly As and a few Bs. I hate the way alcohol makes me feel, I'm terrified of doing drugs, and I have never so much as shoplifted a stick of gum. Throw my mostly situational (but maybe a little bit moral, I haven't decided yet) virginity in there, and I'm practically a poster child for the surgeon general's office.

But Tess doesn't know all that. She doesn't know me at all. All she knows is that my mother abandoned me, my father's name is "none," and I'm going to live with a stranger who took care of me when my mother apparently crapped out on the parental role the first time. I wouldn't blame her for think-ing I might be at risk for snorting household products or running away to join a cult.

There's a light drizzle outside as Tess takes an exit. I'm not sure where we are until I see a green highway sign for Helena Island, the white letters reflecting in Tess's headlights. Which means the expanse of darkness out my window is the ocean. Despite living in a city that borders the Atlantic, I almost never get to the beach. For one, it takes three city buses and more than two hours to get there. And those buses usually have sketchy AC at best.

Helena is one of the coastal islands off the northeast coast of Florida, only a short bridge away from the mainland. Helena and the other small islands are mostly vacation spots for the wealthy, covered in resorts and golf courses and vacation "cot-tages" that are really mansions. A few are historic, and some even have year-round populations, but I've never actually been to one (at least not that I remember, although now it seems as though I spent my babyhood on one).

We turn off the two-lane road and drive over a low bridge that connects the island to the mainland. On the other side, a large, carved stone wall with big brass letters welcomes drivers to HELENA ISLAND in a swooping font.

We drive up a short Main Street, lit up and shiny despite the earlier rain. It's all glossy and landscaped, with each shop and restaurant sign matching like a theme park. There are no golden arches here, no neon signs advertising lottery tickets or two-for-one hot dogs or beer. Tess takes a left around what looks like a town square, and I swear I see an actual bandstand in the middle of the manicured green.

It's nearly dark, the sky a deep purple, but there are people out and about, walking dogs and chasing kids. As we pass a restaurant, I spot a group of kids my age, all in matching school uniforms, clustered around a whitewashed picnic table topped with a cobalt-blue umbrella. It's so idyllic, I feel like I'm driving through a commercial. They look like they've been posed for a promotional shot for better living through plaid and khaki.

One of the guys perched on the picnic table, his long legs folded up with his feet on the bench, glances up at the car as we drive by. I see him squint, as if he knows right away that we're outsiders. He ruffles his blond hair, all cowlicks and curls. I watch in the side mirror to see when he looks away. I lose sight of him before he does.

On the next block, the quaint commercial district gives way to a neighborhood of cottages and bungalows in pastel colors, like beautiful little Easter eggs buried among the green trees draped with Spanish moss. I can almost imagine someone on a ladder carefully placing each piece. Artful lighting beaming up from the lawns makes all the homes look like works of art displayed in a gallery.

The houses are small at first and close together. Still clearly high-end, but nestled neatly side by side, like some architect's idea of what a quaint downtown should be. As we drive farther, they start to spread out. Lush lawns appear, and security gates that guard circular drives and ornate fountains, all landscaped with palms and rock gardens and tropical flora.

And then the landscape starts to change again. The trees get denser, the gardens a little more wild. The houses, fewer and farther between now, look like they predate the rest of the development by a hundred years. The sidewalks are gone, as are the streetlights. And just before it feels like we're about to drive off the edge of the island into the ocean, Tess turns down a nearly hidden driveway.

All along our drive across the island, I've been studying it, scanning my memory for any flicker of recognition, but so far, nothing. As soon as the car bounces up the gravel of the drive, though, I brace myself. Because surely the house, the one I started my life in, will spark something. Maybe it's my mother's influence, years of talk of past lives and connections, but I'm waiting for the *energy* of the place to feel familiar, for the island to reach out and say, *Hey, I know you. Welcome back.*

All I can see of the house is what the headlights illuminate, and even that is mostly obscured by a pair of ancient magnolia trees rising up from the front yard. The house is two stories, with a sloping tin roof rising high and overhanging a porch that encircles the house as far as I can see.

The car stops in front just between the magnolias. The porch light is on, the windows illuminated, making the house look warm and bright in the dark night.

I take a deep breath, inhaling the moment, and try to slow down the pounding of my heart. If what Tess said is true, this woman hasn't seen me in almost sixteen years. Yet when she got a call, late on a Friday afternoon, asking if she wanted me back, she said yes.

And so, it appears, I've come home.

CHAPTER FIVE

THE FIRST THING I NOTICE AS THE CAR pulls up is that Kristin, my foster mother, is waiting out on the front porch. Before Tess has even turned off the car, she's rising from a wicker chair and coming down the porch steps. Her long blondish-brown hair is piled into a messy topknot, and in floral leggings, a black tank top, and one of those comically oversized knit cardigan things, it looks like we've interrupted her evening yoga or one of those other workouts that require weird machinery and deep breathing that only rich people do.

When Tess first said the words *foster mother*, my mind immediately conjured up a kindly grandmother sort of woman, maybe a great aunt, her hair streaked with gray, a few lines on her face, and probably wearing a T-shirt commemorating a holiday or a 5K she volunteered at but didn't run. I certainly never imagined a woman who looks like she stepped out of a picture from one of those lifestyle fashion blogs Lainey likes to read. I can't help but hear my mother scoffing. I've listened to her endless rants on the commodification of everything from organic food to inner peace. She'd definitely see Kristin as a privileged poser.

The second thing I notice is that she's not alone. Still seated in the matching wicker chair opposite her is a middle-aged man. He's got a full head of dark, wavy hair and a pair of black-framed glasses. He's gripping the arms on the chair like he's debating whether to sit or stand. Tess never mentioned a foster *father*, and from the look of him, I think maybe this is new information for him, too. He looks as nervous as I feel.

I climb out of the car and turn to face Kristin. I notice a slight widening of her eyes, a quick drawing of breath. I try to put myself in her shoes (a pair of those hippie sandals with the cork soles that only look chic on a person who is chic already). I try to see me as she must see me, trying to find the two-year-old she knew in the seventeen-year-old standing in front of her. Does she recognize my wavy dark brown hair? Or my green eyes? Did I have the same smattering of freckles across my nose back then that I have now?

I have no idea what's going to happen next, but I know it's going to be big. And in a moment of bubbling panic, I know I'm not ready. So instead of standing there staring and waiting, I take charge and busy myself going around to the trunk of the car to pull out my suitcase. That's when the guy on the porch rises from his chair, taking the steps two at a time, giving me a smile as he practically hip checks me out of the way to pull my suitcase from the trunk.

"I got this," he says, and I wonder if he's reassuring himself more than he is me.

With no other choice, I finally turn to Kristin, who breaks into a nervous smile that looks like it's trying a little too hard.

"I'm glad you made it! Welcome! Oh my gosh, look at you! I'm Kristin! Kristin Stokes! It's so good to see you! Come in!" It all comes bursting out of her, a cacophony of exclamation points. Her smile falters a bit, and she grits her teeth. "Sorry, I've been sitting here trying to figure out what I was going to say first, and it appears I just went with 'all of the above.'"

I can only manage to return a strained smile, though, because I have no idea what to say. *Nice to meet you* seems wrong, since we've met before. But *Good to see you again* doesn't feel right either, because I have no memory of her. *Thanks for taking me in on a whim sixteen years later when I'm practically a stranger* feels like the truest thing, but also the least appropriate.

Kristin takes my silence as a prime directive to uphold both ends of the conversation, and she immediately sets about filling the silence.

"I'm so glad the rain let up. But at least it cooled things off a bit. It's been so steamy lately. Of course, the rain usually leaves a sweatbox behind, so who knows what it's going to be like tomorrow morning. But right now, this feels like the perfect porch weather." She pulls her cardigan around her as she talks. I know I should be saying something, but all I can do is smile and nod. I mean, come on, it's *the weather*.

"Why don't we go inside?" Tess gently suggests, still standing next to me on the gravel drive.

"Oh, right, of course," Kristin says, like it only just occurred to her. Kristin's—I don't know what he is, husband? boyfriend? man friend?—is already ahead of us, standing in the entrance with my suitcase at his feet.

The interior of the house is just like the outside, and a bit like how Kristin seems, sort of in artful disarray. The living room has enormous windows, and any leftover wall space is covered in framed photos of people and landscapes, some black and white and aged, some in screaming color. A pair of overstuffed leather couches and a collection of mismatched armchairs and rugs are scattered around an enormous steamer trunk big enough for me to crawl inside. It's the polar opposite of our apartment, this home so stuffed with memories. I wouldn't be surprised to find Kristin has *two* garlic presses in her kitchen.

Kristin settles onto one of the couches and sort of gestures around like *take your pick*. I sit in one of the armchairs, and Mr. Helpful abandons my suitcase in the hall to take the spot next to Kristin. Tess sits on the other side of the steamer trunk and begins rifling through her bag.

"Okay, well, it's late, so we should probably get settled. I know this is a"—Tess pauses, her fingers twitching as she grasps for an appropriate descriptor of what is happening to me—"*unique* situation. I'm here to help in any way I can. As far as the bureaucracy side of things, I don't have anything official to do tonight. Protocol has me returning for a visit in seven days to check in on things."

Seven days. It's the first time a timeline has been applied to my situation, and it sets my mind spinning. Do I stay here until my eighteenth birthday? Do I stay here until I graduate? What if my mom comes back? Do I go live with her? Do I even get to see her? If I stay here, where will I go to school? Will I get to see Lainey? And (even though I don't want to be *that* girl) Ali?

Tess interrupts my inner breakdown. "Are we all good?"

No. No, no, no, no, no.

"Yes, thank you so much, Tess. I appreciate you working late tonight. And we look forward to seeing you in seven days. I think we'll have no problem getting all settled in in the meantime, right, Maritza?"

I glance up and try to smile, but my whole face feels sort of numb.

Kristin follows Tess toward the door. Tess pauses by my chair and puts her hand on my shoulder. "You have my business card. Call me if you think of anything, any questions. Nothing is too small, okay?"

"Thank you," I reply. There's a tightness in my throat as I grasp the slip of cardstock. I only just met her a few hours ago, and then she was a burden, someone to try and shake or escape. But now, as she walks out, I feel like I want to cling to her hand and beg her to stay. She's walking out with my old life. She's walking out with the last traces of Ritzy and leaving Maritza here in Helena. Sure, Ritzy's life had a crappy apartment and a flaky, absent mom, but at least it was familiar. At least I understood it. At least I felt like I fit there.

But soon she's gone, the heavy door closing behind her with a thud that sounds altogether too final.

"Okay, well, um," Kristin says, clapping her hands in front of her. "How about a cup of tea?"

I nod, trying to look enthusiastic, even though I've never wanted a cup of tea ever, even though I think tea tastes like the ground. But drinking wet yard seems better than sitting here in total silence with two strangers while we all blink and grin at one another.

I follow her back to a kitchen that looks like the "after" shot on a home makeover show. Every surface is white, save for the ones that are shiny stainless steel. I watch Kristin's mystery man friend reach for a yellow teakettle and begin filling it at the sink with a familiarity that tells me he lives here. She hasn't introduced him yet, though, which is annoying, but asking *Um, and who are you exactly?* seems rude.

Kristin moves to a cupboard and pulls out three mugs. She reaches for a lavender tin from another cabinet, rising up on her tiptoes to reach over his shoulder, and he ducks slightly to give her space around his six-foot-something athletic frame. They move around each other in an effortless dance, and it makes me think this must be what it's like to be in the audience of a ballet. Kristin pops the lid off the tin and carefully measures out what I assume is tea, but looks suspiciously like what I clean out of the vacuum filter.

Then all activity pauses as we wait for the kettle, warming on the stove. And we're back to the old silent stares again.

"Oh my gosh!" Kristin exclaims suddenly, her hands flying to her reddened cheeks. "I can't believe I didn't—I'm sorry, Maritza. This is my husband, Peter. Peter Carmichael."

Finally.

"Nice to meet you, Mr. Carmichael," I reply, noting his different last name. So Kristin kept hers when they got married. Of this, my mother would approve.

"It's *Doctor*, actually," Kristin says, with a note of pride in her voice that keeps it from seeming smug.

He leans forward and shakes my hand, a firm, reassuring grip with a friendly smile. "That couldn't be less important. Just call me Pete."

"Okay . . . Pete," I say, trying it out. "Nice to meet you."

"And you can call me Kris."

Pete and Kris. Now would be the perfect time to chime in with my own you-can-call-me, but instead I just give them both a smile. I think it'll be easier to be Maritza here, in this house with these well-dressed, smiling people in their impeccable kitchen. And before I can overthink it, the kettle whistles, like time has run out and the decision's been made for me. Kris sets about pouring steaming water over our little piles of lint, and I'm Maritza now. Maritza who drinks tea.

"So I know this is a strange situation," Kris says as she slides my mug across the counter. "But I just want you to know how welcome you are here, and how glad I am to have you." She pauses, like she's swallowing the end of the sentence, and I wonder if it was *back*, as in *It's good to have you back*. "I don't know how long you'll be here, but I want you to feel comfortable, like this is a home away from home."

"Thanks," I reply.

"I think you'll really like Helena. We've got lots to do. There's the beach, of course, and downtown has some great shops and cafés. I don't know if you've noticed, but we're really close to the square. You could even ride a bike there if you wanted to."

"I haven't ridden a bike in—" I pause, trying to remember when the last time was, but I can't. I end up just shrugging. "It's been a while."

"Well, they say it's just like riding a bike," Pete says, blowing on the rim of his cup, and I laugh in spite of myself. It's such a dad joke, which is weird for me on so many levels. It's going to be strange to live in the same house with a guy, much less one who's supposed to be assuming a role as some kind of father figure for me.

I mirror Pete's actions and blow on my teacup, then take a tentative sip. It's still warm, but the heat isn't enough to hide the bitter, earthy flavor. Turns out no matter how nice your kitchen is, tea is still gross. I try to hide my grimace, but apparently I fail, because without a word, Pete crosses to the fridge, pulls out a bottle of water, and hands it to me.

"Don't worry, it's an acquired taste," he says. "One you definitely don't need to acquire. And if you need caffeine, there's Coke in the fridge, too."

"Oh yes, we've got Coke, orange juice, cranberry juice, lots of bottled water, and of course water from the tap, if you want, but it has this sort of metallic taste to it? And of course, anything in the pantry is up for grabs. There's granola bars and tortilla chips, but we can go grocery shopping tomorrow to get you whatever snacks you want. Are you allergic to anything? The granola bars have peanut butter in them, so if—"

Pete gently places his hand over Kris's, which is pressing into the marble countertop as she leans toward me, offers and information pouring out of her. It's enough to halt her in her wild hostess frenzy. She smiles softly.

"You're probably so tired. I'm sure you've had quite a day," she says, with a smile at Pete. "Why don't I show you to your room and you can get settled?"

I follow Kris back through the house, Pete trailing behind with my suitcase. My mind is on the big thing we haven't talked about. The biggest thing. That I've been here before. That we're not strangers—well, not Kris and me. She didn't bring it up and so neither did I. Or maybe she didn't bring it up *because* I didn't bring it up. Either way, neither of us is talking about it.

Kris starts up the narrow staircase. It leads to a small landing and a long hall with a sloping ceiling. Right at the top of the stairs there's an open door, and inside I see floor-to-ceiling bookshelves and two desks, one neat and tidy with a short stack of books and files perched next to a closed laptop, another an absolute disaster of papers and pens strewn about, books open, laptop open and askew.

"The messy one belongs to this guy," Kris says, nodding over her shoulder. "He's the dean of students at Mercer College." I recognize the name of a small, private liberal arts school located over the bridge and just outside Jacksonville. It's constantly appearing on various "the Harvard of" lists. The Harvard of the South. The Harvard of Small Colleges. The Harvard of Not Harvards. I don't know what a dean of students does, but I know the man is a doctor and has a big-sounding job at Nearly-Harvard.

"Kris is always on me to organize, but she should know better than anyone that studies show a disorganized desk can be a sign of genius," Pete says.

"I'm a psychology professor," she adds, and that's when I realize I'm in the presence of *two* doctors. Toto, you're not in Windridge anymore. My mother would have a field day with the pair of them. For all my mom's interest in reaching a higher power and a deeper understanding, she's always been deeply scornful of therapy and psychology. Maybe because even a poorly trained therapist would tell her to stop trying on different forms of enlightenment and instead just try to live her life in one spot for a change, and that's not exactly what she wants to hear.

It's this thought of my mother that leads me to joke, "You're not going to shrink me, are you?"

"I'm not that kind of psychologist. I'm a researcher. I specialize in the effects on long-term caregivers of Alzheimer's patients, so unless that's you, then no," she says, and turns to side-eye Pete. "But perhaps I should be studying the psychological effects of sharing an office with someone who hasn't thrown away a piece of paper since 2005."

"Always good to be a pioneer in a field," he quips, and they smile at one another in a way I've only seen couples smile at each other in diamond commercials or Hallmark original movies. Good lord, are they always this gooey?

"Okay, this is your room," Kris says, breaking the moment to open a door near the end of the hall. She pushes it open and reaches in to flip the switch, then steps back into the hall so I can go in first.

It's the kind of room that looks like someone just arranged all their old crap around, but if you tried to do the same thing with all *your* old crap, you'd just look poor. I should know. It's what our apartment looks like.

I give Kris a quick glance, trying to determine if she's the sort of person who would hire someone to pick all this stuff out or if all of it is actually hers, acquired over a lifetime of travels and discoveries and stuffed full of memories and stories. Did the wrought iron bed with the big dented curlicues once belong to a grandmother? Or did somebody at a Restoration Hardware factory bang it with a hammer? Was the carved wardrobe, yellow paint rubbed and chipping to reveal a coat of white below, found on the side of the road somewhere? Or did it arrive on a truck with free delivery?

"We're at the end of the hall, so don't hesitate to knock if you need anything at all. Make yourself comfortable in here. Use the drawers and the closet. You've got a bathroom through there." She points to a narrow door that's cracked open. My own bathroom. Never had that before. "We're early risers, but don't feel like you have to be. Feel free to sleep in, and like I said, help yourself to anything in the kitchen at any time. Oh, and the laptop on the desk over there is for you to use. There's no password, and the Wi-Fi should connect automatically, so you're good to go. If you need it, of course."

Pete steps in behind me and lays my suitcase down on a cedar chest at the foot of the bed. It looks out of place in this room, like a booger hanging out of a pretty girl's nose. It makes me wonder what *I* look like in here.

"Okay, well, why don't we let Maritza get settled," Pete says, placing his hands on Kris's shoulders, prepared to steer her away. But before she can move to leave, she practically leaps forward, her arms wrapping around me to pull me into a tight hug. It's so spontaneous that I don't have time to react to it, and instead wind up with my arms pinned to my sides, like I'm being restrained instead of hugged.

"I'm so glad you're here," she says into my hair.

I have no idea what to say to that. None at all. Because while *here* is very nice, and so is she, it all means so much more than a simple place to crash. I don't even *know* what it means yet.

And so I say nothing and instead give the widest smile I can muster as they leave me alone in here. In my room.

———

I glance at the clock on the bedside table, the numbers glowing an angry, red 11:30 P.M. I've been looking at it about every ten minutes for the last hour, and it's really starting to taunt me. I finally reach down below the table and yank the cord from the wall. The red light disappears, but it doesn't help.

I lie in bed surrounded by fluffy pillows and blankets, staring up at the ceiling while I watch the fan spin, hoping it will lull me to sleep. I'm exhausted, after all, a deep, heavy exhaustion that feels like it's radiating out from my soul. Yet despite that, I can't manage to drift off even a little bit. It's not the room or the fact that it's not mine or that everything is different. The sound of the waves could almost mimic the sound of semis rushing up and down I-95 (which never failed to put me to sleep), but there's a rhythmic thwack, thwack, thwack that's breaking through, just enough that I have to listen for it and enough that I can't ignore it.

I climb out of bed and peek out into the hall, but there's no light coming out from beneath Kris and Pete's door. The noise doesn't seem to be bothering them at all, unless they're also lying awake in the dark. Maybe discussing the ways their lives have changed today.

I get back in bed and shut my eyes, but I still hear the thwack, thwack, thwack. Within minutes, I feel like my heartbeat is syncing up to it. I fling the covers off and go to the window, scanning the landscape for the source. The backyard is completely dark, but there's a glow of yellow light coming from the house behind this one.

I creep down the hall and out the back door, closing it with the quietest click I can manage so as not to wake anyone. I don't want them to freak out and think I'm running away, like some bad Lifetime movie cliché.

I cross the lawn, the cool, damp grass tickling my bare feet, until I reach the trees that separate this property from the next one. I get closer and the clearing widens. The light is coming from a tennis court. I'm torn between two competing thoughts: *Who has a private tennis court?* and *Who plays tennis when it's almost midnight?*

I pause just at the tree line, carefully hidden by the strip of a shadow that the tall, narrow pines provide, but close enough to see him. The boy on the court is wearing khaki pants and a white dress shirt, unbuttoned to reveal the undershirt beneath, and his sleeves are rolled up. He's barefoot, a pair of brown leather shoes lined up perfectly with the white line at the edge of the court. He hits the ball with an emphatic smack, and it sails to the back wall, striking just above the painted net. It bounces back, and he slams it again. And again and again, sweat rolling down his forehead, a look of sheer determination on his face.

This continues for several rounds, with me watching from the shadows, until he hits a shot that goes wide. He lunges, and his big toe scrapes the asphalt, one of those tiny little indignities that hurts way more than it should. He stumbles, the ball sailing just past the tip of his racket as he goes down on his hands and knees.

"Dammit!" he spits. He rolls back onto his butt and sends the racket sailing across the court with an incredible amount of force. It slams loudly against the chain-link fence, then clatters to the ground. He stares at it for a long time, his chest heaving, all full of fury. When his breathing slows, I think he's going to stand up and go after the racket, now laying half a court away, with scratches in the red paint that I can see from here. But instead, he leans over, his elbows on his knees, his head tucked low. His shoulders begin to shake, and when he glances up at the night sky, I see tears rolling down his reddened cheeks. He cries like I wanted to back at Tess's office. Like I wanted to before she left me here. Like I want to now, when I'm in this strange place with too many questions and no answers, when all I want to do is sleep but can't.

CHAPTER SIX

I WAKE TO THE SOUND OF RUSTLING around downstairs. The sun is streaming through the open curtains, and when I roll over to check the time, I remember that I unplugged the clock the night before. I finally fumble for my phone and discover it's seven thirty, an absolutely absurd time to be awake on a Saturday morning.

But the moment I burrow back into the pillow to try to go back to sleep, I remember where I am. And why. And then there's no chance of going back to sleep. But I'm not ready to go downstairs to face Kris and Pete and whatever may be waiting for me there yet, so I stall. I snag the laptop Kris left me, a shiny silver Mac, and flip the lid.

I start by emailing Mr. Reynolds at Roasted to tell him that he'll need to cover my shifts for the foreseeable future. Only I'm not quite sure what to say about why. After writing and deleting several versions, I settle on "family emergency" and tell him I've had to go out of town for a while. I leave it open-ended, because I'm still not sure how long I'll be here. My mom could show up again tomorrow. I cross my fingers that he'll say my job will be waiting for me when I get back, but I can't bring myself to ask for that.

Then I open SocialSquare and give my feed a scroll. It's mostly photos of my classmates celebrating the start of summer, either sitting around beach bonfires or toasting with ice-cream cones (and in one ill-advised picture, a giant handle of something brown and probably illegal for people our age to be drinking). I pause on a photo of Ali, who managed to bounce back from our canceled date by joining up with his soccer teammates at Starcadia, one of those arcades that also have go-karts and mini golf. He's holding a fistful of tickets and grinning while Damien Newbery mimes pouring a soda over his head. I stare at Ali's wide, easy smile and feel the usual warm, fizzy feeling deep in my chest. But that's quickly overtaken by a hollowness, because I have no idea when I'm going to be able to see him and finally have that date. I want to text him again so he doesn't think my rain check last night was an excuse or a blowoff. But if I text him before 8:00 A.M., will that make me seem . . . I don't know, as desperate as I actually am?

Instead, I text Lainey, who I know for a fact will be up and getting ready for her Saturday shift at the library.

Ritzy: Long story, but I'm staying with this woman
for a while.

I can't bring myself to type the words *foster care*. It sounds so tragic, and as weird as this situation is, it could be so much worse.

> **Lainey:** Tell me you're not staying with
> Mrs. Sazonov.
> You'll never get the borscht smell out of
> your hair.

I laugh and once again realize just how damn good I have it right now.

> **Ritzy:** I'm on Helena Island. Like I said, long story.
> Maybe we can get together tomorrow so I
> can tell it?

She replies immediately.

> **Lainey:** This I need to hear. Text me details. I'm
> free all afternoon.

I add *Ask Kris if Lainey can come visit* to my mental to-do list, though with how accommodating she's been, I can't imagine it'll be a problem. I could probably invite the soccer team and a biker gang here, and Kris would offer them tea and smother them in conversation.

I manage to stall another half hour with a long, hot shower

in my own private bathroom, the white-tiled stall stocked with lavender-scented soap and shampoo and fluffy towels that feel more like luxurious blankets. I throw on a pair of cutoff shorts and a T-shirt and wind my wet hair into a heavy knot on top of my head.

Downstairs, I find Pete in the kitchen digging through the fridge. He's wearing a pair of those embarrassingly tiny and brightly colored running shorts, and a sweaty T-shirt on top that tells me he's already been out this morning. Which puts his wake-up at, what, dawn? They weren't kidding about being early risers.

"Hey. Sorry, did I wake you?" he asks, emerging from behind the stainless steel door with a carton of eggs and a block of cheese. I try to read his face. Am I intruding on his morning routine?

"No, it's fine. Hard to sleep in a new place," I say, then wish I could swallow the words back, because they sound ungrateful. The bed was ridiculously comfortable, piled high with pillows and covered in sheets that smelled like something herbal.

"I hear that. I'm always a zombie when I stay in hotels," he says, as if that's the same thing. I don't tell him that I've never stayed in a hotel before, but I've always imagined it would be the best sleep of your life. "Anyway, sorry if I was making noise. I'm up early, training for a half marathon in a couple weeks. Runner." He shrugs and gives a sheepish grin when he says it, like he's confessing to being a smoker or something. "Can I make you eggs?"

"Sure."

"Cheese?"

"Sounds good."

"So not a vegan," he says. He turns on the heat beneath a pan on the stove, the blue flame lighting up with a deep whoosh.

"Not a picky eater at all," I reply. I can't be, with my mom's wildly fluctuating nutritional philosophies. We've been pescatarian and vegetarian, vegan and freegan, paleo and low-carb, and once we even eliminated nightshades, though I'm still not clear on what a nightshade is. I've eaten plants raw that I'm pretty sure wouldn't taste good even deep-fried and slathered in barbecue sauce.

Pete cracks eggs into a bowl and whisks them with a fork.

"Noted. I'm not much of a cook. I make eggs and anything that comes in a box. And I can grill a steak without killing it most of the time. It's Kristin who's really good in the kitchen. You'll see soon. I'm sure she can't wait to cook for you." There's pride in his voice, and maybe a touch of something else, like he's trying to sell me on her?

"Are my ears burning?" Kris breezes in through the wide French doors from the backyard. She drops a few canvas bags onto the counter, one of which tips, sending a shiny red apple rolling across the white marble.

"Speak of the devil and her hobbies," Pete replies, and just like last night, their practiced dance begins as they move around each other putting away groceries, Kris stopping at the frying pan to salt the eggs, Pete calling "I saw that!" over his shoulder.

"He never salts them enough," Kris says to me in a stage whisper from behind her hand. "He claims it's a health thing, but I think he just forgets."

"I heard that."

"I'd be concerned about the state of your ears if you didn't," she says with a smile, and he pauses for a kiss as he passes by her en route to the pan. They seem like newlyweds, all gushy and mushy, but also like they've been together forever. I wonder how long they've been married. I spied a wedding photo on a table in the entry hall, but it was hard to place the date. Kris was wearing a flowing, gauzy thing with lace and ribbon, her hair cascading down her shoulders in effortless blond waves. Pete had on a navy suit, the collar on his crisp white shirt open. If I didn't know them, I'd think they were the models who came with the frame.

When Pete's safely ensconced at the stove, poking at the scramble with a spatula, Kris turns her attention to me. "Sleep okay?"

"Fine. Great!" I reply, and I notice Pete give me a side-eye over his shoulder. But he doesn't spill my secret.

"Is there anything I can do to make things better than fine?" She's so hopeful that I search my brain for a task I can give her. Then I remember my to-do list.

"Would it be okay if my friend Lainey came by tomorrow?"

Her eyes brighten. "Of course! Tomorrow's supposed to be

gorgeous, one of the last comfortable days before the heat of the summer kicks in. You guys could go down to the beach." She glances out the wide window of the kitchen, where beyond the lawn is the beach. She drums her fingers on the counter and bites her lip. "Which brings me to today. We have this . . . *thing* tonight."

It just hangs there in the air for a moment, this statement that seems loaded with something, but no one wants to touch it. Finally, Pete deposits a plate of steaming cheesy eggs in front of me along with a fork. "C'mon, honey. Can't we skip that?"

She shakes her head, a quick, short motion. "Sadly, no, as I am on the board of this particular event, and you agreed to take a shift with the silent auction."

Pete groans. "Which means I'm going to have to stand at that table for an hour listening to George go on and on about that boat of his."

"There are other people for him to talk to."

"Yes, and yet somehow he always finds me. It's like he put a GPS tracker in my shoe."

I watch their verbal ping-pong while I attack my eggs, hungrier than I thought I was. It's strange to be in a house with so much conversation. Mom is always talking, sure, but it's usually more talking *at* me, not *to* me or *with* me. Most of our time together involves her treating me to a monologue on whatever her new passion is, be it knitting or basket weaving or essential oils or crystals. There's always someone who got her "turned on" to whatever the hobby du jour is, and I have to listen to that person's résumé, which usually takes the form of a "spiritual journey." I've long since learned to tune it out, which makes our apartment, so full of my mother's chatter, manage to feel very quiet.

"We're going," Kris says to Pete, and then turns to me. "As I was saying, we have this charity event tonight at the country club. It's cocktail attire, so I was thinking that if you didn't have anything to wear, maybe I could take you shopping downtown. My friend Heather has this cute boutique, and I know we could find something perfect."

"Oh, you don't need to do that," I say, though as I'm saying the words, I know that the answer is *yes, actually, you do.* Because I don't have anything that could even come close to being described as "cocktail attire." I have exactly one dress, a pale-yellow sundress that I wear anytime I have to dress up for a school thing. I wear it with flip-flops (they're black, so I figure they can double as dress shoes, right?). "I could just stay here."

A look passes between Kris and Pete, one I think they don't want me to see, but I can't miss it. It's loaded, and it reminds me that I'm not just a houseguest. Even though they don't fit the stereotype of foster parents, as far as they know, I'm just your average foster kid, ready to break into their liquor cabinet and steal whatever's not nailed down.

"You should come," Kris says. I can hear her need to sell me on the event so that I'll say yes. "There will be a bunch of island kids there your age. It'll be good to meet people. And honestly, I love shopping for people. You'd be doing me a favor."

Ritzy would insist on staying home. I'm seventeen, after all, and until yesterday, I'd been home alone for two weeks.

But now I live in a place where someone else cooks me eggs to order, and the grocery shopping is done in sustainable canvas bags. I live in a place where people use the phrase *cocktail attire*. This is where Maritza lives, and so I just smile and thank her and say it sounds like fun.

Kris claps her hands in delight. "Awesome! Well, finish your eggs, and we can head out."

By the time we arrive, downtown is buzzing with activity, like a very well-dressed beehive. A line of people are waiting in front of a café, the sidewalk tables already full of diners downing pancakes and eggs. They wear straw hats and ball caps, their eyes hidden behind designer sunglasses as they stare down at their phones. We pass a woman with a fleet of tiny, well-groomed dogs wearing bows and bandannas, and a man on a bike wearing neon spandex and sport glasses like he's in a Nike commercial. Everyone is clean and put together, as if they were put on the street with the same care as the landscaping.

I follow Kris across the street, weaving around shoppers and dodging joggers in brightly colored fabric. I don't even notice what store we are going into until I hear the tinkle of a bell as I follow closely behind Kris. Everything inside is bright white and glossy, and somehow even my sneakers make a click-clacking sound on the marble floor.

"Morning, Kris!" a voice calls from deep within the glitter and gloss. "I'll be right out!"

"Look around, take your time, try stuff on, okay?" Kris is talking to me, but she's already rifling through a rack of T-shirts. I figure this is encouraging. At least she's not worried about me shoplifting. "Swimsuits are in the back." She points toward a wall where I see brightly colored strings and straps on hangers. On the way over, she'd managed to pry out of me that I'm also in need of a swimsuit. My last one finally fell apart in the wash a couple weeks ago, and though I tried my best to brush her off, already feeling awkward about letting her buy me a dress, she insisted. It seemed easier to just say yes, and my goal while here so far has been to make things as easy as possible. Don't make waves.

I ease past more racks of flowing garments, things with sequins, the kind that can afford to be decorative instead of utilitarian. I'm pretty sure everything in this store has to be dry-cleaned, a thing with which I have exactly zero experience. I have no idea what dry cleaning even *is*. It might be witchcraft. Or a very elaborate scam. DRY-CLEAN ONLY is a warning strictly forbidden in my world. A garment might as well say, *Buy this, then light a twenty-dollar bill on fire once a month.*

When I arrive at the swimsuits, I flip over the first price tag I see. It's attached to a green-and-yellow-striped triangle top that I have absolutely no interest in, as the colors would make me look sort of sick, and the flimsy straps don't look like they'll hold anything in place. But this is my standard practice anytime I go into a new store. All I need is one price to act as a barometer. I always know right away if a store is going to be for me, and from the number of digits on the tag for this tiny triangle top, I know I won't find *anything* here. Not even a 75 percent off closeout sale can make any of this stuff practical, even if someone else is paying. If I had all the money in the world, I wouldn't buy a $125 bikini. No, scratch that. I flip over the tag attached to the matching bottoms: $125 for a bikini *top*.

"With your skin, I'd recommend the warmer colors. That green's gonna make you look sick." The voice comes from a shelf of leather bags. I turn and see a short woman with a blond pixie cut wearing the exact kind of expensive, flowing fabric decorating the racks throughout the store.

This price is gonna make me be *sick*, I want to say, but instead I duck my head and move to the back corner. I reach for a one-piece suit, black with a pattern of little gold starfish. The straps come up in a halter over a sweetheart neckline, and ruching along the sides comes all the way down to the hip. It looks like the kind of suit someone would wear in 1945, while they were waiting for their beau to get home from war.

"Now *that* would look fab on you," the salesgirl says, and I jump. She saunters up behind me and pulls it off the rack, thrusting it into my hands. I don't even have a chance to check the price tag. "So many girls come in here without the required curves to really rock that suit. You *have* to try it on. With that mermaid hair and a bright red lip, you'd look positively pinup."

Who wears a red lip to the beach? I want to ask her, but she's already herding me like a collie toward the dressing area. I look around for Kris, but she's all the way at the front of the store, and calling for help seems a bit overdramatic. The salesgirl tosses back a heavy black velvet curtain and places the suit on the hook just inside the door. "You're an eight, right? I'll bring you some things."

Without the prying eyes of the most persistent salesgirl in the world, I venture a glance at the tag. The $165 price is crossed out, and $99 is written over it in a hasty red pen. *A bargain*, I think, shocked at how quickly it all becomes relative. Not even one day here and I'm starting to experience a new normal.

I catch a glimpse of myself in the mirror. I threw on a pair of cutoff shorts and an oversized T-shirt, a Goodwill score that's been washed just enough times to make it perfectly soft, but not so many times that it lacks the structural integrity of a T-shirt. I wouldn't be surprised to find a shirt like this one sold brand-new in this very store, but for about fifty times the three dollars I paid for it.

I study myself for a moment, my long brown curls that the salesgirl called "mermaid hair," and my boobs and hips that she referred to as my "curves." If she hadn't said it with such a warm and friendly smile, I'd think maybe she was insulting me. Still, I pull off my T-shirt and start to slip into the suit. I'm just about to tie the halter neck when a handful of suits come over the top of the curtain.

"Try these," comes the salesgirl's sugary voice. I reach up and take hold of the hangers she's dangling over. They're all reds and oranges and a mustard-yellow bikini.

"Heather, leave her be," I hear Kris say.

"She's with you?"

"Yes, that's Maritza. She's staying with me for . . . a while."

I hear a low "ooooohhhh" and then some whispers. My name must mean something to Heather, which irks me. This salesgirl knows more about my history than I do.

"Do you have it on yet? Let's see!"

"Heather!"

I choose to remain silent as I tug the straps and adjust my boobs into the cups. When I look in the mirror, I understand what Heather meant about curves. She actually *was* being complimentary, because this suit looks bomb on me. The ruching around the hips makes it look like I have an hourglass figure, and the sweetheart neckline is really flattering without letting my girls fall all over the place. I tuck my hair behind my left ear and feel the inevitable tug of a smile. I still would never, ever in my life pay this much for a bathing suit, but I understand the allure. The fabric feels solid, not like it will pull and pill from sitting on a pool deck. The straps feel like they'll hold everything in place with a perfect curve and fit, and I don't get the sense that the elastic will be snapping anytime soon. So *this* is what ninety-nine dollars buys you.

"Everything okay in there?" Kris asks, and without even thinking about it, I push the curtain aside. Kris is standing in the little waiting area with an armful of dresses, and Heather is beside her holding even more. Kris smiles, and Heather's mouth drops open in a scarlet O.

"That's perfect! Don't even try on the others, that's the one," Heather squeals at a pitch that gives me goose bumps. Then she holds up a long finger. "Oh, there's a cover-up that will look great with that! Lemme grab it."

"I don't need—" I start to say, because I have plenty of oversized free T-shirts from school events to serve as cover-ups, but Kris cuts me off.

"Sorry about her. She's really enthusiastic. I've known her since we were little, and she's always been really, well, *familiar* with people." Kris takes the stack of bathing suits Heather brought and turns to put them on the return rack outside the dressing room. "Let's just say this is the perfect job for her." She rolls her eyes, but I can't ignore the affection for her friend. "So, do you like it?"

I finger the price tag. "It's kind of expensive."

Kris reaches out and flips over the tag dangling below my armpit. "It's on sale. Forty percent off."

"Yeah, but forty percent off a lot is still a lot."

"True," Kris says. "But it's a really well-made suit. That'll last you years if you take care of it. Makes the cost per wear a lot lower."

I chew my lip, doing a little math in my head. Ninety-nine dollars is probably more than I've spent collectively on every swimsuit I've worn in my entire life, but Kris is right. And she's offering. Still, I don't know what accepting that will come along with. Helena is a different world for me. I have no idea what kind of strings people here could attach to something like this.

Kris must read my hesitation all over my face. She steps into the dressing room with me and pulls the curtain shut.

"Maritza, I don't want to make you uncomfortable, and I'm happy to take you somewhere else to shop if you want. But I want to get that suit for you, if you want it."

I steal one last glance at myself in the mirror, realizing that I do want it. The thought of putting it back stokes a little fire of what feels like desperation. Suddenly I want it *bad*.

"Okay," I say. There's a fizzy feeling in my stomach as I accept, equal parts excitement and nerves. I'm trying not to do the math on all the things that ninety-nine dollars could buy, but I remind myself that it's not my ninety-nine dollars to spend. It's hers. And it seems to make her really happy, which is nice. "But please don't make me wear that." I point at Heather, approaching fast and armed with a gauzy, fringed thing that looks like a grandmother's whisper.

Kris glances over her shoulder, then back at me with a grimace. "Deal."

⸻

It takes several minutes of convincing before Heather gives up trying to dress me like Vacation Barbie, but eventually we leave the store with my new bathing suit, a pair of big black vintage-style sunglasses that I only agreed to because they were ten dollars, and a dress for tonight's "event," as Kris keeps calling it. The dress is black lace and sleeveless, with a V-neck and a flared skirt to the knee. Kris assured me I would get a ton of use out of it, and it was one of the cheapest options in the store (which wasn't saying much). And I have to admit, it does look pretty great on me. Both Heather and Kris tried to wrestle me into a pair of shoes, but after discovering that Kris and I are both a 7.5, Kris agreed to let me borrow from her instead. Even after minimizing the damage as much as possible, the total still came close to a month's rent.

Back out on the sidewalk, our purchases wrapped in butter-yellow tissue paper and placed carefully in individual lavender shopping bags, Kris cocks her head at a store a few doors down.

"I have to stop in to Reuger's before we head out," she says. "I have a prescription to pick up that wasn't ready earlier."

I follow her to a sort of general store with wide windows. Inside is a long, silver café counter along one wall. An older couple in tennis whites sits on red vinyl stools sipping cups of coffee and trading sections of a newspaper. There's a wall of clear containers filled with candy, silver scoops sticking out of a bucket of paper bags. I can't tell if they're decorative or if the candy is actually for sale. These are not problems you have when shopping at the Dollar Tree.

"If you need anything, toiletries or whatever, just grab them and meet me back at the pharmacy counter, okay?"

I make my way toward the aisles in the back of the store, scanning the signs until I find hair care. I pick out a new brush from the shelves, a wide wooden paddle with bristles on it that doesn't look like a fancy brush, but which must come with some superpowers if the price is to be believed. Still, it's the cheapest one they carry that won't immediately break off in my thick hair. I also grab a package of hair ties, the big black ones that I can wear on my wrist for the inevitable hair emergency that happens when your hair is long and thick and you live someplace with a constant ocean breeze and 100 percent humidity. These, at least, are a price I recognize. Still, I could kick myself for leaving my old brush behind at the apartment.

"Mom! They have Merlin! On a towel! Can I get it? *Please?*"

I look up to see a kid barreling down the aisle toward me, a towel wrapped around his shoulders and trailing behind him like a cape. I step out of his path just in time to keep from being little-kid roadkill, my hip knocking into a shelf of shampoo bottles. I reach out to grab one, but I miss, and they all cascade to the floor as the image of a brightly colored cartoon dragon flutters past.

"Ryan, slow down, buddy," a voice calls. It's low and slightly gravelly, and there's the tiniest hint of a southern drawl in the way he says "Ryan." It comes out as almost a single syllable. Suddenly there's a shadow over me as the owner of the voice bends down to retrieve the white bottles from the floor. "Sorry about that. He loves that damn dragon. I swear, if it was printed on a bottle of milk of magnesia, he'd want it."

"Sounds like Disney's really missing out on a key marketing opportunity." I glance up as I place the last bottle on the shelf before standing up to my full height. Which is a head shorter than this dude. He's instantly familiar in that nagging way that you worry you'll never place, but it hits me after only half a second. The curly blond hair isn't weighed down with sweat, the cheeks aren't red. And there are no tears. The tennis guy.

Before I can say anything, or wonder if he saw me last night, too, the little boy and his towel reappear. This time it's clutched in one hand, the tail of it trailing behind him on the tile floor.

"Mom said if I want it, I have to buy it with my own money," he says, a distinct pout appearing on his lower lip. He has the same sandy, shaggy hair as his brother, only with less-contained cowlicks, and a metric ton of freckles across his face. He slings the towel back over his shoulder, and that's when I notice that his right arm, the one not clutching a towel, is only half as long. There's the crook of his elbow and what looks like a fist, and then nothing. I quickly avert my eyes to avoid staring, looking first at the shampoo bottles, then up to his big brother, who is grinning down at his little brother.

"Okay, that sounds fair."

"But I don't *have* money."

"Ah, and there's the rub," he replies with an exaggerated Shakespearean inflection.

The little boy cocks his head, his freckled nose wrinkling in confusion. "The what?"

His older brother laughs. "I'll tell you what. You apologize to this poor girl who you nearly flattened, and I'll spot you." He reaches into his back pocket for a wallet as he turns to me. "And your name is?"

I'd been so busy observing them like a little stage play that I'm almost shocked at the moment the fourth wall breaks and I'm brought in. "My name?"

"Yeah. If Ryan is going to give you a proper apology, he should know your name." There's that charming smile again, and I swear I see him wink at me. Dude is *smooth*, and I'm not sure I'm a fan. If I were in Jacksonville, I'd simply turn my back and walk away. But this place feels too small for that. There are definitely different rules here, and I need to start learning them. Fast.

"It's Maritza," I say.

"Maritza," he says, the slight southern lilt putting a long, syrupy emphasis on the middle, an effect that must usually work really well for him. "Nice to meet you, Maritza. I'm Spencer, and this is Ryan, who is now going to apologize to you."

The little boy shuffles his feet, then peers up at me from underneath the longest, blondest eyelashes I've ever seen. "I'm sorry I almost ranned you over, Maritza."

"Ran," Spencer corrects.

"Right. Ran. I'm sorry I almost *ran* you over." Then he holds out his hand to his brother. "Can I borrow the money now?"

Spencer slaps the cash into Ryan's hand like a slick high five, a grin on his face. "It's only considered borrowing if you plan to pay it back," he says, but the little boy is already streaking up the aisle toward the register, all warnings of slowing down gone from his mind.

While Spencer puts his wallet back into his pocket, I take a moment to study him. He isn't acting like a guy who'd spent the previous evening crying on a tennis court. And he certainly doesn't look like the guy who has something to be crying about. From his expensive shoes to his perfect orthodontia smile, it seems like life is going just fine for him.

When he looks up at me, a grin breaks across his face, but then Kris appears at the end of the aisle carrying a small paper pharmacy bag. She looks lost in her own head as she kneads at the paper in her grasp. It's not until she spots us that she puts on a smile, like she's flicking a switch.

"Oh, Spencer! Is your mother here?" Kris asks.

"I think she's getting coffee at the counter."

"I see you've met Maritza." Kris turns to me. "Spencer lives in the house behind ours. His mother is a good friend. Speaking of, I'm going to find her. We need to talk about the Fall Festival committee."

I notice she doesn't give Spencer any information on who I am in her life. She's leaving my explanation in my own hands, and I appreciate it. I doubt this guy has ever met a foster kid before, and I don't want whatever stereotypes his mind would conjure up applied to me.

"I'm staying with Kris for a while" is what I go with, and Spencer accepts it without question. I wonder if he's curious, or if it's just his good southern manners that keep him from asking more questions. Or if, his mother being such good friends with Kris, he already knows. I could have been a discussion over the breakfast table this morning. *That poor girl. A foster kid. Showed up in the middle of the night.* Accompanied by the low "oooohhh" of Heather's reaction in the store. I wonder if his mother had to explain to Ryan what a foster kid even *was.* People with their own tennis court probably don't have a whole lot of interaction with the foster care system.

"Cool," Spencer says, and I can't find anything in his tone or his expression that says he knows anything about my situation. "Kris is awesome. She makes the *best* chocolate chip cookies. Seriously, there's some witchcraft and wizardry involved in those things."

"Spencer, we're going. You coming?" says a tall blond

woman in workout gear with her hair braided down her shoulder. She's standing at the end of the aisle with Kris. She shares Spencer's blue eyes and the perfect ski slope of a nose. Ryan appears next to her, a bag containing his dragon towel dragging at his side.

"Yup," Spencer replies. He reaches down, picks up the last bottle of shampoo that I missed, and passes it to me. He gives me a half smile paired with a full twinkle in his eye. "See you around."

"Yeah," I reply, cradling the shampoo in my arms like an idiot. Ugh, this guy is entirely too much.

Kris pays for my hairbrush and hair ties, and I add the brown paper bag to my collection. This is probably the most shopping I've ever done in one day, and I feel buoyed by the purchases, each one a new opportunity, a fresh start. I never really understood people who acted like shopping was some kind of recreational activity, but I think now I get it. I'm starting to understand why people call it "retail therapy." Of course, that feeling is followed closely by one that I think might be what those same people call "buyer's remorse," because the guilt of all this new stuff that I didn't pay for also makes my bags feel way too heavy.

CHAPTER SEVEN

KRIS DISAPPEARS INTO HER OFFICE TO finish some last-minute event prep, so I grab one of the paperbacks from my suitcase and head down to the water. I manage to kill the entire book and four hours with my toes buried in the sand.

Back up at the house, I find Kris with an armful of shoes for me to try and an offer to help me with my makeup. Her enthusiasm is infectious, and when I finally slip into my new dress, I'm surprised to find myself actually excited for tonight's festivities. Sure, my mom would probably disown me if she knew I was looking forward to spending the evening at a country club, but she already abandoned me, so she doesn't get a vote.

When Kris and I head downstairs—she's in a bright pink shift with a halter neckline and some delicate folds along the bodice that make it look as expensive as I suspect it was— we find Pete waiting at the bottom of the stairs in a tuxedo.

He gives Kris a wide smile and a kiss on the cheek, then turns his attention to me, nervously adjusting his glasses on his face. I feel for him, because he clearly has no idea how to talk to me. We get into the car and drive in silence for a while, then turn off the main road onto a drive that winds between dunes dotted with seagrass. I adjust the straps on my dress and give my bra a good hike so I won't have to do it in front of people. I climb out and get a look at the Island Club for the first time. It isn't as grand as I imagined when Kris first mentioned where the event was being held. I pictured a lush country club, something sort of *Gone with the Wind*–like with verandas and balconies, a gently rolling golf course with endless greens and artfully arranged landscaping dotted with bright, colorful flowers.

Instead, it's a low beige stucco building with a terra-cotta roof. What it lacks in height, it more than makes up for in square footage, running in either direction on the shoreline for what looks like a few blocks. The front doors are wide and squat and look heavy like a castle entrance, and I wonder if I'll be able to open them without grunting. I don't get to test that, though, because as we approach, a uniformed attendant steps out from behind a potted palm and pulls the door open for us.

I follow Kris through the entryway, our shoes clicking on the tile floor. I keep catching glimpses of my reflection in decorative mirrors that dot the walls we pass. Kris glides down the hall effortlessly despite her impossibly high heels, her hand resting gently on Pete's arm. I tromp unevenly behind her, my black dress swishing around my legs, accentuating my awkward gait. I don't even have the high heel excuse. Kris had presented me a few choices to go with my dress, and I opted for a pair of simple ballet flats, figuring tonight isn't the night to learn to walk on stilts. I'll be out of place enough without also falling into a chocolate fountain or something.

It isn't until we emerge from the building and onto the back deck that the Island Club begins living up to my imagined hype. It's immediately clear that whoever designed the place knew instinctively that no one would care about the interior building, because laid out before me is a wide view of the blue ocean at sunset, the sky dappled pink and orange and purple.

"Gorgeous, right? We always plan these events for sunset," Kris says. "Nothing gets people happy and ready to write big checks like a glimpse of that."

"Well, the sunset and an open bar," Pete adds with a wink.

"Kris! I'm so glad you're here!" A woman in a skintight coral cocktail dress comes running up to us. Or more accurately, she scurries, since I'm pretty sure between her sky-high heels and the way her dress binds her thighs together, running is not a possibility. When she's finally in front of us, I notice her blond hair is slightly fried and her kohl-lined eyes are starting to go wild. "One of the bartenders called in sick, so we need to do some staff restructuring; otherwise, there's going to be a *huge* line at the bar."

She's breathless, and her tone escalates with each word. You'd think she was describing the approaching apocalypse, but I guess if Pete is right, any kind of roadblock at the bar might decrease the size of the checks. Still, it's hard to take her seriously as she frets about a missing bartender with the same level of distress one might apply to a fast-approaching hurricane, but Kris is either really good at faking it or is also appropriately horrified. She turns to me.

"Do you mind if I—" she asks, but Pete cuts her off.

"We'll be fine. Go. Problem solve," he says, giving her a soft kiss on the cheek.

Kris and the coral woman hurry off, leaving us standing on the landing looking out over the entirety of the party. There's a small, wide staircase leading down to a large stone landing, with tall cocktail tables covered in pristine white cloths where well-dressed people congregate and rest drinks and small plates of appetizers. Another flight past that leads to another patio, this one with a small jazz band set up and a mostly empty dance floor. Beyond that, down a third flight of stairs, is the largest space, a stone patio surrounded by tiny white fairy lights. There's the warm red glow of a heat lamp where a man in white is carving some giant hunk of meat, a long buffet stretched out in gleaming silver beyond him. Waiters in white and black carry silver trays with tiny bites of food, gliding silently among the crowd as people pluck them from the trays.

"So, shall we get something to drink? The bartender will

put as many cherries in your Coke as you want," Pete says. He's got a smile on his face, but I notice he keeps digging his hands into his pockets, then pulling them out again.

"Can't beat that," I reply, though my stomach is jumping a little too much to add carbonation to the picture.

"Shit. Incoming," he mutters, and before I can ask *what* exactly is incoming, I hear a deep, gravelly voice roar, "Peter!"

A very large man with a salt-and-pepper beard is barreling through the crowd toward us like he's being pulled by a homing device. His white shirt strains over his ample belly, his bow tie slightly askew.

"Hello, George," Peter replies. "This is Maritza."

George's eyes flick over to me for a split second, but it's immediately clear he has no interest in me. He's got his conversation already lined up, and it appears that nothing and no one is going to stop him from having it. "Did you hear about the docking fees down at the marina? A ten percent hike! It's highway robbery! For that price, your excursion should come with a happy ending."

Pete's cheeks flush, and I have to bite back a laugh. This is apparently the infamous George of the miserable boat talk.

"Well, no, I hadn't heard about that, George, as I don't *have* a boat docked at the marina. Or a boat at all, as a matter of fact," Pete says, his tone dripping with sarcasm that sails right over George's head. The man is so involved in the conversation he's decided he's going to have that he doesn't appear to care if someone is actually having it with him.

"Yes, well, I'm thinking of looking at docking over on Amelia instead, but then who wants to drive across the bridge to get to their boat?"

He sputters on, a litany of indignities related to the care and keeping of his boat. As a waiter passes by me with a tray of shrimp, Pete turns and lunges for one, taking the moment to whisper, "Get out while you can. I'll fall on this grenade."

I bolt at his tone but am immediately sorry. Sure, listening to George sputter about swabbing the deck or whatever was boring as all get-out, but at least it was a thing to do. I pivot on my heel to go back, but then hear another weird maritime sex joke escape George's mouth and decide I'm better off going it alone.

If I'm going to be by myself, it's probably best to keep moving, like a shark who keeps swimming so as to avoid dying a social death. I start down the stairs. I pass the cocktail tables and the dance floor, then weave through the revelers until I'm at the far edge of the crowd. I pause, wondering if this is a good spot for invisibility or if I'll just look like a wallflower without an actual wall. I head off toward a corner of potted palms, my eyes on a low ledge where I can probably sit and wait out some of the party. On my way, I spot a bar, and thinking back to the apocalyptic predictions about a line, I figure I ought to go ahead and get a drink.

"What can I get for you, miss?" asks the waiter, a handsome guy who looks like he'll be headed to a fraternity party after this.

"Coke, please," I reply. "Two cherries," I add, remembering Pete's advice. I can't help but think back to my Sonic score just yesterday. Jeez, was that yesterday? It already feels like a life-time ago, when I had my feet up on Lainey's dash, bopping along to oldies while fishing cherries out of a Styrofoam cup. Now here I am watching middle-aged people bob their heads to jazz or some such background music while a guy in nicer clothes than I usually wear serves up as many cherries as I request. For free.

"Coming right up," he says. He fills a glass with ice and soda, then drops three cherries in. I guess two just isn't indul-gent enough in this crowd. "For you."

Popping the first cherry in my mouth, I turn and head back to the corner I scoped out earlier, but when I get close, I see that it's already occupied. A small group of people around my age are there. A guy in a suit is seated on a low wall and has a girl in a slinky red dress draped across his lap. Another girl in a silver strapless dress tosses back a drink, and I'm just about to turn and seek another hiding spot when the tall guy with broad shoulders turns, shaking his blond hair out of his eyes.

"Hey, you're from this morning," he says. It's Spencer.

"Oh, um, yeah. Hi," I reply, completely fumbling the greeting.

"Hey, guys, this is Maritza," he says. "She's staying with Kris."

"Oh, I love Kris!" coos the girl in the red, her arm slung around the neck of a guy with buzzed dark hair. "She made the *best* cupcakes for a bake sale I ran. You know, the one for the after-school program?"

"This is Bennett and Avery," Spencer says, gesturing to the couple seated on the wall, the names running together like a celebrity duo, Bennett-and-Avery. "And this is Ryleigh."

The girl in the silver dress grins at me, her red lipstick accentuating a wide mouth and a longer face. Her dark hair is already falling down from the delicate updo it must have started in, and her dress seems to be making a break for it both from above and below, as she keeps tugging at her cleavage and pulling on the hem.

A waiter sweeps by with a tray of something tall and bite-sized, artistically arranged on a cracker but bearing no resemblance to any food I've ever seen. Ryleigh reaches out and wordlessly plucks one from the tray, popping it into her mouth like a tortilla chip. As soon as she bites down, though, she makes a yuck face and swallows hard.

"Ugh, dill! I hate dill," she moans, then reaches for my glass and takes a long sip, swishing it around in her mouth. Her nose wrinkles for a second time. "Is this just Coke?"

"Yeah," I reply. *Just* Coke? I suddenly feel like I should apologize, even though *she* was the one who took *my* drink without even asking.

"Rookie mistake," Spencer says. He reaches into his jacket

pocket and produces a silver flask, something I've never seen outside of a James Bond movie. He expertly unscrews the cap with his fingers while holding it in his palm. "You want?"

"Don't be stingy!" Ryleigh says, reaching for the flask before I can say, *No, I definitely do* not *want.* She pours a hefty splash into the glass, stirs it around, and then takes a long pull. "Ah, that's better."

She passes the glass back to me like she's bestowing an enormous gift upon me, but now all I want is to get it out of my hands. Not only do I not drink, but I'm worried what might happen if Kris or Pete or anyone else catches me with it. Just holding it, I can smell the alcohol wafting from the ice.

"I, uh, need to go find Kris," I say. Spencer nods, but no one else even looks at me. They're already deep in their own conversation of in-jokes and friendly banter. It makes me homesick for Lainey. I miss our jokes and our easy conversation. Right now, I'd give anything to be on the couch watching *The Brady Bunch* with her. Will I ever get back there?

I tiptoe away slowly before turning and hustling through the crowd and up the stairs, taking deep breaths to steady my emotions. I will not cry. Not here. Not now. Not in front of these people. I distract myself by looking for someplace to stash my drink, finding it on top of an empty café table. I leave it behind like a spy doing a dead drop and quickly walk away. But I don't get far before I'm stopped again.

"Maritza, right?" A woman in a gorgeous emerald-green sheath smiles at me, and it only takes me a moment to place her as Spencer's mom, the activewear-clad woman from the store earlier. She has the same friendly smile and sparkling eyes, though tonight they're rimmed with some kind of shimmering makeup, her lips a pale pink.

"Yeah," I say, then realize I sound kind of trashy. I clear my throat. "Uh, yes."

"I'm Kate Ford," she says. "It's so nice that you could come."

"Oh, well, it was nice to be invited," I reply, though really, it was unofficially mandated that I be here. My name is definitely not on any list anywhere in this facility.

Mrs. Ford gazes around the party with a beatific smile, exuding the kind of calm, relaxed persona that I always associate with the people who take spa vacations.

"It's a *really* good cause," she says. She nods to a row of tables behind us loaded down with gifts and prizes, people scrawling bids onto auction sheets. I spot Pete standing behind a gilt-framed painting, George still beside him yammering on, oblivious to the pained expression on Pete's face. "The Jacksonville Community Clinic does *such* important work."

She launches into her talking brochure explanation of the clinic and their services, but I stop listening. I don't need to hear it. I've been there. Without health insurance, it's where I'd gone when I needed my MMR booster or a tetanus shot. I'd been in for strep a couple times, and bronchitis, and that time I stepped on a yellow jacket sophomore year and my foot turned all red and swelled up with hives, giving it the appearance of angry hamburger meat. I can practically smell the mix of linoleum and disinfectant in the waiting room, the buzz of cartoons on a TV overhead just barely distracting the kids from their long wait.

Still, I smile and nod like this is all new information, like I haven't been the recipient of the funds raised at events just like this. That the people drinking and dancing and bidding on rounds of golf and framed art aren't the reason why I got a prescription for amoxicillin just last month.

"Oh, excuse me, I see someone I really need to talk to," Kate says, nodding toward a woman in the crowd who is frantically waving her over.

"Sure, of course," I say, but she's already drifting away. Everyone here seems to be doing an awful lot of talking, but no one seems to be particularly connected with the person they're talking *to*. It's like they all arrived with an agenda, a script, and a mandate to tick all their boxes before climbing into their luxury SUVs and driving home. It's the least social social event I've ever been to.

I reach into my purse and glance at my phone. When I see that I've only been here less than thirty minutes, I realize this is going to be a long night, and all my attempts to blend in have left me spit out on the other end. I'm back at the top of the stairs, still alone, and I don't even have a Coke in my hand to show for it. It may be time for some good old-fashioned hiding out in the bathroom.

Which I do, for a good half hour. I listen to women drift in and out, having shockingly candid conversations for a public restroom. I learn that someone named Angela caught her husband with the nanny *again*, and she's starting to think she'll have to fire her. I overhear a woman fumbling through her purse, searching for a spare Xanax. I know that's what she's looking for because she literally says *out loud*, "Now where is my *fucking* Xanax?" I hear two women discuss the point at which they'll finally break down and send their teenage daughters to weight-loss clinics with the same intensity that I usually associate with college admissions.

By the time I decide I can't hide any longer, I'm thoroughly disgusted and thinking that maybe my life, though shabby and unconventional, isn't actually that bad. Would I really want to trade what I have, crappy apartment and all, for nice clothes and obnoxious neighbors? Maybe my mom, though flaky, was right whenever she railed against consumerism. If she could see me now, she'd probably sigh and shake her head. *That dress is nice, Ritzy*, she'd say, *but is it prescription-drug-addiction nice?*

Eventually I leave the bathroom and wander deeper into the Island Club. I wind down hallways covered in photos of golf teams, a plaque celebrating all the holes in one (hole in ones?) dating back fifty years. There are framed portraits from ladies' luncheons and a couple autographed pictures of celebrities I vaguely recognize toasting on the patio or hitting golf balls. I keep going until the wood and carpet gives way to linoleum and the light fixtures take on a neon glow overhead. I pause in front of a corkboard covered in notices, none of them aimed at club members. There's a page advertising uniform ordering and something with instructions on clocking in. There's a list of health code violations and the required workplace safety placard.

And then a pink flyer catches my eye.

HIRING FOR SUMMER
DISHWASHERS
SERVERS
LINE COOKS
$12/HR

There's an email address and a phone number, and the bottom is cut into those little pull-off strips. I flash back to the email I sent to Mr. Reynolds at the sandwich shop, and the smell of the Del Taco drive-in fills my nose, equal parts melted cheese, grease, and gasoline. Sure, this is still food service, but it's classy food service, right? And with no update on when I might be leaving here, it would probably be a good idea to try to line something up. It would be nice to have my own money in my pocket instead of letting Kris buy me things, and that might make it easier for me to get comfortable here.

"Sucks, all the good jobs are already taken."

Spencer's wandering down the hall toward me, a glass in

his hand, his tie loose, his hair still characteristically askew. I can't see exactly what's in his glass, but the redness in his cheeks and the lazy amble of his gait point to the contents of his flask.

"Good jobs?" I ask.

"Lifeguard, camp counselor, beach attendant, that kind of thing. People start lining those up around spring break."

It takes me a moment to realize what he's saying. "Do *you* work here?"

"Yeah. I teach tennis lessons a few days a week," he replies, reminding me of his mid-court meltdown the previous night. "Avery is a pool attendant, Bennett is a lifeguard, and Annie works at the kids' camp."

"Really?" I say.

He arches an eyebrow at me. "You're surprised?"

I pause, wondering how honest to get, and then I figure, *Hell, just go with it.* The less honest I am, the more I become like the people here, and then I'll have completely lost myself. "It didn't occur to me that any of you guys would have summer jobs."

He smirks. "Ah, so you pegged us rich kids for obnoxious layabouts glomming off our parents' money?"

"No, it's just—" I say, then pause, the mental dominoes falling into place. Somehow, he's got me pegged for *not* a rich kid.

He shrugs. "I know your deal. Kris and my mom are good friends. And word on the street is, you and I built sand-castles together when we were babies," he replies. I hate the familiarity in his tone. Whatever his mom told him, he definitely does *not* know my "deal." He doesn't know anything about me.

"Well, I'm sure you have plenty of stereotypes in your head about me," I reply.

"None, actually," he says, his eyes on me like a challenge. He reaches up and plucks one of the strips from the bottom of the flyer and presses it into my palm. "Dining room jobs suck, but you might as well apply. At least the tips are good."

He turns to go before I can say anything, but halfway down the hall he pauses. "And then we could hang out this summer. Maybe try our hand at that sandcastle thing again."

I stand there stock-still in front of the corkboard, the strip with the email and phone number growing increasingly damp in my hand. What just happened? Was he flirting with me? Or just being friendly?

I wait for him to get far enough away so it won't look like I'm tailing him through the club. I give myself nearly to a hundred Mississippi before I make my way back to the party. When I emerge onto the patio, I run into Kris.

"I'm so sorry I was busy, Maritza," she says with a heavy sigh. "I saw Pete still being held hostage by George. Why that man has latched onto my husband, I'll never know. But what do you say we go rescue him and get out of here?"

"Are you sure? I mean, if you need to stay . . . ," I say, though I do desperately want to get out of here.

"I did my duty, Pete did his, and now we're done. Plus, I'm dying to get out of these shoes." Hearing that her time on four-inch heels wasn't as effortless as it looked has me feeling better about my own inability to walk in a fancy dress, which makes me smile the first genuine smile I've had since we arrived.

The drive home isn't as silent as the one to the club. Kris tells me tales of party-planning disasters and speaks wryly about her compatriots on the committee that put on the event. It sounds as though Kris lives among them but is also somehow apart from these women, somehow different, though I can't yet put my finger on how. Maybe it's the same thing that spurred her to take in a foster kid and care for her as her own for nearly two years. Maybe it's the same thing that brought her onto that porch last night, waiting for me sixteen years later. But it does make me feel like living with her isn't the same as living with the fat-camp moms or the drugged-out ladies from the bathroom would be. It makes me think maybe my mom's snap judgment of her wouldn't be right.

As we pull into their driveway, Kris twists around in her seat to face me. "So, is your friend coming over tomorrow?"

The thought of Lainey here gives me that last push toward feeling better about tonight.

"Yeah, I just need to text her details."

"Great! I look forward to meeting her." She turns back to face forward, but the smile on her face is practically audible.

I quickly pull out my phone and text Lainey.

1423 Bayshore Drive, Helena. Bring a bathing suit.

Arriving home, I spot lights on over at Spencer's house. No light on at the tennis court, though. Maybe I'll actually be able to sleep tonight.

CHAPTER EIGHT

BARNEY ARRIVES JUST BEFORE LUNCH, shuddering to a stop, something under the hood doing its usual clunk, clunk, crank after the engine shuts off. It's a testament to how much Lainey and Barney are soul mates that the car is still running even when odds say he should fall apart in the middle of the road. He just keeps chugging for her. Barney has never broken down, never even had so much as a flat tire. I swear, someone bewitched that car.

A perk of Barney's noisy arrival is that I can rush out onto the porch to greet her. Lainey climbs out of the driver's seat, an oversized tank top covering her bathing suit, then leans over to pull her beach bag off the passenger seat. She slings it over her shoulder, tucks her sunglasses into the messy bun on top of her head, and saunters up onto the porch.

"Well, look at you, Miss Fancy Pants," she says, winking, before throwing her arms wide and enveloping me in a hug.

"Whatever," I mumble into her hair as we rock back and

forth. I breathe in the familiar peachy smell of her favorite body lotion that she drives all the way to the Galleria across town to buy. Tears prick my eyes, because even though it's only been a day and a half, I've missed her.

She pulls back just in time to see me wiping my eyes, which I'm sure are growing redder by the second.

"Oh, you stupid sap, suck it up! Besides, you've gotta tell me what's going on, and I don't want to have to figure it out between sobs, okay?"

"I don't even know where to begin," I reply.

She gestures to the porch, the yard, the blue of the ocean glittering in the sun, just visible in the backyard. Then she throws an arm around my shoulder and pulls me in again. "Maybe start with all this?"

As I lead Lainey into the house, I try to see it again for the first time, this time without the terror and confusion of my initial arrival. Lainey keeps her cool, but I see her eyebrows rise as we walk into the kitchen, where Kris is tapping away on her laptop at the island. I can already hear her mind churning about tile and flooring and cabinetry. She watches entirely too much HGTV.

"You must be Lainey," Kris says, looking up over the top of her laptop. She's smiling, but not nearly as effusive as she was when I arrived. She seems distracted, her eyes going from us to her computer, even as she greets Lainey. Her smile doesn't reach her eyes.

"Nice to meet you," Lainey replies. She's even better with

grown-ups than I am. I've seen her charm even our sternest of assistant principals.

"Welcome to Helena, Lainey. Beach chairs and towels are in the garden shed, and help yourself to any snacks you want. Let me know if you need anything." She's rattling it off like a cruise director.

"Thanks," we reply in unison, and I grab Lainey by the hand and drag her out the back door before she can start in on a conversation on the perks of gas versus electric stoves.

The garden shed turns out to be more like how I'd envision a pool house. The walls are painted a light aqua, with gleaming white molding around the room. A workbench takes up one entire wall, as organized as the kitchen and the office (at least, Kris's side), not a color-coordinated tool out of place.

In the corner, a shelving unit contains a stack of fluffy yellow beach towels. We each grab one along with a white folding lounge chair from the rack next to it.

"I've never actually been to a country club, but I feel like these amenities are nicer," Lainey says. "Which means you basically *live* at a fancier country club."

"Okay, well, I have now been to a country club, though I can't speak for the amenities. But remind me to tell you about it when we get down to the water."

"Fancy indeed," Lainey singsongs in an exaggerated British accent.

We set up on a patch of white sand, the waves lapping lazily at the shore. I pull off my T-shirt and cutoffs, dropping them in a pile next to my chair, then slip off my flip-flops and turn them sole side up to keep them from heating up like a skillet in the afternoon sun (a trick every Floridian learns after the first time they cook their feet as a kid).

We settle into our chairs, and the silence settles right around us, thick like the humidity. I can tell Lainey is waiting for an explanation, but I wasn't kidding when I said I didn't know where to start. Because the real beginning is the note in the kitchen and my mom disappearing. Only I missed the window to tell that part of the story. I didn't mean to lie to my best friend. It just sort of happened, and now I have to undo it.

Lainey huffs out a sigh. "Ritzy, just talk, okay?"

I swallow the lump in my throat. "So, a couple weeks ago my mom went to Mexico to study, like, transcendental mind reading or something, and I have no idea when she's coming back. Which is apparently a big deal since I'm not eighteen yet, so technically I'm in foster care. This is foster care."

Lainey's eyes grow wide. "First of all, this is not foster care. This is damn lucky," Lainey says, her eyes taking in the blue horizon. "Second, *why didn't you tell me?*"

"I don't know," I tell her. "It's just, it just happened, okay? I mean, I wasn't sure if she really left. And then I felt sort of crazy, and the longer it went, the harder it was to say, *Hey, my mom abandoned me.*"

"That doesn't make any sense, Ritzy."

"I know. I feel like nothing has for a while. I'm sorry."

The silence settles back between us, and I rack my brain for something to say to make things okay. I just need to know that we're still friends, that she's not going to leave me, too.

"Young Ryan Gosling on your right," Lainey says, her voice low.

Oh, thank god.

Lainey and I are pros at spotting celebrities. It's our favorite game. No, not actual celebrities. They never show up at Covina Beach. They're probably all at places like this, come to think of it. Private beaches and strips of sand, away from prying eyes.

No, Lainey and I are champions at spotting celebrity doppelgängers, from the A-list Oscar winners all the way down to the Z-list reality TV competitors and stars of regional commercials. On any given day, we can find Beyoncé in the parking lot, wrangling two tote bags and a rolling cooler; Ben Affleck in the lifeguard chair; and the weatherman from the community access channel sunning himself in a neon-green Speedo (although that may have actually been him).

And now this moment of normalcy, of familiarity, feels like a warm blanket. I lower my sunglasses on my nose and follow Lainey's gaze down the beach. A tanned, shirtless guy in a pair of black running shorts is jogging toward us, his stride labored as he charges through the sand. His blond hair, drenched with sweat, flops over his left eye, bouncing with each heavy step.

Spencer.

As he gets closer, I wonder if he'll stop and talk. I hope he does, because that'll *definitely* get Lainey talking. I'd love to hear her trademark cutting response to Spencer's showy personality. But he's nearly upon our chairs, and his stride doesn't slow. Instead, he raises his hand to his forehead and gives us a little two-fingered salute, accompanied by a huffed-out "Hey." And then we're watching his glistening, muscled back as he jogs away.

Damn.

Lainey turns and lowers her sunglasses dramatically down her nose. "Hold up, do you *know* young Gosling?"

I hope the heat of the afternoon masks the blush I can feel creeping into my cheeks. "Yeah, I mean, I met him yesterday. He's really . . . friendly?"

"You mean flirty," she says, reading between the lines.

"It doesn't seem flirty. It's more . . . asshole-ish?"

"That's not a word."

"You know what I mean."

Lainey's gaze is fixed on the last dot of Spencer as he disappears down the beach. "Yeah, I think I do."

The silence descends again. It feels awful. I miss my friend more than ever now that she's finally sitting right next to me.

"Ali says to tell you hi."

I suck in a salty breath. "You talked to him?"

"Yeah, a bunch of us crammed into Francie's mom's minivan and hit the drive-in last night."

I'm jealous. While I was feeling out of place at a country

club, all my friends were hanging out with my number one crush.

Lainey looks at me sideways. "Have you heard from him?"

"No," I reply. "But that might be because I haven't texted him?"

"Ritzy!"

"What? I don't know what to say! The last time I talked to him, I was canceling our date to pack up and get in the car with a social worker. I mean, he got all the way to my house before I even remembered. He's got to think I blew him off. How do you come back from that?"

"Um, by telling him the truth?"

"What do you mean?"

She gives me a look. "C'mon, Ritzy. Tell him what happened. Tell him about your mom, and that you're staying here. He'll understand why your head wasn't on the date, so he won't think you blew him off."

My heart practically stops.

"Does he think that?"

"He didn't say that, but he definitely seemed bummed that you guys didn't get to go out."

"Okay, but what did he say *exactly*?"

Lainey sighs. "Just that you said there was a family emergency. And he made air quotes when he said that, which leads me to believe maybe he thinks it's a line? I don't know, I told him you really did have something going on."

"Did you tell him where I am? Or why I'm here?"

"No. Because if you recall, *I* didn't know." She gives me a look, and I know I'm not totally forgiven. "Seriously, just tell Ali the truth. The whole truth. He'll totally get it."

I shake my head. "His parents are, like, storybook married, running the restaurant together. They'll probably die in each other's arms when they're ninety-five. I don't want him to see me as, I don't know, *troubled*."

"He's not going to think that, but if that's your decision, then I'll say whatever you want me to say," she says, her voice heavy with the advice she wishes I'd take. "But still, text him anyway. Just to say hi, you know? I mean, I'll totally come pick you up and bring you into Jax if you want to try to set up another date with him."

"Ugh, *I* have to be the one to set up the date?"

"That's what happens when you cancel. Time to be a modern woman and ask the dude out," Lainey explains. "Come *on*, it's Ali. He's, like, the nicest guy in the world, and he already asked you out once. You know he's interested. This will be the easiest ask-out in the history of ask-outs."

I shrug, and she lets me leave it at that.

We stare out at the ocean for a few minutes, silently watching the waves roll in.

"Seriously, though. Why didn't you tell me?" Lainey finally says.

"About Ali?"

"No, about your mom," Lainey says. "She's been gone a while, but you didn't say anything. I don't want to make this about me, but what the hell, Ritzy? I could have helped or something. You could have come to stay with me."

I sigh. It's a question I've asked myself a thousand times, one I hoped Lainey herself would never ask. "I wish I had a good answer. I don't know. Maybe I figured she'd be back? It was just so embarrassing. Like, whose mom just disappears?"

"Yours, apparently," she replies. "I know what you mean, I guess. Your mom's always been sort of weird, but I never figured she'd do something like this."

"Yep. Psychics and yogis and gurus, sure. But walk out on her kid? I never saw that one coming."

"Still, you shouldn't have lied to me."

"I didn't lie."

She arches an eyebrow at me, a lethal look that I wish I could replicate. "You didn't tell me the truth."

I'm quiet, because I don't have anything else to say. She's right. I might as well have lied. To my best friend, who definitely would have helped. But I kept my mouth shut like an idiot.

"I'm sorry," I whisper, tears welling up in my eyes.

She stands up out of her chair and comes to lean on mine, throwing her arm around me. "I'm not trying to make you feel guilty, Ritz. I promise. Just . . . no more secrets, okay? Especially with you living all the way out here. We've gotta be honest with each other."

I nod, returning her hug with a squeeze of my own.

We spend the few hours in the sun composing the perfect

text to Ali that I promise I'll send to him later when I've worked up my nerve, then coming up with plans for what Ali and I could do on the date. Lainey fills me in on the stories from her usual library patrons, including her impression of the eighty-year-old woman who comes in to browse Christian singles sites, but always needs assistance with "the interwebs." It has me laughing until tears are practically squirting out of my eyes. We speculate on what level of famous people might spend their summer on Helena (we land on maybe some of the second stringers from the Jaguars. It seems more like a standard rich-people haunt as opposed to a celebrity getaway). By the time we're done, we've both got questionable tan lines and sore abs from laughter.

"Hey, so I should probably get back soon. My mom has the night off, so we're going to go to the Chinese buffet for dinner. The one with those amazing garlic string beans."

When we get back to Barney, Lainey tosses her bag on the front seat and turns to give me a hug.

"Let me know if you need a ride anywhere, okay? Anytime, no questions asked."

"Thanks," I say, pulling away before I start to cry. "And you can come out here whenever. I don't know how long I'll be here, but we can totally hang on the beach. Anytime, no questions asked."

"Oh, I will. As long as the sun's shining, at least," she says with a wink.

"You are *literally* a fair-weather friend."

"Keep me posted on what's going on with"—she pauses, then sweeps her arm around the expanse of the property—"all of *this*. And no more secrets, okay?"

I nod. "Okay."

"Seriously. I'm just a text away. You can even *call*, like the olden days."

She pulls me into another hug. I get another whiff of her peachy lotion and feel tears prick my eyes. I'm glad she came. But I wish she didn't have to leave.

CHAPTER NINE

A WEEK. I'VE BEEN HERE A WEEK, AND after the awkward charity event, I'd decided it was probably safer to stay close to home. Which meant a week of sitting by the beach making my way first through the books in my suitcase, and then into the stash of romance novels Kris keeps in the corner of her office. It was a week of polite, surface-level chitchat with Kris, who was always trying to cook me something or plan an outing, and Pete, who talked to me like I was a running buddy. A week of trying unsuccessfully to work up the courage to ask Kris about our shared history or ask Pete about *any* of his. A week of chickening out.

I'm exhausted from trying so hard to be relaxed.

On Friday afternoon, I come trudging up to find Kris in the kitchen, just like every other day, paging through cookbooks or prepping ingredients for the evening's meal. Pete was right, Kris is definitely the chef of the family, and in the week that I've been here, we haven't eaten a single meal she hasn't made from scratch. No boxes, no jars, no powdered flavor packets. Today she's attaching a metal monstrosity to her pristine countertop that looks like an instrument of torture meant to extract information from a murder suspect.

"I'm making pasta," she says, as easily as if she'd said she was making a peanut butter sandwich. To me, "making pasta" means opening the box of spaghetti or penne if you're feeling fancy. Until this very moment, it hadn't even occurred to me that pasta was *made* anywhere but the factories of Barilla, Mueller, or Kraft.

Kris has her hands deep in some dough when the phone rings. "Can you grab that?"

"Hi, Maritza," comes the voice from the other end, perky and professional with a hint of southern twang.

"Hi, Tess." My heartbeat starts to accelerate, slowly at first, then all at once into a great pounding rhythm. Because this could be it, the answer to my uncertain future. Have they found my mother? Is she coming back? "How's it going?"

"Oh, busy, busy, as usual," she says, and in the background, I hear what sounds like a crying baby and some clattering around. "Listen, I'm calling to fill you in on a few things. Do you have a minute?"

I nod, then remember that it's a phone call and she can't see me. "Yeah," I say. I pull out a chair at the kitchen table and plop down, turning my back to Kris, who I can tell is listening but trying not to.

"Okay, so we've got a hearing scheduled for Monday. You'll

go before a judge, mostly just to update everyone on where we are in this process. It won't take a long time."

"Have you heard from my mom?"

"We reached out to the, uh—" I hear some rustling of papers in the background. "The Bodhi Foundation? Yes, that's it. We called, but they refused to give out any information about their guests. We also sent a letter, so maybe that will wind up in her hands, if she's still there."

"Do I need to wear anything? Like, is this a dress-up thing?"

"You can wear whatever you want, but I think it's always a good idea to present yourself how you wish people to see you."

I can tell that's social-worker talk for *Wear nice clothes so people think you're nice, but I don't want you to feel bad if you don't have nice clothes.*

"Is Kris there? I've got a few things to discuss with her."

"Yeah, she's right here."

I turn and see that Kris still has her hands buried in pasta dough, which she must have been kneading this whole time.

"Tess wants to talk to you," I say, and hold the phone out to her. She practically leaps toward the sink, where she rinses the flour and goo off her hands, then takes the phone.

⁓

The hearing takes place at the county courthouse in Jacksonville. I figure I need to look presentable, so I'm wearing my only pair of khaki pants, along with a tank top and a cardigan, the borrowed black flats from Kris back on my feet. I keep running my hands over my hair, trying to smooth the curls and tame the frizz, but it's becoming a nervous habit and I'm worried it's just making the whole situation worse.

Kris and Pete are also dressed up—Pete in a suit and tie, Kris in a floral sundress with a blazer on top. They look like Sunday-school teachers, and I wonder if they're worried about what impression they'll be making, too.

"All parties in the matter of Maritza Reed please report to courtroom four." The voice crackles over the intercom, and the noise of everyone waiting in the lobby lowers to a hush as we all strain to hear if our case is being called. We've apparently all been given the same arrival time, but the order in which we are called seems totally random, like someone back there is just drawing names out of a hat. Hearing my name is a relief, but it also sends me into a panic. Immediately I feel sweat start forming under my arms. I hope I won't have damp spots on my sweater when I'm standing in front of the judge. Suddenly every little thing feels like it could make a difference in what happens to me in there. What will the judge think if I'm sweaty? What will he think about the tiny moth hole at the hem of my cardigan? What will he think of my messy hair, my shaking hands, or my voice, which will be sure to quiver or crack when I'm forced to speak?

Tess is with us, too. She's dressed in her sassy professional clothes, her overstuffed leather bag heaved over her shoulder as she stands and cocks her head for us to follow. We push through the door to find a windowless room painted gray, with gray institutional carpet. It doesn't look anything like on TV, where the courtrooms all have dark, carved wood and big windows, with the lawyers' feet click-clacking on the shiny wood floors. The only thing that looks remotely judicial is the black robe on the judge, who is sitting at an elevated podium at the front of the room. Tess leads me up to a table near the front, where a young guy in a suit is already seated, a folder on the table in front of him.

"Maritza, this is Justin Fellows," Tess says, and Justin stands and holds out his hand to shake. "He's your court-appointed lawyer."

"Oh, okay," I reply, my voice halting. This guy looks like he's maybe seventeen, like he had to get a pass out of homeroom to be my lawyer today.

"Don't worry, having a lawyer doesn't mean you did anything wrong," he says with a warm smile, and though he looks young, he sounds self-assured, so I try to relax. "I'm just here to represent your interest. I can answer any of the legal questions for you when we're done."

"Okay," I say again.

"It's going to be easy," Tess says for probably the tenth time this morning. "Remember, just answer the questions when the judge asks. It'll be very clear."

"Okay." I wish I had more to contribute, but my heart is

pounding too hard for me to come up with anything else to say.

The judge slams his gavel on the desk in front of us, sending my heart into my throat. But before I can really start to panic, he smiles a nice, wide smile. He's old, someone I'd describe as a grandpa, though I really never know if someone like that is fifty or seventy. He's got bushy gray hair and little wire-rimmed glasses. He looks like he's about to ask me what I want for Christmas.

"Welcome, everyone. We're here to do our preliminary hearing for minor child, ah"—he glances over the top of his glasses at a stack of papers in front of him—"Maritza Reed. Maritza, that's you, I take it?"

"Yes," I say. "I mean, yes, Your Honor."

He laughs. "Don't worry about formalities, Miss Reed. Just talk to me like I'm normal people, okay?"

"Okay. I mean, yes." I cringe. I've been saying "okay" so much it's like I don't actually speak the language.

Then the hearing begins, and there's a bunch of technical jargon that sounds vaguely like something I've heard on TV. I only sort of understand what they're talking about. Everyone gets introduced, including Justin, Tess, Kris, and Pete. Tess tells the judge my story and answers a few questions. And then there's a long silence.

Because they're waiting for me to talk. Everyone is looking at me.

"I'm sorry, what was the question?" I ask. Of course I'm screwing this up already.

"I just wanted to hear, in your words, what happened, Maritza," the judge says.

"Oh, well, okay," I say, wondering where to begin. How much context does he really need? Do I need to explain about my mother's constant search for inner peace or whatever? But he must do this a lot, because he smiles again and says, "Just start with the last time you saw your mother."

"Right. Well, it was about two weeks ago. She said she was going to stay at this place, the Bodhi Foundation? I think it's this school for meditation or something, and she said she was going to go study. And the next day she left."

"Did she tell you when she'd be back? Or if she'd be back?"

"She said she could be there for up to six months, but she wasn't super clear, no. I don't really know the details."

"That's just fine, Maritza." He shuffles some papers on his desk. "And what attempts have been made to find Marybelle Reed?"

Tess opens her folder. "Ms. Reed does not have a cell phone, so we're forced to rely on alternate methods of communication. On Monday, I called the number listed for the Bodhi Foundation, but was unable to reach Ms. Reed or even confirm if she was there. That same day I sent a certified letter regarding the DCF case. I followed up with a letter regarding the hearing information. I have yet to receive any communication from her or confirmation of her whereabouts."

The judge nods, a little V of concern forming between his eyebrows. "Okay, well, in the absence of the custodial parent, we're looking at an abandonment case under Florida statute. So let's go ahead and create our permanency plan with the idea that Ms. Reed will reappear, noting that if there has been no contact within sixty days, parental rights will be severed."

He continues talking, with Tess and Justin chiming in about future hearing dates and details, but I completely stop listening as soon as I hear the part about parental rights being severed. Sixty days? That's it? By the end of the summer, if my mother doesn't emerge from whatever meditative trance she's climbed into, she could wind up not being my mother anymore?

I have that distinct dizzy feeling that accompanies waking up from a very deep sleep and not knowing where you are. A week ago I was getting ready for summer and looking ahead to senior year. I had a job and friends and a date with my crush. I had a mom. Now I'm standing in a courtroom while a judge talks about turning me into a legal orphan.

Where is she?

It was one thing when staying with Kris was just a temporary, if extended, solution. But to hear that it might very well become permanent? I don't trust my mom to answer a letter within sixty days, even if she wanted to. That's just not her style. And that could wind up costing me my only parent. I want to scream out, *Wait! You don't understand! This has all gone way too far!* But before I know it, the gavel slams and a security guard is ushering us back through the door. In the lobby, another group stands as they hear their case being called over the intercom.

"Well, I'll see you all in thirty days for our next hearing," Tess says. "Of course, I'll be in touch if I hear anything from Maritza's mother, and you're welcome to contact me at any point with any questions."

"Tess will get in contact with me if there are any legal issues," Justin adds, passing Kris a business card. "But of course you can always reach out to me as well. Otherwise, I'll see you back here next month."

"Thank you," Kris says, and all the adults shake hands. Then they all smile at me, and I realize once again everyone's waiting for me to speak.

"Thank you," I say, a sort of sweeping blanket expression of gratitude to the group. It's the best I can do.

I follow Kris and Pete back to the parking garage, climbing into the back seat of the Prius. Pete starts up the car, which makes no noise. Kris twists around in the front seat.

"Do you have any questions?" she asks.

I have a million questions, all circling me like a cloud of gnats. But I can only take a swipe at one.

"Sixty days? If they don't hear from her in sixty days, legally she's abandoned me?"

Kris takes a deep breath. "That's what the judge says."

That doesn't seem like enough time. My mom said she could be at that foundation place for six *months*. And if she doesn't pick up a phone or answer a letter, that's *it*.

"So I'm sort of in limbo for sixty days?"

"No! I mean, I guess legally, yes. But you live with us. And you'll stay with us as long as necessary. No matter what happens, you'll always have a place with us here. It's important to me that you know that."

Pete shifts in his seat, but he doesn't say anything. Instead, he puts the car in reverse, then pulls quietly out of the parking garage. Damn these stupid hybrid cars and their silent engines, making it blatantly obvious that there is a gaping silence between all of us. I wonder if Pete realized when I showed up at the house on Friday that he might just be gaining something like a daughter. The thought makes *me* squirm; I can't imagine what he must be thinking. But Pete seems to specialize in saying nothing at all.

CHAPTER TEN

I'M OUT OF BED EARLY ON SATURDAY MORN-
ing, despite having stayed up far too late the night before. I
shower and head down to the kitchen, where I find Kris and
Pete. He's still in his running gear, attacking a plateful of
eggs. She's paging through a thick binder, a highlighter in her
hair and a pen in her teeth. At my appearance, they both stop
what they're doing and look up, their faces full of questions. I
know how they feel.

"How are you doing?" Kris asks as I pull a bowl from the
cabinet and a box of granola from the pantry.

"I'm okay," I say. I decided last night, as I lay in bed not
sleeping but doing a whole lot of thinking, that I'd stop being
so "on my best behavior" all the time and try my hand at being
more honest. Frankly, the act is exhausting. "Yesterday was . . .
not the greatest."

"I'm so sorry, Maritza," Kris says, closing her binder. She
caps her highlighter and places it on top of the binder, perfectly

lined up with the title on the front: *Issues in Alzheimer's Care*. "Like I said last night, you are always welcome here, so don't feel like that's in any way unstable."

"I don't," I say, and I mean it. Before I went to bed last night, I pulled everything out of my suitcase, putting my books on the shelf by the window and my clothes in the drawers. I took all my toiletries out of the shopping bag I'd brought them in, placed them on the counter and in the cabinet, and threw the bag away. I slid my suitcase, now empty, under the bed.

I moved in.

I pour myself a bowl of granola, but before I drench it in the fancy organic milk Kris buys that comes in a glass bottle, I pull the slip of paper from my pocket. It's crumpled, but you can still make out the phone number and email address on the pink paper.

"I think I'm going to call about a job at the Island Club," I tell them. There's a pause as they share a glance.

"You really don't have to do that," Kris says. "We're happy to provide whatever—"

"I know you are, and I appreciate it. And I'm sure I'm still going to need a lot from you. But I would feel better having some of my own spending money. I also think I'll get bored lounging around all summer. Having a job will give me something to do outside the house. And maybe I'll even meet some people."

Pete looks impressed. "I think that sounds like a great

idea," he says, then pauses, gazing at me expectantly. "You look like you have more to say?"

"I do." I nod. "I'm going to need to go pack up the rest of the stuff in my old apartment. There's not much, but the landlord's not going to hold it past the end of the month."

"Well, I'd be happy to go with you and do that," Kris says.

"I know, but I think, if you don't mind, I'd like to do it with Lainey."

I see Kris's brow furrow, but again, Pete comes to the rescue. "We can clear out some space in the attic to store boxes. You pack everything up, and if you need help transporting it all, you let us know. Otherwise, I'll be here to carry them up."

"Thanks. I want to get it done today. My friends back in Jacksonville are having a beach day, so I figured I could go do that, and then after that, Lainey and I could pack up."

Kris looks like it's killing her not to have a job in all this other than to agree, but it's a testament to her desire to help that she's willing to give me that.

"Just call me your fairy god-friend!"

Lainey opens Barney's trunk to several shopping bags filled with packages of paper towels and what look like cleaning supplies.

"There are a bunch of boxes underneath that I flattened, but we can get more. The guy at the liquor store around the corner from my house was fine with me scavenging," she says. I want to hug her, because I hadn't thought to pick up any of this stuff. "We are getting that deposit back if it kills us."

"You're my hero. Seriously," I tell her. I load my arms up with the plastic handles of shopping bags, while Lainey scoops up a giant stack of cardboard boxes in her arms. "We can use trash bags for the clothes. Too many boxes will be hard to cram in the car."

"Yup, I picked up a box of the giant black ones," she says. "They're in one of the bags."

We cross the hot blacktop and head up the stairs to 12C, my home for the last year and a half. But I guess this will be the last day of that. I unlock the door, shoving it open with my knee as my arms start to shake with the weight of the bags. Inside, the familiar smell of dust and something burnt from Mrs. Sazonov's apartment fills my nose. I'd forgotten about that smell, or maybe I'd just stopped noticing it. But living at Kris's, which always smells like essential oils and baked goods, suddenly makes me realize how noxious the odor is in here.

"Okay, so game plan," I say, dropping the grocery bags just inside the door. "Clothes in black trash bags, bulky stuff in the boxes. Use the white trash bags under the sink for actual trash, so we know what goes in the dumpsters versus what goes in the car."

"Aye, aye, captain," Lainey says. She gives me a quick salute, then digs in a plastic shopping bag for a roll of packing tape, setting about taping a box to prepare to fill it.

While she does that, I find the box of black trash bags, ripping it open to pull one off the roll. Then I head straight back to my mom's room. I want to get that one done as soon as possible. When I open the door, the room is pitch-black, the shades drawn tight. When I try to flick on the light, nothing happens, and I wonder how long the bulb has been out.

I cross the floor and open the shades, clouds of dust spinning in little tornadoes in the sunbeams now streaming in. My mother, never much of a housekeeper, at least contained her mess to her own room. Which is an utter disaster. There are clothes strewn about from one end to the other, with no indication as to what's clean and what's dirty. It looks like the "after" scene in a movie makeover montage, where the main character tries on everything in her closet and tosses it around while some boppy pop song plays in the background. I shake out the trash bag and start scooping and dumping, not caring if things are inside out or zipped, or if shoes are winding up with their mates. There are several half-finished knitting projects still on needles, big skeins of yarn dragging behind them like anchors. I dump them into the bag, needles and all. Just get it packed, that's my only goal.

I fill one trash bag, then two. I'm midway through the third when I've cleaned everything off the floor and bed and swiped everything out of her closet. There's so much strewn about that it almost doesn't occur to me to check in the dresser drawers. No one who kept her clothes in such a state used her dresser, right? Still, I know it'll nag at me if I don't check, so I start pulling out drawers. As I suspected, they're mostly empty. A few lone socks waiting in one (their mates woefully absent), a ratty old T-shirt that probably only had life left as a dustrag in another. Still, I toss everything in the third bag, because I don't know what has meaning to her, and besides, I have room before I close this one up. I tell myself that's the reason, and not because there's any lingering part of me that thinks she might come back.

When I open the bottom drawer, I find the only thing in the entire room that is folded up. It's an old beach towel, the colors once vibrant, I imagine, but now faded, the edges frayed. I reach for it and find that it's folded around something more solid. I unwrap the towel and find an oversized manila envelope, crinkled and worn. On the front, hastily scrawled in an unfamiliar hand, is my name.

I glance over my shoulder, like my mother is going to pop out and chastise me for going through her things, but of course I could just yell back, *You're in Mexico and also a figment of my imagination! Plus, this has my name on it!* Then I flip the envelope over and pop open the little metal prongs on the closure. They don't bend that easy, and I have to use a fingernail to get under one side, telling me that this envelope is very old and hasn't been opened very often. I peek inside and find a stack of paper and more envelopes, these white like bills.

I turn the entire thing upside down and let the contents fall onto the carpet in front of me. My birth certificate is there, along with my Social Security card. I set those aside immediately, knowing they'll come in handy, especially if my mother never comes back. There's a brown file folder, the kind with the bracket inside to hold the papers in. As soon as I open it, I see the words FLORIDA DEPARTMENT OF CHILDREN AND FAMILIES. My hands start to shake, my breath catching in my throat. The top looks like a standard biographical form, the kind you'd fill out to register for school or a gymnastics class. There's my name and birthday, and an address I don't recognize: 865 Walker Road, Jacksonville. My mother's name is there, my father's name blank, as usual.

At the bottom, folded up into a little square, is a piece of newspaper. I have to be careful as I unfold it, because age has made it tissue thin, the folds ready to let go at any moment. I smooth it out on the back of the file folder, careful not to smudge the ink.

LOCAL ORGANIC FARM RAIDED
by Susannah Womack, staff reporter

Acting on an anonymous tip, police and agents from the Drug Enforcement Agency raided Plough and Stars, an artist colony and cooperative farm, in the early hours of Friday morning. Police, accompanied by agents with the Drug Enforcement Agency, raided the property at 865 Walker Road after reports that the farm was growing marijuana for distribution.

The property, owned by commune leader Joshua Boland and his wife, Louisa, features several small homes and approximately twenty acres of farmland.

More than 40 adults and 12 children, ranging in age from six months to 13 years old, were said to be living on the property. The minors were taken into custody by the Florida Department of Children and Families, where they will be placed in foster care until an investigation can be completed. The adult residents were processed by the Jacksonville Sheriff's Office. Several have since been released on bail.

Plough and Stars can regularly be found at farmers' markets around northeast Florida selling organic fruits and vegetables. Several members of the commune are also noted artists, with works displayed at local galleries.

"At this time, we're interviewing members of the commune and trying to determine who knew what and who is culpable," Detective Lance Brown said. "We're working cooperatively with the DEA, DCF, the Department of Agriculture, and others to get the facts and ensure the minor children are cared for."

I read the article six or seven times, trying to pull out as many facts as I can. The address on the DCF form matches the address in the article, and the dates line up, too. And this artist-colony-meets-organic-farm sounds like exactly the kind of place my mom would want to live. Which makes me the six-month-old in the article, the youngest of the kids living at a place called Plough and Stars.

I search through the stack of papers and shake the envelope again to make sure there's nothing else stuck in the corner, but there's no follow-up article. There's nothing to tell me if my mom knew there was pot growing there, nothing to tell me if she thought it was a good idea to have her six-month-old baby around a drug operation. Though it tells me something that I don't find this all particularly surprising. What I find most surprising is that this is the first I've ever heard of it. My mom, the paragon of honesty and openness, who spent more time trying to be my friend than my mother (with brief stints attempting to be my spiritual guru), never told me that she was arrested or that I was taken away from her.

I don't know what I'd expected when Tess told me that I'd been in foster care before, but it wasn't this. A drug raid? I drop the papers and read through the article again, my palms starting to sweat as my hands shake, tears beginning to well up. This is all so much worse than I could have imagined.

"Ritzy, you okay?" Lainey's voice trails off as she pokes her head into the room and takes in the scene before her. And hearing her voice pulls me back to reality and sends the tears tumbling down my cheeks. All I can do is shake my head. *No.*

Lainey rushes across the floor, dropping to her knees next

to me and pulling me into a hug. I cry into her curly hair, a million thoughts racing through my head. I'm so mad and so confused and so *hurt*. I have some answers, but they've only brought up more questions, and the one person who can answer them all for me isn't here.

When I finally catch my breath, I sit back and swipe at the tracks of tears on my cheeks. Then I push the newspaper article, still resting atop the file folder, toward Lainey so she can read it.

"Holy crap," she says. She points to the mention of the six-month-old. "This was you?"

I shrug. "That's my guess, though who even knows, right?"

"There's someone else you can ask about this, you know," she says, passing the envelope to me. I clutch it to my chest, the only evidence of my history I have so far. Lainey is right, of course. I could ask the person who took me in. I could ask the person who gave me back. I could ask the person who was there for all those beginnings and milestones, the one who wasn't my mother but certainly acted like it.

Without a word, I carefully fold the newspaper article and place it inside the file folder, then stack my birth certificate and Social Security card on top. I put the whole thing back into the envelope.

"We should finish," I say, clutching the envelope to my chest. "I don't want to miss the beach."

Lainey looks like she wants to say something more, but

she keeps her mouth shut and nods. She reaches for the third bag, the one I hadn't quite filled. "This ready to go?" she asks. When I nod, she ties it off with the red plastic handles and hauls it over her shoulder. "I finished up the kitchen. Give it a look to make sure I didn't leave anything behind, okay? Then we'll do your room."

It takes another two hours to finish up in the apartment. We throw everything we can in boxes or trash bags, though thankfully most of the apartment's contents belong to the complex. Most of what we have are clothes and bedding, with a few stray books from my shelf. I leave the garlic press in the drawer with the scratched-up silverware that came with the apartment. And I tuck the envelope into my purse so it doesn't wind up lost in the trash bags that contain my life. Once we get everything packed, Lainey and I give the whole place a cursory scrub. I know Mr. Benson will have it professionally cleaned after we leave (and take the money to pay for it out of our security deposit, if I had to guess), but it can't hurt.

When we're all done and Barney is loaded, Lainey drives me to the little building at the front of the complex that holds the leasing office. There's no one inside, so I take one of the forms from the plastic tray marked MOVE OUT. I slide my apartment key into the provided envelope, along with the one my mom left behind. I fill in Kris's address in the space for a forwarding address, just in case there's anything left of the security deposit. Then I drop the whole thing into the metal lockbox on the desk and turn to Lainey.

"Welp, I don't live here anymore," I say. The apartment sucked, but it was home. "Let's go to the beach."

The drive is silent, though it feels like my thoughts are shouting at me the whole way. I'm surprised Lainey doesn't have to tell me to keep it down. By the time we get to Covina, I'm already drenched in sweat, and it's only partly from the heat. I think Lainey can sense that I'm wound up, because she turns the music up loud and lets that be the reason we don't talk.

Lainey pays three dollars to park, and we only have to circle the sandy lot for a few minutes before we find a mother loading up a tantruming toddler into the back of an SUV. Lainey puts her signal on and waits.

"So, are you okay?"

"Fine."

She arches an eyebrow at me. "Okay, but just so you know, everything about you says, *Lainey, I am feeling a lot of things, but* fine *definitely isn't one of them.*"

I look over at her, still clutching the wheel as she studies me. I know that of all the people in the world, Lainey is the one to confide in. But right now, I just want to go lay on the beach and let the sun fry me into oblivion, maybe climb into the waves and let the push and pull of the tide distract me.

And Ali. Thinking about his big dopey smile tugs just a little bit of the foulness out of my mood.

"I'll *be* fine," I tell Lainey. "I just need to detach from all this for a while."

She shrugs. "Okay. Well, then let's hope this Gwyneth Paltrow wannabe gets her organic offspring into that car seat soon before I sweat to death waiting for this parking spot."

It's almost one o'clock, and the sun is high and bright in the summer sky by the time we trudge out onto the sand. We're the last of the group to arrive. Ali and the soccer boys have already staked out a spot not far down the sand from the entrance, a giant rainbow umbrella marking their spread. When Lainey and I shuffle up with our bags, we see that the soccer girls have also joined in on beach day. Zoe Pike is laid out on a towel, her bleach-blond hair in a high ponytail, her barely-there black bikini complementing her glistening skin. Next to her is Gwen Wilson in a sporty red two-piece, who gives us a wave as we drop our bags into the sand.

"Welcome, ladies!" she says, jumping up to give Lainey a hug. Gwen is awesome, one of those girls who are pretty and smart and popular and *not* an asshole. I'd hate her if she wasn't so damn nice. "Make yourself at home, but mind the hacky sack." She nods toward the boys standing in a circle playing some kind of full-contact hacky sack that has them sandy and red-faced, tackling one another with reckless abandon. I try not to stare at Ali, who's pumping his arms in victory after taking down Colin Calloway. For the first time since discovering the envelope in my apartment—my *old* apartment—I feel a moment of happiness as a chill races through my body. A soccer player, Ali is lanky, but lean, his muscles outlined in sharp relief. He must feel my eyes on him, because his gaze sweeps across the sand and falls on me.

"Hey, Ritzy!" he calls, giving me a wide grin and a wave. "Come play!"

I have never in my life wanted to play hacky sack before. I don't even know *how* you play hacky sack, other than flailing at that little fabric ball with your feet. But I'm willing to try anything if it means escaping this mood and getting closer to Ali. So I drop my beach bag in the sand next to Lainey, shed my shorts and T-shirt, and trot over to the boys. I catch Ali looking at me in my new suit before quickly darting his eyes away, and it warms me more than the afternoon sun.

When I get to the circle of guys, I linger on the outside until Ali reaches out and grabs my hand, pulling me in next to him. "Just try to keep it from hitting the ground. You can use anything but your hands or arms, like soccer," he says, flashing me a grin before lunging to catch the little knit bag on the top of his head, then flinging it across the circle to Waylon Roberts. I'd be impressed if I wasn't still stuck on the warmth in my palm from when he pulled me into the circle. It feels like electric sparks are radiating up my arm and coming out of my ears. I'm so dumbstruck that I don't notice the hacky sack flying toward me, where it connects with my chin, then lands on the sand with a muffled thump.

The other guys dissolve into laughter, but Ali just smiles. "Okay, so you didn't use your hands, which is good," he says. He bends down to pick it up, and I let my eyes linger on his lean shoulders. "Try again?"

I think I respond with something like "Umphyeah," but I can't be sure between the heat and the embarrassment over taking a hacky sack to the face. As Ali tosses it across the circle, I square my shoulders and prepare for the next attack. I will not embarrass myself this time. And so when the ball comes back to me, my left leg shoots out like a missile, and I launch it back at Waylon, this time beaning *him* in the face.

"Ha! Nice shot," Ali says, arm up for a high five. And so we continue, kicking and lunging and laughing, trading high fives and smiles that make it feel like something more than a hacky sack is flying between us. When I get temporarily blinded by a giant grin from Ali, I nearly miss an incoming sack. I lunge too late and wind up in a pile of arms and legs in the sand. Which turns out to be worth it when Ali bends down and offers me his hand. He pulls me up with a surprising amount of strength for such a lanky guy.

I take a deep breath, breathing in the smell of burgers from a nearby grill, which mix with the salty air to send my stomach growling. Either it's loud enough for Ali to hear, or he just smells the burgers, too, because he nods over toward the top of the beach. "Wanna grab a bite?"

"Yeah," I say. "Lemme get my flip-flops."

I trudge back through the sand to where Lainey is now

propped up on her elbows on a towel, paging through a giant workbook.

"Did you do that problem set?" she asks, and when I turn, I see Ali coming up behind me.

"Indubitably," he replies.

Lainey raises her eyebrows. "Well done, Mr. Anikhindi. Points to you."

"Though I'm struggling on the analogies. Perhaps I can check out your datum?"

"Latin! Bonus!"

Ali licks his finger and marks an invisible point on a scoreboard in the air. Meanwhile, I'm just standing there, wondering how I can get into this verbal ping-pong, considering I have no idea what they're talking about.

"Ali and I are in the same SAT prep class at the library," Lainey explains as soon as she catches the look of confusion on my face.

"Our teacher is this British guy who pretends we're on a game show and gives us points every time we use an SAT word in conversation," Ali adds. "He's a total dork, but it's kind of awesome."

"Yeah, says the guy with the photographic memory for vocabulary and a million points."

Ali shrugs, an impish grin on his face. "What can I say? I'm good with the lexicon."

Lainey sticks her tongue out at him, but Ali just laughs and starts toward the snack bar. "You coming?" he calls over his shoulder to me, and I have to jog to catch up. We walk back toward the boardwalk, where families are showering the salt and sand off before heading home. Just past the bathrooms is Wahoo's, the beach snack bar. We get at the end of the line, which isn't too long. Then we stand there in silence, me racking my brain, wishing I could capture the witty banter that he and Lainey had going on. Or, if nothing else, that someone would toss a hacky sack at my face.

"So, is everything okay?"

"What?" I ask, yanked out of my mental panic.

"It's just, you said you had a family emergency, so . . ." He trails off, and I realize he's talking about our original date, just over a week ago.

"Oh! Yeah. Yeah," I say, trying to figure out how I'm going to fill him in. Lainey said to tell him the truth, but now, standing here in front of him, I just don't think I can say the words. "My mom actually had to go away for a while, so I'm staying with, um, a family friend." It has the virtue of being in the neighborhood of the truth, and Ali nods.

"Cool. Glad to hear it. Hey, what do you want to eat? My treat."

"Oh, thanks. Um, hot dog with ketchup and a Coke."

"You got it."

I step aside so he can order, letting my thoughts wander, surprised that they amble toward Spencer. He's nothing like Ali, who is so nice and cool. Everything doesn't seem like a performance from him. I let myself imagine what might have happened if my mom hadn't left, if I hadn't been sent to live with Kris. Would we have had another date? Would we have kissed by now? Would he be my boyfriend? Would I be in that SAT class, too, laughing about our dopey professor and practicing ten-dollar words in conversation?

Ali is back and handing over a hot dog in a little paper boat, a Coke already sweating in the summer sun in his other hand. We walk away from the counter to the railing of the boardwalk, where we balance our cups on the edge and dive into our food. As he reaches for a cheese fry, I notice a piece of green string tied around his wrist that I've never noticed before.

"What's that?" I ask, nodding toward his arm.

He glances down. "Oh, my little sister tied it on me the other day. She told me to make a wish, and said when it falls off, the wish will come true."

"Ah," I say, because my mom's hippie friend Rose sold colored strings like that in her shop, usually with cheap little charms on them and some silly poem to go with them. "What did you wish for?"

He pretends to be offended, sucking in a breath, his hand on his chest. "Well, I can't tell you *that*," he says, his eyes wide. "Then it won't come true!"

I laugh. It's cute that he played along with his sister. But I *do* wonder what he wished for.

"So have you started the summer reading yet?" he asks.

I shake my head. "Not yet." And only partly because I'm not sure I'll be at Southwest next year, which I don't tell him.

"*Man's Search for Meaning* was pretty awesome, but *Tess of the d'Urbervilles* is putting me to sleep," he says between bites. "I think I'm going to have to look at CliffsNotes or something. Lainey actually showed me this great site that she found that helps you understand the classics."

"Auntie M's," I reply. Lainey discovered it freshman year when we were trying to slog through *The Scarlet Letter*, which, I'm sorry, is basically a literary nap.

"Yeah, and since it's some lit teacher in Canada who created it, I don't really feel guilty for looking."

I can't put my finger on why, but I feel a case of the shitty kitties coming on, a phrase my mom used to use when she was feeling negative. I have no idea why I'm suddenly a shitty kitty. I'm standing here talking with my crush, who bought me lunch, which practically makes this a date. But it's *not* a date. And somehow, he seems more excited to be talking about my best friend than he is to be talking with me.

"So, hey, um, question," Ali says, interrupting my spiral.

"Yeah?"

"Are things settled enough where you're staying that maybe we could have that date?"

And just like that, the shitty kitty goes into hiding. A grin spreads across my face.

"Yeah, that would be great," I reply.

Ali meets my smile with one of his own.

"Awesome. I've gotta work the restaurant this week. My brother is off at basketball camp so I'm doing his shifts and mine, too. But how about Friday? I could pick you up around five?"

It's six days away, which is about five days too long, but I still accept happily.

"Cool. I'll plan something fun, okay?" Ali says.

"Definitely," I reply. "I'll text you the address."

He wads up the paper from his hot dog and tosses it, free throw style, toward the trash can behind me. I turn to see it bank off the side and hit the ground. Ali looks sheepish, then hustles over to pick it up, dropping it into the trash can. He looks up and grabs for the green string on his wrist, giving it a tug until the knot unravels. I raise an eyebrow at him, and he just shrugs.

"My wish came true."

CHAPTER ELEVEN

FIRST THING MONDAY MORNING, I CALL the number on the pink slip of paper. There's a harried-sounding woman on the other end of the line, and it takes me three tries before I catch that her name is Libby, she's the hiring manager at the Island Club, and her day is completely screwed.

"I've had three servers call out today, all claiming they've got mono, but I suspect they're on their way to that EDM festival in Tallahassee. If they're not bright-eyed, bushy-tailed, and Visine'd first thing tomorrow, then they're all fired."

"Actually, I think I can help," I say when there's a moment for me to break into her monologue. "I saw that you were hiring for the dining room?"

But she barrels on as if she hasn't heard me. I wonder if she even realizes she answered the phone.

"You wouldn't think it would be that hard to find people to work for twelve dollars an hour *plus* tips, but oh my god,

I swear this kitchen has a revolving door on it. It's like they'll take the job, and then suddenly there's a Renaissance Faire and I'm down two line cooks."

"I could—"

"I mean, I'm going to have to find a freaking white shirt and a bow tie and suit up myself tonight if this keeps up. Thank god it's Monday and not Friday—"

I let her talk for another minute or so, the words coming out in a tumble. I don't want to get on her bad side by interrupting her. I need this job. I need the money, I need to fill my time, and I need to distract myself from the bridge between my new life and my old one that seems to be smoldering behind me.

I hear a moment of silence on the other end of the line. Libby must finally be taking a breath, so I jump in.

"I'm calling about the server job," I say. "I would like to do that job."

"Oh! Well, great! Haven't you just answered all my prayers? Can you be down here at noon for an interview?"

"I'll be there."

Libby's office looks just like she sounds on the phone. That is to say, it's crammed full of information with only a vague attempt at organization. Not that she has much choice. The space seems to be a former closet of some kind. From the linoleum tile, windowless walls, flickering neon light, and vague scent of industrial cleaner, I'd say this used to belong to housekeeping. Now it houses a small wooden table that's attempting to be a desk, one battered rolling office chair, and a metal folding chair that's listing to one side. The walls are covered with those plastic slots that hold flyers and brochures, the kind you usually see in a guidance office.

"I could ask you if you have experience, but the truth is it doesn't matter. So long as you can smile and not drop drinks in someone's lap, you're golden. And honestly, I can train you out of the drink dropping in a night," Libby explains. She blows a frizzy curl out of her eye, but it falls right back.

"I'm a hard worker," I tell her, which is basically my only serving qualification. "And I'm not into live music or living history."

"Good," she says. "Sorry that we don't have anything better available."

"Better?" I ask.

"Yeah. You know, pool, tennis, kids' camp. Most of the island kids want those jobs, but you sort of missed the boat on those."

I nod. Spencer had said as much at the fund-raiser. Frankly, I'd be happy doing just about anything for twelve dollars an hour, and with the prospect of tips, I don't care a bit if it involves wearing a bow tie. Not that I'm looking forward to working in the dining room. Hauling around heavy trays and coming home covered in the daily special is not really how I was hoping to spend my summer, but hey, it's better than working at a drive-through.

Libby reaches into one of the slots on the wall behind her desk and pulls out a collection of forms.

"Fill these out, and then you can get started tonight, if that works."

She's searching through the mess on her desk for a pen when I hear someone stomping down the hall outside the office. I look over my shoulder just in time to see a tall, thin blond girl appear in the doorway, a look of pure, unadulterated rage on her face. She's wearing a crisp white polo shirt bearing the logo of the Island Club over her heart and a khaki miniskirt, a pair of sparkly flip-flops on her feet.

"I *cannot* do this. I told you I couldn't do kids' camp. I told you I don't do children. I told you I wanted to work at the pool. But did you listen? *No!* And now *look at this!*"

The girl reaches back for the end of her ponytail and shakes it, hard enough that it takes me a minute to see what she's talking about. Actually, I smell it before I see it, that sickly sweet, fake grape scent, which is emanating from a wad of gum that is tangled in her hair.

"I quit, effective immediately, so I can make an emergency visit to my stylist, and Abel Marcus's mother *will* be writing me a check!" And then without another word, she pivots on her heel and stomps away.

Libby turns back to me and plasters a bright smile on her face, though the sheer panic in her eyes betrays her.

"Okay, so we have an opening at the summer camp. Elementary schoolers. You interested?"

It takes me less than five seconds to say yes, and that's before I find out that the camp jobs pay a whopping eighteen dollars an hour. A little grape gum doesn't scare me.

The acceptance is barely out of my mouth before Libby is pulling a walkie-talkie from a charger on her desk. "Annie? Can you meet me in my office once you get the kids settled?"

There's a crackly bit of static before a voice comes back over the speaker. "Will do."

"You fill these out, and Annie will be here shortly. She'll give you a little orientation. Unfortunately, I can't let you start right away, since you'll need a background check for camp. Probably not tomorrow, but maybe Wednesday?" I nod. "Now if you'll excuse me, I need to go make sure the rest of my servers are showing up tonight."

She leaves me alone to fill out forms. I finish quickly, and with nothing else to do, I pull out my phone and start scrolling through SocialSquare. Right away I spot a shot of Lainey. She's leaning over an enormous pepperoni pizza. Waylon is there and Gwen. And sitting next to Lainey is Ali. They're all grinning and giving thumbs-up to the camera, which Waylon is holding out in front of them. The tag says they're at Gino's Pizza, the photo taken last night. *I thought Ali had to work.* Before I can talk myself out of it, I comment, "Looks fun!" And within seconds, my phone buzzes with a reply from Lainey.

Wish you were here! Last-minute pizza date isn't
the same without you :(

Last minute. Which I can't do because I live all the way
the hell out here.

A blond head pops around the doorway, catching me mid-
frown. "Hey, I'm Annie. Your tour guide?"

Annie is tall but stocky, like she plays a contact sport. She's
also wearing the white Island Club polo, hers with khaki shorts
and a pair of sneakers. She looks friendly, or at least more
friendly than the last girl who stood in this doorway.

"Yeah, I'm Maritza." I stand and shake her hand. "I'm the
new camp counselor."

"And not a moment too soon," she replies wryly.

"Yeah, um, I saw the other girl. She seemed . . . fun."

"Aubrey is the worst. I should totally buy Abel a bag of
Skittles for the favor he did me in getting rid of her," she says,
cocking her head to get me to follow her out into the hall. "So,
have you been to the Island Club before?"

It's a simple question, but one that's definitely loaded. I can
hear it in her voice. If the island kids are the ones who usually
take these jobs, and the island isn't that big, then Annie would
know me (and whether or not I'd been to the club before). But
since she doesn't know me, I'm from somewhere else. I'm an
outsider.

"Once. For the clinic fund-raiser the other night," I explain. "I just moved here."

"Well, welcome to Helena. Which house?"

"End of Bayshore? I'm staying with Kris Stokes," I say, because Kris seems like the kind of person most people around here know.

"Oh, that's great! Kris is great. Is she your aunt or something? Wait, I'm sorry. Don't answer that. I'm trying not to be so nosy. My friends are always telling me I'm hella nosy."

And I let it go at that, because if there's one thing I've learned about Helena Island, it's that someone else is bound to fill her in.

"Okay, well, let's go for the grand tour, shall we?" We set out from the office. "You'll spend most of your time in the kids' clubhouse behind the pool, but members tend not to designate between anyone's jobs, so if you're wearing the logo, you're gonna get asked questions." She taps at the little palm tree on her polo shirt.

As I suspected on the first night we pulled up to the Island Club, the property is a little bit like Mary Poppins's bag. It's much bigger than it looks. She shows me the main dining room and the kitchen, where I learn that if I show up post-banquet I can raid the buffet leftovers, but not a moment before or Pablo, the head chef, will totally go ballistic. She shows me where the member locker rooms are, just down from the small spa, where apparently people go to sit in a roomful of hot steam (which pretty much sounds like walking outside in August in Florida, but I guess it's only good if you pay for the privilege?). The golf pro shop is at the far end of the building, opening up onto the first hole of an expansive golf course.

"That's, like, its own kingdom, so don't even worry about going over there," Annie tells me, and I don't understand what she means, but from the look of all the stern older men in starched polo shirts strolling around, I'm happy to avoid it.

When we get to the tennis courts, I spot a familiar face on the bench just outside the fence, hunched over on his knees, his head in his hands.

"Ryan, where's your brother?" Annie asks him.

Ryan rolls his eyes and points to the far court, where Spencer is hitting balls at a gaggle of adorable little kids in tennis whites. "His lesson is going over, even though I *told* him camp gets out at twelve thirty. He never listens to me, though."

"Sorry, bud, that's how it goes for the little brother," Annie says, ruffling his hair.

"How would you know?" Ryan grumbles. He's clearly in a mood.

"Because *I'm* the little sister," she says. "Same rules apply."

We leave them behind, but I can't stop myself from glancing back at Spencer on the court. He's showing a little boy how to grip his racket. And even though the boy takes a wild swing and sends the ball sailing three courts away, I see Spencer smiling and patting him on the back before making a few adjustments. Once we're around the corner, Annie shakes her head and sighs.

"Poor Ryan. He's mostly pissed that his dad said no to golf

camp," she explains. "He's totally an outdoor kid. He's got zero interest in the arts and crafts and theater stuff we've got going on at the general kids' camp."

"Why won't his dad—?"

Annie holds up a hand to stop me mid-question, like it's one that everyone's been asking. "It's not even worth it. I just try to keep him moving as much as possible so all that energy doesn't explode all over the rest of the campers," she says. "Of course, that means that my co-counselor needs to keep a good eye out on the rest of the kids, which is why Aubrey wound up with gum in her hair."

"She wasn't watching?"

"Oh, she was watching," Annie says, rolling her eyes and gesturing to the pool, now in front of us. "She was watching the lifeguards set up the lounge chairs for the afternoon."

There's a collection of buff, shirtless guys in red swim trunks standing around the pool, their skin tan, their hair sun-lit, fashionable sunglasses giving them all the look of movie stars trying to avoid paparazzi. They're stationed at various points around the pool and have their eyes out scanning the water like they're searching for the last survivors of a shipwreck.

"Pool dudes take themselves way too seriously," Annie explains, shaking her head. "It's worse than golf."

We take a quick jaunt down to the beach, where Annie introduces me to Ray and Dave, two aging hippies with skin that looks like beef jerky who manage the cabana and beach chair rentals. We pass Ryleigh, she of the metallic dress and distaste for dill, this time in a red bathing suit and sunglasses, perched on a lifeguard chair, scanning an empty ocean. I guess when most of the people on the island have their own private beach, there's not much need for the one at the country club ("Best job on the island!" Ryleigh drawls as she pulls a magazine out from under her chair).

We finish up the tour in the staff lounge, a room barely twice the size of Libby's tiny office, only this one has a single window and a couch crammed into it.

"Time clock," Annie says, gesturing to a keypad on the wall by the door. "Your ID number will be your Social. Don't forget to clock in and out; otherwise, you have to fill out a correction form with Libby, and she'll make you sit in her office and listen to her complain for at least fifteen minutes as penance."

I'm double-checking my forms when Spencer wanders in. The staff lounge is so small that his lanky frame takes up my exit, and I end up plopping down on the couch to wait for him to clock out.

"Where's Ryan?" Annie asks.

"What?" Spencer glances up, his hair sweaty and clinging to his forehead. "Oh, uh, he's waiting for me out by the court."

"Spencer! You're not supposed to leave kids unattended."

"He's not a kid. He's my brother." Spencer goes back to squinting at the keypad, entering his ID number like he's solving a complex equation.

Annie sighs. "Hey, are we doing food tonight, or no?

Because last time I didn't eat before, and there was no food and it was bad news for me." It takes me a second to realize she's talking to Spencer and not to me.

"I think Eli said he's picking up pizza."

"Thank god," she says. She crosses the floor and playfully hip checks Spencer away from the time clock, then seems to remember that I'm there. "Oh, Maritza, are you doing anything tonight?"

I shake my head. "Not that I know of."

"Great! We're getting together out at the Pen. You should come."

I've never heard of the Pen or Eli, but since my friends are all hanging out without me, I need to make my own plans; otherwise, I'm just going to be sad and pathetic and lonely. Thanks, Mom.

"Yeah, that sounds great," I say. "But I don't, uh, I mean . . . where?"

"Oh, the Pen is this spot on the southern tip of the island. There's this little peninsula, so we call it the Pen. Eli tried to make the Fjord happen, but it didn't stick."

"Can I bike there?" I ask.

Annie bites her lip, contemplating the distance. "It's kinda far, and in the dark, the roads out there can be a little sketch," she says, and then her whole being lights up with the glow of an idea. "But oh! Spence can drive you!"

She elbows him, and Spencer looks up, first at Annie, then at me. He looks barely present, and I'm not sure he's actually heard any of the conversation that's been happening around him.

"I don't know," I say to Annie, not wanting Spencer to get voluntold to be my chauffeur.

"Oh, come! Avery and Bennett just got back together, so there probably won't be any crying this time. It'll be fun!"

I glance at Spencer, who nods. "Yeah, I can totally drive you," he says. "It's cool."

I almost—*almost*—believe him. But even if it is a forced offer or a pity offer, I'll take it.

"Yeah, okay. That sounds fun."

"My house at seven," he says, and then he's out the door and gone.

CHAPTER TWELVE

I ARRIVE AT SPENCER'S HOUSE RIGHT AT seven and am met by Ryan. He flings the door open, his hair stuck up at all angles, a temporary tattoo on his right arm, just above where the rest of his arm should be.

"I can juggle!" Ryan declares, as if I've come over just to find out if this is true. He has three small, multicolored balls clutched in his right hand. He immediately starts tossing balls into the air in a carefully paced rhythm. I expect them all to bounce to the floor, not because he only has one hand, but because in my experience most people, especially small children, *cannot* juggle. Anytime you hear the phrase *I can juggle*, you're about to get hit in the face with a ball.

But to my surprise, the balls arc through the air, coming down with just enough time between them for Ryan to pluck them from the air and toss them again. Up and around they go, until finally he gives one a slightly-too-hard toss and it bounces on top of his head before landing on the floor.

"That's amazing!" I exclaim, and there's barely any forced enthusiasm there. I really am amazed.

"Percy Andrews can juggle one-handed, which I can obviously already do. I only *have* one hand." He shakes his left arm, as if this is new information for me. "I'm gonna have to learn to, like, one-footed juggle or something if I wanna beat him."

I figure he's joking, but he furrows his brow like he's seriously considering the logistics of juggling with one foot. Then he nods like he's accepted the challenge and is on his way to formulating a plan. He runs off without a word.

I'm only left standing alone in the foyer for a moment before Spencer appears at the top of the stairs. He's wearing a pair of gray shorts and a loose, long-sleeved rugby stripe shirt, the collar sticking up part of the way in the back. His hair is a puff of cowlicks and curls, with obviously no attention or product paid to it. He takes one look at me in my cutoff shorts and tank top and frowns.

"Did you bring a sweatshirt or anything?"

I shake my head.

"It can get kind of cool down by the water at night," he says.

It can get kind of cool in here, I want to say, reacting to his chilly delivery.

He reaches into the hall closet and pulls out a navy zip hoodie with a white crest screen-printed on the back. THE HARPER SCHOOL, it says. I wonder if it's his, but as soon as I gather it in my arms, I know it is. There's the smell of salt and sand and a hint of pine that I didn't realize was all Spencer until just now.

"Thanks," I say, tucking it under my arm.

I hear heavy footsteps falling, and Spencer springs into action, grabbing my elbow and guiding me toward the door. "We should go," he says, his voice suddenly library quiet.

"Spencer?" a deep voice calls from the top of the stairs. It's Spencer's dad. I recognize him immediately, even though we've never met. He looks like one of those age progressions of Spencer and Ryan. Same blond hair, only the cowlicks and curls have been tamed by a short haircut and some kind of shiny product. And Mr. Ford's face is more severe. Sharper angles. Harder and more hollowed out.

"Don't forget about tomorrow," he says, but his gaze is mostly on the small screen in his hand. "I want you in a clean shirt. Ironed."

"Yes, sir," Spencer says, giving a two-fingered salute.

Despite his lack of eye contact, Mr. Ford catches the gesture and glances up from his phone. "That's right, get it all out of your system now. I don't want any attitude with Coach V."

Spencer rolls his eyes in my direction as if to say *dads*, but the muscle in his jaw is tensing as he grits his teeth.

"Be back by curfew. I want you rested."

"As if you know my curfew," Spencer mutters as he turns to head out the door. I have no choice but to trot after him like a stray puppy. I guess introductions won't be happening, so I give Spencer's dad a smile and small wave over my shoulder as we go. He doesn't even notice, though. His focus is back on his phone.

Just before we make it out the door, Spencer's mom pops out of the kitchen clutching a Ziploc bag full of cookies. "Take these with you," she says, striding down the hall for the hand-off. "Oatmeal chocolate chip with pecans. Did I hear your father?"

She glances up the stairs, as if he might still be standing there, but he's gone.

"Nothing like being parented by the top of someone's head," Spencer says to his mom, miming staring down at an invisible phone.

She ruffles his already-mussed curls.

"You know he's working," she says. "Don't be out too late."

"You want me back by my *curfew*?" He hooks his fingers into sarcastic air quotes.

"Keep being a smart-ass and I'll be happy to give you one. In the meantime, use the judgment I worked so hard to instill in that thick skull of yours, okay?"

While Spencer and his dad's exchange was all acid and sharp points, Spencer and his mother have the kind of easy rapport I've seen on family sitcoms. It's so familiar, even though I've never experienced anything like it myself. Most conversations with my mother felt more like New Age sales pitches. *Oh, Ritzy, you really should give crystals/oils/underwater meditation a try. It'll change your life!* Mom was never clear on what about my life needed changing. When it came to the more utilitarian side of parenting, things like appointments or curfews, I'd been largely on my own, which is what had made my earlier conversation with Kris so surprising.

As I was heading out the door, waving good-bye, she stopped me and started giving me the third degree. *Where was I going? Who would I be with? Who was driving? And when would I be home?*

"Oh, uh, I'm not really sure," I'd said with a shrug, eager to get out the door. I didn't want to leave Spencer waiting, and I also didn't like having to explain myself like that. "Spencer's my ride, so I guess whenever he heads back."

Kris wrung her hands, like she was trying to work herself up to a dare.

"What's up?" I asked, inching closer to the door.

"I'd like you home by midnight," she said, and I don't think I could have been more shocked if she asked me to please skip home while singing "Memory" from *Cats*. A curfew? I was getting a curfew?

"I don't know what time Spencer . . ." I trail off, because I don't know how to end this conversation. Am I supposed to just say okay? Or is this a negotiation? What if Spencer isn't leaving at midnight? What if his curfew is later? Do I just make him take me home?

"Just tell him you'll need to be home by midnight," she

said, and there was something final in her tone that told me this would not be a negotiation.

But now I have a perfect in to bring it up.

I smile at Mrs. Ford. "Um, Kris said I needed to be home by midnight, so I guess we both have a curfew tonight," I say with a shrug.

Spencer gives me a sideways look, but his mother just smiles, then points at me. "I like her," she says.

Spencer's car is a tiny vintage sports coupe, a two-seater painted powder blue with a brown leather convertible top and cracked brown leather seats.

"You don't mind the top down, do you?"

I shake my head, thankful I pulled my hair back, or I'd probably collect every bug on the island in it.

"Good, because I can't actually get it to go up. I've been working on this car for two years. Finally got it running reliably this summer, so I can start on the bodywork next." The driver-side door creaks as he pulls it open, and I have to give the passenger side a good heave with both hands before it finally releases itself to me.

"You fixed this car?"

"Yeah. It's amazing what you can learn from watching YouTube videos," he replies with a shrug. I take my seat and try to shift around so the cracks in the leather aren't cutting into the backs of my thighs.

The car roars to life. Or should I say, groans. After a few wheezes, the engine turns over, and Spencer throws it into reverse. We back out of the garage, the engine sounding like a bunch of soda cans in a dryer. I worry that I'm riding in a teenage boy's high-stakes Lego set, but after a minute or two, the engine seems to calm down and sink into a familiar rhythm.

We follow the edge of the shore around the island. It's getting dark, and things are quiet, the only lights coming from the few homes set far back from the road, half hidden by sand dunes. I sneak a glance at Spencer. His left elbow is resting on the edge of the open window, his left hand draped over the bottom of the steering wheel. His right hand rests on the gearshift. The wind is whipping his blond curls, but his face is still as stone as he appears to be staring fifty miles down the road ahead.

I settle in for the drive. In minutes, Spencer downshifts and turns on a dirt road that winds through the dunes. We pull to a stop next to a brand-new white Range Rover and a sporty black BMW sedan.

We get out of the car and approach a small campfire, around which sit a handful of people about my age. I recognize the couple from the charity party because once again they're draped over each other, sharing a single seat atop a flat rock. I also recognize Ryleigh the lifeguard, but the other guy, blond and attractive in that fresh-faced surfer kind of way, is new.

Spencer takes an open seat on a log, and though I keep waiting, he never introduces me. Finally, Annie elbows him hard in the ribs.

"Oh, right," he says. "Guys, this is Maritza. Maritza, the guys."

"Well done, Spence." Annie rolls her eyes at him.

"I met you the other night!" says the silver-dress girl, who is now wearing a pink-and-green shift dress so bright it practically glows in the dark, with neon-pink lipstick to match and a pair of comically oversized sunglasses perched atop her head despite the inky blackness of night. "I'm Ryleigh." I bite my tongue to keep from telling her that this is actually our *third* introduction.

"You met Avery and Bennett the other night. And that's Eli," Spencer says, pointing to the blond surfer guy. "And you know Annie."

"Better known as Annistyn," Eli quips. "With a *y*."

"Where?" I ask.

"Does it matter?" Annie groans. "Please. Just call me Annie."

"Her parents were firmly Team Jen," Ryleigh drawls.

"It's a family name, if you must know," she snaps at her friend, then turns to me. "They have entirely too much fun teasing me about my name."

This is the part where I'd normally pull an Annie and give

them a "call me Ritzy," but I'm not going to. Ritzy was the girl back in Jacksonville, the girl with only one good friend and a flaky mom, the girl who wore ratty clothes and never had enough cash. But Maritza? Maritza is a girl who hangs out on the beach and works at a country club and has a curfew. Maritza is a girl surrounded by perfect parents who cook dinner and bake cookies. Maritza rides in vintage sports cars and has a whole group of friends with silly rich people names who are both popular *and* nice. Maritza fits in. Why would I want to bring Ritzy into that?

"You wanna drink?" Ryleigh asks.

Annie reaches for the lid of a cooler and flips it open. "We have beer, and Avery swiped a bottle of champagne from her parents' fridge." Across the circle, Avery hoists a black bottle that glistens with sweat.

"It was left over from my sister's graduation party," she says, like having champagne lying around your house is normal.

"We also have Coke," Annie says. She lifts the lid on the cooler, which is filled with brown glass bottles of beer and clear glass bottles of soda.

"It's *Mexican* Coke," Ryleigh says with a flourish, and Avery elbows her hard. "*What?* I just mean it's made with cane sugar. You know, instead of chemicals or whatever."

"I'm sure that still has plenty of chemicals," Eli says, hoisting his beer. "Unlike *this*, which is downright natural."

"Please, beer is not natural."

Eli turns the bottle in his hand, clears his throat, and reads aloud. "Yeast, hops, and malts."

"I'll give you a thousand dollars if you can tell me what any of those things actually are," Annie says.

I accept a bottle of Coke, which Spencer opens by smacking the lid on the edge of a rock, a move that I've never seen outside of a television set. I take my seat on a vacant log around the fire and wonder what I'm going to say to these people. But I quickly realize the answer is, not very much. They have a boisterous shorthand full of inside jokes and continued conversations that leave very little space for a new person to jump in. It feels sort of welcoming, like I can know their secrets and be part of their club, even if I can't get a word in edgewise.

And so I sit, clutching my glass bottle of ethnic soda, and listen to them talk. The focus of tonight's conversation appears to be college applications, which is at least something I can understand. At Southwest, they started talking to us about college apps last year. We practiced writing essays in English class, and we all had to pay a visit to the guidance counselor to discuss our "options." My guidance counselor, Ms. Silverstein, sat there on the other side of the desk, batting her overly mascaraed eyes at me while she waited for me to answer the *And what do* you *want to do?* question. By the time I walked out of that half-hour meeting, I had a list of schools (all public and in state) and deadlines, the names of three teachers who could write me recommendations, and a packet of information on financial aid. That's what I knew college planning to be. But these kids? These kids approach college planning with the strategy and skill of an NFL draft. Apparently, Bennett's mom has hired someone to come help him apply to college and is insisting he apply to ten schools. Avery groans, not because ten is too many, but because *her* college consultant is making her apply to fifteen.

"One dream school, four reaches, five targets, and five safeties," she says, and I'm not sure if the nasally impersonation is meant to be her mother or the consultant. "As if I'd go to any of my safeties. Please. I'd take a gap year first."

"I'm taking a gap year," Annie says.

"Your parents are cool with that?" Ryleigh asks with the same shock you'd expect from someone hearing her best friend is getting a face tattoo.

"Yeah," Annie replies with a shrug. "I mean, I'm not even sure what I want to do with my life yet. I need time to explore."

There's a moment of heavy silence while the group contemplates deferring college for a year, and before I know what's happening, I hear the words coming out of my mouth.

"What's a gap year?" I ask.

Six pairs of eyes swivel toward me, a mixture of surprise and a little bit of pity.

"It's when you defer college for a year. Some people get jobs, some people volunteer or do mission trips. A lot of people travel."

"Or if you're Alexis Antonini, you sit on your couch

blogging about reality shows and claim you got internet famous when one of your tweets goes semi-viral," Ryleigh says, and my question is quickly forgotten as they start cracking jokes about Alexis Antonini, which then becomes a series of jokes about other classmates, which becomes Bennett complaining that his lacrosse team's regionals win means a trip to the state tournament, onto which his mother is tacking a tour of Florida State.

They're such champagne problems. That's what my mother would say. "Them's champagne problems." Sometimes it would be with a deep, syrupy southern accent or sometimes with this twenties-style gangster affectation. She said it when I cried over missing the fifth-grade safety patrol trip to Washington, D.C., because I had to go on a yoga retreat with my mother's ashram. She said it when I had to miss tryouts for the spring play because we were at a drum circle for peace. She said it every time I complained that her essential oils were giving me headaches:

"Them's champagne problems."

But the thing was, I never told her that those didn't feel like champagne problems to me. They just felt like *problems*. And now, sitting here listening to these otherwise very nice people whine about summer programs and Ivy League schools and literally *too much winning*, all while drinking actual champagne, their luxury cars parked just a few yards away, I want to scream. Or laugh. Or scream with laughter.

"Where's Spencer?" Eli asks as the fire starts to die down

and we can get better looks at one another across the lowering flames.

"I thought he went to take a leak," Bennett replies, but then I hear the familiar groan and rattle of the engine. Spencer. Is leaving.

"Oh crap, that's my ride!" I jump up from the log and start jogging toward the car just as the rear lights turn white. He's thrown it into reverse. I wave as I approach the car, partly so he won't leave me and partly so he won't run me over. "Spencer! Hey, Spencer!"

The brake lights illuminate red, and the car stops. He turns over his shoulder, sees me, and makes a face I can't quite read in the darkness.

"Oh yeah, I'm supposed to give you a ride home," he says.

I climb into the car without a word and settle into the passenger seat, stretching the seat belt across me and fastening it with a metallic click. He doesn't say anything else as we peel out, sand spitting from the back wheels. It's not until we're at least a mile down the road that Spencer shouts over the wind.

"Sorry for being kind of a dick tonight," he says. He shrugs as he says it, a crooked smile on his face, and I can tell that he's gotten himself out of stuff before by being *aw shucks* charming. But I'm not buying it.

"*Kind of* a dick?" I fire back. "You nearly left me there!"

"It's not like you'd have been stranded," he replies. I guess the apology portion of this conversation is over. "Anyone would have taken you home."

I narrow my eyes. "It's actually less about the ride and more about the fact that your head was so far up your own ass that you forgot about the existence of the other human being you brought here in your car."

He pauses for a moment, then nods. "Yeah. Sorry." He looks over and gives me a crooked grin before focusing his attention back on the road. "It's really not about you. I owe you one."

He tosses it off like it's nothing, like he says it all the time. And I bet he does. I'm starting to realize that people on this island trade in favors. It's their currency. Sure, Lainey and I have had an elaborate series of IOUs over the years, but we're talking a few dollars for a breakfast burrito or a movie ticket, a tank of gas at the very most. But the stakes feel higher here. It's easy to owe when no one doubts your ability to pay. When no one is going to ask for more than you can give in return.

———

Spencer was silent for the rest of the ride home. He didn't even drop me off at Kris's house, instead pulling into his own driveway, leaving me to walk across the dark lawn. I glance at the dashboard clock just before I get out and see the time:

12:29 A.M. In one night I've had my first curfew and blown my first curfew.

As I cross the lawn, I start wondering what's going to happen when I get inside, and the look on Kris's face when I find her at the kitchen table with a mug of tea tells me it's not going to be good.

"You're thirty minutes late," she says as soon as the door shuts behind me.

"Sorry. We got to talking and I lost track of time." I'm ready to shrug it off when I notice the stony look on her face.

"I called you and texted! The only reason I didn't call the police was because I called Kate. She said you guys were still at the beach."

I remember Spencer, who'd been quiet all night, firing off a text, and I feel a second flare of anger at him. He knew I was supposed to be home, and he knew Kris was looking for me, but couldn't be bothered to do anything about it. What a guy.

Not that my anger at Spencer does anything for me now. I pull my phone out of my pocket, but I don't see any missed calls or texts. Not from Kris or anyone else. And then I notice the little letters in the top corner that read NO SERVICE.

"I'm sorry, my phone looks like it's not working," I say. "I guess I should have called, though."

"You *guess* you should have called? Maritza, right before you walked out of here, I told you that I wanted you home at midnight. You agreed. So when you don't show up, and you don't call or text, all I can do is worry."

"I figured since everyone else was out so late, it was probably fine. You really didn't have to wait up for me."

"But I was worried, don't you get that?"

"I'm sorry," I reply, but even I can hear the exasperation in my voice. Jeez, I was only half an hour late. It's not like I stayed out till dawn.

Kris takes a deep breath. "This might have been different if your phone had worked. Then I could have reached you, and then at least I wouldn't have been envisioning you dead in a ditch somewhere. But your phone *didn't* work, and you didn't have the sense to try to check in or let me know what your plan was."

Kris walks to the sink and deposits her mug, rinsing it thoroughly first, then turning to me.

"We'll talk about it more in the morning. And we'll figure out what's going on with your phone. For now, let's just get some sleep."

Kris waits for me to head for the stairs first, and she trails after me, as if I might make a break for it instead. She doesn't even say good night as I head into my room, which is how I know she's *really* mad.

And then *I'm* really mad. Because the whole thing is just monumentally stupid. She knew exactly where I was, because I *told* her, and because she called Kate, who confirmed it. So I wasn't in by midnight. That was a completely arbitrary time anyway. I've made it seventeen years without a curfew. I lived for two weeks without any adult supervision at all, and I was just fine. Yet I come to Helena Island and suddenly I have to answer to someone else? This is all such a joke. When Mom left, she told me to follow my own path, but so far it feels like I'm being led around by other people.

CHAPTER THIRTEEN

MY MORNING STARTS WITH A CALL FROM
Libby, who sounds like she's talking to me from a war zone.

"I've got to make this quick," she says, her voice rising
above the chaos happening around her. I hear a crash, then
a shriek. "Your background check won't be done until tomorrow, which means I'm filling in with the tiny humans today.
You better not have a jewelry heist in your background that
will prevent you from doing this job, because I am *not* cut
out for it."

"I'm clean, I swear," I tell her.

"Thank god." Then another crash, and I hear her mutter
what starts out as a swear, but quickly morphs into the more
family-friendly *fudge*. "Gotta go."

With no work, my day is wide open. I wonder if Lainey
could come back out, but after last night's tense talk with Kris,
I'm not eager to ask her permission. I'm not sure what kind of

trouble I'm actually in. Is this a thing that cools off overnight? Or am I grounded? What does that even mean?

I ponder the possibilities as I pour myself a bowl of cereal. I'm slowly picking out the marshmallows from the organic interpretation of Lucky Charms that Kris buys at the health food store when Pete strolls into the kitchen. Instead of his usual running attire, he's in a pair of jeans and a button-up shirt, the sleeves rolled up. He looks casual but official.

"First day of work?" he asks.

"Not yet. They're still waiting to find out if I'm a felon or not."

"Well, keep us posted on the results," he says with a wink. He pours himself a cup of coffee from the pot Kris has set to brew each morning. He adds a spoonful of sugar, then pauses before adding another. "So, no plans today?"

"You're basically looking at my whole agenda," I say, gesturing to my bowl of cereal.

"Kris had some errands, so she's already out. I have to head into campus to sign some expense reports. Want to come?"

Do I? I haven't spent any time alone with Pete since I got here. He's been more of a sidekick to Kris, who is the star of this foster parent show.

"We won't be out long. You could see campus. It's really pretty this time of year."

I'm not totally sure this sounds like the rip-roaring time he thinks it is, but I can't really think of a nice way to say no, so I shrug. "Okay, let me get dressed."

Half an hour later, we're in Pete's Prius cruising across the bridge. Mercer is a twenty-minute drive, but the first five of them feel like a freaking eternity. Pete and I seem to have no idea what to say to each other, and after the last minute clicks by like Chinese water torture, Pete gives up and turns on some music. Some twangy singer-songwriter situation that sounds very *dad* plinks out of the speakers, but at least it fills the awkward silence between us.

When we pull onto campus, I recognize it immediately. Not because I've been there, but because I've seen the brochure. There's a whole stack of them in the guidance office at South-west, and they're handed out to the most promising students. I remember paging through it, admiring the diverse array of faces and the beautiful brick and ivy of the grounds. It just *looks* like what college should look like. And it looks like something I'd never be able to afford.

I've spent a lot of time trying not to wish for more than I have. Like Lainey says, *Wish in one hand, spit in the other, then see which fills up faster.* And so I've worked hard and picked goals that I could achieve. State school with a good financial aid package was something to work toward, something it seemed possible to achieve. It's a goal that probably won't lead to disappointment. But being here and seeing all this, there's a glimmer that wonders if I could be so lucky. Could I be hurrying across these paths between buildings and trees, a bagful of notebooks and pens and books slung over my shoulder?

Pete locks the car. "My office is over there, in the main administration building," he says, pointing to a three-story building with ornate windows and spires and a grand set of stairs leading to the enormous wooden doors.

"What does a dean of students do, exactly?" I ask.

"It can vary from campus to campus, but here at Mercer I oversee all aspects of student life, from student activities to housing to conduct. I'm also the middleman between student organizations and the rest of the administration."

I nod, piecing together what that might mean from what I know about college, which is mostly what I've seen on television.

"I also handle the student life budget, which is why I'm here today. I have to sign a bunch of expense reports. It's a glamorous job, really."

He pulls open the door to the administration building, and I step into what I'm pretty sure is Hogwarts. There's a double grand staircase leading up to a second floor, where there's a fireplace on the landing so big I could walk inside of it. A chandelier the size of a small SUV hangs overhead, and it reflects the light streaming in through several ornate stained glass windows.

"Dang," I say as we start up the stairs, my sneakers squeaking on the polished mahogany.

"Yeah, it's not a bad life, I gotta say. Certainly makes up for the years I spent working in housing breaking up drunken freshman dorm parties and trying to find out who kept drawing penises on the whiteboards." He laughs to himself, then at an office door. DR. PETER CARMICHAEL is painted in delicate gold on the frosted glass window of the door.

Inside, there's an enormous desk that's large enough to double as a life raft for the both of us. Behind the desk, a set of enormous windows look out onto the leafy green quad, where I imagine when it's not summer, there are students reading and tossing Frisbees or whatever else they do that winds up in a photo in the brochure.

I take a seat in one of the leather chairs across from his desk, while Pete settles in to sign a folder full of papers on his desk. A stack of brochures is sitting on the corner, the same ones that were in our guidance office. I pick up one and start paging through it, reading about Mercer's liberal arts curriculum, their brand-new student center, and their recently remodeled residence halls. I flip to the back, to the section on academics, and start to read about their teacher education program. I'm not totally sure what I want to be, other than a college graduate, but teaching has always seemed like something I could be good at. I like kids, and I like school. And I definitely like a job that I understand and one that offers a steady paycheck and benefits.

"Have you thought about where you want to go to school?" Pete asks, looking up from his forms.

"Yeah, I'm probably going to apply to Florida and Florida

State. Maybe Central Florida. And I'm not ruling out doing my gen eds first at Florida State Jacksonville," I say, repeating the plan I'd worked out with my guidance counselor.

"Do you have any reach schools in mind? Maybe someplace smaller, private? Mercer's a great school," he says with a grin.

"I think paying for college is going to be my reach," I say, trying to play it off like a joke. "That FAFSA thing is going to be my toughest application."

"There are lots of ways to pay for college, Maritza. And if you have the grades, you should definitely look at some other schools. You want to find the right fit. Someplace like Mercer could be it."

I don't tell him that the right fit is one I can pay for, because that sounds snotty, but it's true.

"Besides, dependents of faculty get free tuition here," he says, returning to his stack of forms.

My head snaps up from the brochure. "I'm not your kid," I say, the words out of my mouth before I can stop them. Then I suck in a breath before I can do any more verbal damage.

Pete's pen pauses mid-signature, his cheeks turning red. "No, of course not. I would never—I just mean, I mean, in case things . . ." He trails off, then sighs. He takes his glasses off and sets them down on the desk, rubbing his eyes. "Maritza, I don't really know what my role is with you. This is all new to me, and I want you to know that I support you and want to help you, but I don't want to be anything you don't want me to be. That's why I've been sort of staying out of the way."

I nod, not sure what to say. Because if he's waiting for me to tell him what his role is, he's going to be waiting a long time. I have no idea.

"Here's the thing, though. Kris isn't trying to be your mom, but like it or not, she definitely considers you family. And it's really hard for her to walk that line, so maybe you could give her a little bit of room to make some mistakes, okay? Just cut her a little bit of slack."

I wonder if he's talking about last night and the curfew. Last night Kris was definitely trying to be a parent, and I was definitely not interested. I didn't want to make her feel bad, but I also don't want her to think she can roll up in my life at the age of seventeen and try to parent me. And if Pete thinks the offer of free fancy college is going to make it easier for me to let that happen, then he's sadly mistaken.

But I don't say any of that. Instead I nod, then go back to the brochure, which suddenly feels like a brick in my lap.

———

The drive home is more radio and no talking, which I'm glad about, because it gives me time to sort through my conversation with Pete, who isn't trying to be my parent, and Kris, who definitely is. He's probably right, I do need to cut her a little slack. But I also don't want to let go of my freedom, of who

I am and who I've been, just to make her feel good about being a fake mom.

When we pull up to the house, I realize it's the absolute last place I want to be. I can't tiptoe around this house and pretend it's home right now. I want out.

I try Lainey first.

"Sorry, dude, Barney's got a flat, and I can't make it all the way out there on the spare," Lainey says when I call her for a ride. "Plus, I've got work. Where do you need to go?"

I know that if I tell her, she'll figure out a way to get out here, and I don't want her feeling guilty, not when she has her own stuff on her already-overflowing plate. I'll fill her in later.

"Oh, I just wanted to hang out," I say, pacing my room with the landline pressed to my ear. My cell still says NO SERVICE. "I miss you."

"Miss you, too, dork," she says. "I gotta go. I volunteered to lead toddler story time this afternoon, and I will *not* survive that without caffeine. Hang out soon?"

I wish Lainey good luck with story time and toss the phone onto the bed, then fall back onto the comforter. Could I call a cab? That would cost a fortune, money I definitely don't have without asking Kris, and where would I even go? Maybe a bus? But in all the time I've been on Helena, I've never seen any kind of public transportation buzzing around the island. You can walk most places, and everyone here has a luxury car or two at their disposal.

I'm starting to spiral when I hear a familiar thwack, thwack, thwack.

Spencer.

He owes me. He said so last night. And I'm about to cash in.

Before heading out the door, I rifle through my bag to find an old Sonic receipt and a pen. I scrawl a quick note to Kris in hopes of avoiding the same kind of scene we had last night. Then I stuff my useless phone into my purse, sling my purse over my shoulder, and creep down the hall. Kris's office door is closed, a top forty radio station blasting through an old stereo she keeps in the corner. I pause to see if she heard me, but either the music is too loud or she's still mad at me and giving me space. Pete, as per usual, has disappeared out on a run.

I cross the lawn, my sandals still in my hand, until I emerge from the trees to find Spencer practicing. Just as I did on that first night, I pause between the trees to watch him. Now he's wearing a pair of gym shorts and a loose tank top, tennis shoes on his feet. He stands next to a wire basket full of brand-new bright green tennis balls, serving each one over the net with impressive force. I watch the way his body moves, fluid and practiced, his arm rising and then dropping as he tosses the ball, his racket following behind him to make contact. I can see the muscles in his arms and legs, built up from years of doing exactly this motion, a task as second nature for him as brushing your teeth.

Unlike the first night, this morning I step out of the trees and toward the opening in the fence surrounding the court. With his eyes trained on the white line on the opposite side of the court, his brow furrowed in concentration, it takes him a moment to notice me standing there. In fact, he doesn't notice me at all until I finally speak.

"Hey."

His head turns only a fraction, his eyes sweeping across the court to me. Then he turns his body back to the net, a ball held low on the racket in front of him, preparing for another serve.

"What's up?" he asks, then tosses the ball and hits it with another impressive thwack.

"I need a favor."

"Okay." Thwack.

"I need a ride."

"Okay." Thwack.

"Now."

He's halfway to another serve when he stumbles forward slightly, the hand holding the ball dropping. He pivots toward me, letting the racket fall to his side.

"You owe me," I remind him.

He lets out a sound that falls somewhere between a sharp exhale and a laugh, then shakes his head.

"Where are we going, exactly?"

"I don't know," I say, digging my toes into the grass, trying to avoid his gaze. "I just want to leave here. I need to get out, okay?"

I don't know what about that convinces him, but he immediately drops the ball in his hand. "Yeah, okay. Lemme get changed. Meet me at the garage."

He disappears into the house, and I head toward the garage to wait for him. It only takes a minute or two before one of the doors starts its mechanical groan, and a black Range Rover begins to back out. I immediately duck behind an oversized hydrangea, thinking this will be Spencer's mom, or worse, his dad, but the car comes to a stop and the driver taps the horn. Spencer.

"This yours, too?" I ask as I heave myself up and into the passenger seat.

"It's my dad's," he replies. "I use it sometimes. I don't know if you noticed, but the MG isn't good for inclement weather, and I usually smell like gas after I drive it."

"Isn't your dad going to miss it?" I ask, but he only shrugs in response. He has his reasons, but he's not sharing them with me.

We set off down the road, the sky covered in a thick blanket of gray clouds. There's enough mist in the air that Spencer has to keep activating the windshield wipers, but not enough to keep them going automatically. It becomes almost like a nervous tic as we navigate off the island and onto the highway. Every few seconds he reaches for the windshield wipers and flicks them to clear the moisture.

I take a moment to appreciate the car as we drive. The tan leather of the seats is buttery soft; the dashboard—which looks like a tiny command center—is accented with shiny chrome. The car is wide, which provides for ample space between us, unlike the MG, which had us brushing elbows the entire drive.

The silence stretches as wide as the six-lane highway we're driving on. Spencer bobs his head as if to a beat, but there's no music playing. I want to turn on the radio, but I'm not sure what the etiquette is in his—er, his *dad's*—car. With Lainey, the rule is the driver controls the tunes, which means I pretty much never get to pick. Which is fine, because Lainey never bothers me about gas money, which I can only offer her sporadically.

"So you're sneaking out, huh?" he asks, finally cutting the silence.

"How do you know I'm sneaking?"

"Um, because you arrived at my house carrying your shoes and acting all weird?"

He has me there, but I keep my mouth shut.

"So do you do this often?"

"Never," I reply, because it's true. It's not like I had to sneak out with my mom, and even if I did, I never really had anyplace to sneak off *to*. The only place I ever go is Lainey's.

"Seriously?"

"Never had much need to."

"So you don't have an overprotective mom?"

"My mom left three weeks ago to study a transcendental

pyramid scheme. She left her house keys and a very nice note instructing me to follow my own path. So no, not an over-protective mother."

Spencer is quiet, his eyes glued to the road. I wonder what he must think of me now that he knows the truth.

I shrug. "Well, now you know my secrets."

"I hate my dad," he replies. "There. Now you know one of mine."

I owe you. I guess he was serious about being even.

"Why do you hate your dad?"

"Poor-little-rich-boy reasons," he says. He shakes his head. "He's planned out my entire life, basically trying to mold me in his image." He adopts a stern, clipped tone that I recognize as his father's. "Tennis scholarship to Duke, where I'll double major in economics and political science. Then a dual program in law and business at Vanderbilt. Then I'll join him at his firm doing finance and law or some shit that I don't understand and don't care to."

It doesn't sound like a bad plan to me. A top college with a scholarship, a graduate degree, and a guaranteed job with a guaranteed big fat salary? If these are champagne problems, crack me open a bottle, please.

"So you don't want tennis or Duke or Vanderbilt?" I ask gently, trying not to let the judgment in my head seep out into our conversation.

"Or finance or law," he replies.

"Okay, then what *do* you want to do?"

"I mean, the tennis is fine, I guess. When my dad refuses to pay for wherever I do want to go to school, hopefully tennis will cover that."

"And what do you want to study when you get there? Philosophy? Art? Underwater basket weaving?"

He laughs. "What I really want to do is design prosthetic limbs." The corner of his mouth quirks up in a smile, the first I've seen on him all day.

This surprises me. Usually when someone wants to rebel against their parents, they pick something like art or theater or writing the great American novel. But this seems like a perfectly reasonable, respectable plan to me. "Would you be a doctor?"

"No. I think I can major in biomedical engineering. I might not even need a graduate degree, though I'm open to whatever I need to do. I'm going to make an appointment with Ryan's PT so I can ask some questions and go from there."

I bite my lip, rolling his plan over in my mind. "So you want to give people who are missing limbs new limbs. And you think your dad won't like that?"

"I *know* he won't like that," he says, practically spitting the words.

There's a heavy silence that hangs in the car. Nothing he's saying makes sense to me. Sure, my mom's never really encouraged my college plans either, but at least I knew enough to know that her indifference to my college plans was unusual. Most parents I know, like Lainey's and Ali's, are all about the college plans, and they encourage whatever dream their kid has that takes them down that path. So to imagine a parent dismissing something requiring a degree in biomedical engineering seems outright absurd to me. But then again, there's not much about Spencer's relationship with his dad that I understand.

"And what does your mom think?" I ask, because that's a relationship that seems to be on more solid ground.

"She thinks that I should do what will make me happy, and my dad will get on board because he loves me." It sounds completely reasonable, though somehow he delivers it like it's absurd.

"But you don't think so?"

"If history teaches us anything, then I'd say it's highly unlikely," he replies. "But enough about me." He takes his right hand off the steering wheel and mimes holding a microphone in his fist. "What is it you want to do with your one wild and precious life, Miss Reed?"

"I'm not sure. Maybe a teacher? I like kids. I'm pretty good with them. And it's a steady job with a good paycheck."

"Children are the future," he says.

"That's what they tell me."

We ride along in silence for a bit, and the whole drive I'm sifting through all the things I've learned about Spencer in the short time I've known him. He's charming and funny. He's got a great smile and lots of friends. His mom seems nice, his dad seems like a total dick. His brother is a hilarious ball of energy. But there's something that's nagging at me that I can't quite place in the sphere that is Spencer.

Maybe it's the moment of honesty earlier, the one I gave him and the one he gave me in return. But somehow now feels like the time, especially since he's driving a car and we can avoid eye contact.

"I saw you crying on the tennis court."

He doesn't say anything at first, but his hands grip the wheel a little harder, and he lets out a short, hard burst of air.

"When?" he finally asks.

"You've done it more than once?" But immediately I feel like a jerk. This clearly isn't something we can joke about. "My first night here. Last weekend."

He lets out a breath, nodding slowly.

"Fight with my dad," he says through gritted teeth. "I didn't know anyone was out there."

"I couldn't sleep, and I heard you playing tennis, um, *angrily*? I went to investigate."

"Well, aren't you the little Nancy Drew." His sarcasm feels like a deflection, but a halfhearted one.

"Do you want to talk about it?"

I can tell he's really thinking about it. He puts an elbow up on the window and leans into his arm, running his fingers through his messy hair. It's a gesture I'm starting to recognize as one of frustration or confusion from him, so I stay silent, letting him work it out.

"Maybe some other time."

"Okay," I reply. I settle back into my seat and watch the road disappear beneath us. "Where are we going?"

"You said you wanted to get away? From all this?"

"Yeah," I reply.

"I know just the place."

CHAPTER FOURTEEN

THE PLACE TURNS OUT TO BE THE PARK-ing lot of an abandoned Kmart filled with rides and lights and colors. Spencer says we passed it on the way here, but I have no memory of it. The sun is out now, and it's hot as a nova, but the pavement still smells damp. It's not very crowded, what with it being lunchtime on a Tuesday. The park is mostly peppered with tired-looking moms corralling toddlers and pushing fat babies in strollers, and a couple different camp groups in matching T-shirts.

"This is your plan?" I ask.

"No," he says, pointing down the midway to a giant green dragon. "That is."

The ride is called the Dragon's Curse, and it consists of a giant green dragon with rows of seats on its back. When activated, it swings on a metal arm like a pendulum, first forward, then back, higher and higher, until it finally swings 360 degrees, pausing before plummeting back toward the earth to slow its swing to a stop. The ride is almost empty, since nearly everyone at the fair right now falls beneath the YOU MUST BE THIS TALL TO RIDE line (as demonstrated on a plywood sign with a crudely spray-painted dragon holding up his arm). An operator stands at the ready, should anyone show up for the ride. Although "ready" might be a stretch. He's leaning against the metal railing surrounding the ride, his eyelids at half-mast, his greasy hair falling into his eyes. It looks like he's mastered the art of sleeping with his eyes open.

"No *way* I'm riding that," I tell Spencer.

"Why not?"

"Um, because until recently, that thing was folded up into tiny pieces and hauled around on the back of a truck across interstates. And it was put together by *that* guy," I say, pointing at the youngish dude working the controls, "who looks like the only math he can do is calculating whether or not what his dealer sold him is the appropriate weight."

"Come on, live a little," Spencer says, poking me in the side.

"A *little* living is all I'll have left if I board that thing. Carnival rides only end in vomiting or death, and on bad days, both."

"You said you didn't want to think, and I'm pretty sure you won't when upside down on the Dragon's Curse. What are you, chicken?"

"What are you, five? And yes, I *am* chicken," I reply, but I snatch the strip of red tickets from his hand and march toward the hulking green monstrosity. Because I think he's right, and hanging upside down on a creaky death trap might be the only way to get my mind to shut the hell up for a little while.

As I buckle into the seat, the stoner carny dude asks me if I have anything in my pockets that might fall out and kill someone below, and I start to have a touch of regret. But I swallow it, and then the ride is groaning and protesting as it begins to swing.

"This sounds like your car on steroids," I call out to Spencer, trying to joke through my terror.

"Let's hope it wasn't assembled with YouTube videos," he says.

And then we're swinging. Up and back and up and back, higher and higher each time. I feel my stomach start to catch just before we swing back, the drop feeling more and more intense with each motion. I'm clutching the safety bar so hard I wonder if it's possible I'll leave finger-shaped indentations in the metal.

"You gotta let go!" Spencer calls out as we get closer to being upside down.

"Are you crazy?!" I shout back.

"Come on, you gotta!"

We swing forward and back and forward and back, until suddenly we've reached the apex. We are completely upside down. My thick hair falls from my neck and reaches toward the ground. I feel Spencer looking at me, and I crack my eyes open just enough to see his stupid, upside-down smiling face.

"Let go," he says, but this time he doesn't yell. He leans close to my ear and whispers, sending a chill up my spine.

And just before we tip and fall back to the earth, I do. I pry my fingers from the safety bar and let my arms drop over my head, hanging free, the bar across my knees the only thing keeping me from the effects of gravity.

And when the dragon goes over and we are rushing toward the ground, I open my mouth as wide as it will go, and I scream.

We ride the dragon twice more, then hit up the Scrambler (four spinning cars attached to each of four long metal arms that are also spinning in circles), a rickety old-school roller coaster (with cars shaped like pirate ships), and the fun house (where we stare at ourselves in progressively more warped mirrors). Sometimes I've felt fear (on the Dragon), sometimes I've felt sick (on the Scrambler), and the rest of the time I've just felt free.

When we've had enough of the rides, we head over to the midway to get food. We use our remaining tickets to buy corn dogs and sodas and a funnel cake topped with so much powdered sugar it looks like a miniature replica of the Alps on top.

"Do you see a free table?" I ask, balancing the funnel cake on top of my cup of soda, a corn dog in my other hand and a straw between my teeth.

"No, but I see something better," he says. "Follow me."

"Okay, but for the record, I'm not eating this food while sitting on the Scrambler, so if that's your plan, get another one," I reply, taking a bite of my corn dog.

He doesn't respond, just takes off down the midway between junk-food vendors and those rigged carnival games where, if you manage to outsmart them, all you walk away with is a scratchy stuffed animal or a half-dead goldfish. I follow as fast as I can, little puffs of powdered sugar wafting into my face with the breeze. I hear voices over a tinny, ancient sound system, and as we get closer I realize that they're singing something. It's not until we're right at the stage, with a few rows of hay bales laid out as seating, that I realize it's a singing duo performing children's songs (at the moment, a very energetic rendition of "Turkey in the Straw").

Spencer takes a seat on a hay bale in the last row, setting his Dr. Pepper down by his foot. He pats the empty space next to him. Onstage, the duo finishes up their song, the prerecorded music swelling to a crescendo as they execute a little square dance move. The guy is wearing overalls over a blue plaid cowboy shirt, his sleeves rolled to the elbow and cowboy boots on his feet. The girl has on a matching plaid shirt atop a voluminous pink skirt made of tulle and some kind of metallic material that catches the couple of struggling stage lights pointing down on them. The girl's hair is up in pigtails that stick straight out from the side of her head and flow down in golden waves, and the boy's hair is the same color of late-summer wheat fields.

"Hi! I'm Taffy, and this is Joe, and we're so glad you could join us today!" the girl says into the microphone in an exaggerated singsong. She looks like she's in her midtwenties, though she seems to be trying hard to convince us they're both teenagers.

"Taffy and Joe?" I whisper to Spencer.

"Which one do you think is a stage name?"

"Do you think they're related?"

"Either that or they're boning," he says.

I shudder. "Dear god, I hope it's not both," I reply.

Up onstage, they launch into an up-tempo remix of "Twinkle, Twinkle, Little Star" that somehow involves a hip-hop beat. Taffy bounces and spins, swishing her skirt around her knees with both hands.

"You know they hate each other," Spencer says, ripping off a chunk of the funnel cake from the plate and stuffing it into his mouth.

"Yeah, because Taffy's skirt is always pulling focus from Joe's sick harmonies," I reply.

Spencer launches into a fussy, angry southern accent. "Goddammit, Taffy, if you swish that skirt one more time," he says in an impression of a fictional Joe.

I muster my best Taffy, a prissy southern belle with a voice full of nails. "I'm just trying to bring the heat, Joe. Maybe if you tried a little harder we'd have worked our way up to Disney by now."

"Do *not* throw that in my face, Taffy. You *know* how much I wanted that Peter Pan audition."

"I can't believe you didn't get it, considering you never seem to *grow up.*"

"Shut up, *Taffy.*"

"Hit your harmonies, *Joe.*"

A mother in front of us with a sleeping baby in her arms turns to glare at us, and I notice the dried remains of what looks like spit-up on her shoulder. I mouth a "sorry" to her, and she turns back around.

"We need to get out of here before they start pelting us with burp cloths," I whisper to Spencer.

"On it," he says.

He takes the funnel cake plate, now just a pile of greasy powdered sugar, and tosses it into a nearby trash can. When he returns, he picks up his soda, passes me mine, and then takes my hand and drags me away before we can wake anyone's child or ruin anyone's show. And even though I try to brush it off like the excess powdered sugar decorating the front of my shirt, I feel a touch of electricity pass between us when our palms meet.

By the time we're back on the interstate heading toward the island, the afternoon traffic has picked up and we can't fly unimpeded down the road. A few fender benders cause slowdowns, and by the time we're driving back over the bridge onto Helena, it's four thirty, which is past the time I should have been home from work at the Island Club. I pull out my phone, but it still shows NO SERVICE, and all I can do is pray that Kris isn't freaking out. I worked so hard to leave behind the pain I felt earlier. I don't want to lose *this* feeling, this happiness mixed with a sugar coma.

"That was fun," I say, watching the ocean out the passenger window. "Which is not a thing I'd figured I'd say about today."

"I'm glad I could help turn it around," Spencer says.

"Thank you," I reply. "I owe you one."

CHAPTER FIFTEEN

KRIS IS SITTING IN A CHAIR ON THE porch, and as soon as she sees the car approaching, she jumps up.

"Why does she look mad?" Spencer asks.

I gulp. "I'm not sure, but I think I'm about to find out."

He pulls the car to a stop, and Kris doesn't move a muscle. Her mouth is set in a firm line, her jaw full of tension.

"Good luck with that," he says.

"Yeah, thanks," I reply. It's all I can say, even though I want to say so much more about the fun I had with him. I'm a little peeved that I have to jump out of the car and face whatever this is without a proper good-bye.

"Welcome back," Kris says, then turns on her heel and heads into the house. She doesn't say it, but I know I'm supposed to follow her.

I follow Kris up the porch and into the house, my heart thudding quicker and quicker with each passing second. For a ridiculous moment, I actually try to remember what kids on TV would do in this situation, what they would say. But no catchphrase is going to get me out of trouble.

Kris heads straight for the kitchen, and I stay right behind her without a word. She pulls the kettle from the stove and immediately starts filling it while I take a seat on one of the barstools at the island. Great, on top of getting in trouble, I'm going to have to drink tea again. But she only takes one mug from the cabinet. Instead, she pulls a bottle of water out of the fridge and slides it across the counter to me.

"Where were you?" she asks, her tone level.

"I was out with Spencer," I reply. "I left a note."

"Oh, right. You mean this one?" She holds up the crumpled receipt, then reads aloud. "Out with Spencer. Won't be too late."

"Um, yeah. That's the note."

"I'm trying not to thoroughly lose my shit right now," she says, then turns back to making tea, a heavy silence hanging over the room. It's the first time I've heard her swear.

"What's the big deal?"

"Excuse me?"

"I didn't have any plans, Spencer asked to hang out. I left you that information. I'm sorry you were worried, but I don't see why you're *this* upset."

"Well, first of all, I had no idea *where* you were or how long you'd be gone. If something had happened to you, if—god forbid—you'd been in an accident, I wouldn't have had any idea where to start looking for you. But aside from that, we *just* had this very conversation last night, so don't act like it's unreasonable that I need to know where you are," she says, clearly winding up. "I would have thought that after last night, you would have realized that you can't just run off without telling me where you are. That you can't just disappear."

"I didn't just disappear," I say. "I didn't know where we were going. And I was back before midnight."

"What does that have to do with anything?"

"Isn't that my curfew?"

"Maritza, a curfew isn't a blank check to disappear without any explanation."

"I left a note!"

"That contained no information! And you still don't have a working phone, so I had no idea where you were or what you were doing!" Her voice is growing shriller by the second.

"What does it matter where I was or what I was doing?"

"Maritza, don't you get it? I'm responsible for you. When I can't find you, I get worried."

"Look, I wasn't doing anything bad. You're not going to get in trouble."

She pauses, cocking her head like she's trying to translate what I'm saying into a native tongue.

"You think I'm worried because *I* might get in trouble? I care what happens to you. I care *about* you," she says. Her voice trembles slightly at the end, causing something to crack open inside me. How can this woman who barely knows me act more like a mother than the woman who gave birth to me? Why am I so annoyed with her for caring, when I'm pissed as hell at my mother for doing the exact opposite? I look down at my hands, which are fiddling with the hem of my shorts. If I learned anything today, it's that Kris is all I have left.

I feel the tears start to well up. I try to swallow the tremor in my voice, but when I open my mouth to speak, it all just comes tumbling out with the tears. "I just needed to get away, okay? I just needed to feel like *me*." I drop my head into my hands, trying to hide the tears.

"Oh, Ritzy," Kris says, her voice cracking. I hear the mug thud onto the countertop, then a rush of steps as she circles around the island to get to me. Her arm loops over my shoulder, her hand warm on my arm as she pulls me in close. But that isn't what makes me sit up, swallowing the sob that's making its way up my throat.

Ritzy.

"Who told you to call me that?" I ask, my eyes boring into hers, searching for an explanation.

She blinks back in shock. "What?"

"Who told you that's my nickname? Because I didn't tell anyone who could have told you. How did you know?" I can hear myself getting hysterical over a stupid nickname, but I can't stop. "Why did you call me that?"

Kris bites her lip, stepping back from me slightly. "I'm sorry," she says, though it's clear she doesn't know what she's apologizing *for*. How could she? She doesn't know that I was guarding that name, that I'd put up a wall between it and her. Between it and *here*. "It's what I called you when you were little. It just came out."

And with the one final, whooshing wave, I feel everything leave my body. The anger and the hurt and the sadness, until all that's left is just confusion. I suck in a breath and hold it like a promise, until I worry I might pass out, and then I let it out long and slow.

Kris's fingers twitch like she wants to be holding on to her mug right now, but it's across the counter and she's still facing me. "Do people still call you that?"

"Yeah," I say. "My mom calls me Ritzy."

Kris nods, like she's thinking hard, turning something over in her mind. She takes a seat next to me. She leans forward on the countertop. Then she opens her mouth and says, "I think there are some things we should talk about. Some things we probably should have talked about when you first got here.

"You showed up on my doorstep when you were six months old. You were absolutely the tiniest, most delicate thing I'd ever seen, and I was sure from the moment I took you that I would break you. I'd only just finished my foster parent training program. I'd been called once before to take in a child, but whatever the situation was had resolved before that kid showed up. So you were the first.

"I didn't know anything about your situation. And I didn't know how long you'd be with me. It was just this wide-open gulf, and you were this tiny baby in my arms. I tried not to fall in love with you, because of course you could be leaving anytime. But as the days turned into weeks, turned into months, turned into a year, how could I not? I was raising you, and as much as I knew you had a mother already, I still felt like one to you."

She pauses, glancing at me to see if I have any questions, but I'm glued to her every word.

"Do you know anything about why you came to stay with me the first time?"

"I didn't even know I was with you to begin with," I say. "I found some stuff when I was cleaning out my mom's room at the apartment. A newspaper article about a farm or something?"

She nods. "Right after you were born, your mom went to live at an artist colony, I think it was. I don't know much, just that she didn't have anyone around after you were born, and she needed help. She had some friends who lived there, and they had kids, and she figured it would be a good place for her to have some extra hands and eyes on a brand-new baby. What she didn't know is that the couple in charge of the place were also growing quite a lot of weed on the property, which is how they had the money to keep it going in the first place."

"So she didn't know?"

"She had no idea. But of course, the state and the police and all these other people had to investigate that thoroughly first. That process dragged on for about six months and only ended because the couple eventually confessed. So your mom didn't have to go through a trial or worry about having a record. Still, it was a long process to get you back. Remember the whole permanency plan from your hearing?"

I nod, thinking about all the things the judge said my mom would have to do to get me back. It had sounded insane, particularly when you considered that my mom wasn't even present to get started. Parenting classes? Counseling? Right.

"Well, she had to do all that stuff and more. Because of the pot, she had to do all these drug rehab programs, which was ridiculous because she wasn't even involved. Anyway, she did it. It took nearly a full year *after* the criminal charges were dropped, but she did it all. And all that time, you were living with me.

"I tell you all that because here's the thing. I wanted to keep you. I so desperately wanted to keep you. I tried, in fact, probably harder than I should have. But your mother, she wasn't going to walk away from you. She did everything the court required. She attended every DCF meeting. She jumped through every hoop, followed every rule. And it wasn't easy. They really don't make it easy, especially with kids as young as you. She really had to prove herself to them. But every challenge they laid, she met it, and so just after your second birthday, you went back to her. 'Family reunification,' they call it. I wasn't there to see it. I don't think I had the strength to endure it. But you have to know that for nearly two years your mother fought for you. She never stopped being your mom, and she fought to make sure the court knew it. She didn't leave you, Maritza. She went away, but she never left. Trust me on that."

The kitchen is silent. Tears are still rolling down my cheeks, falling onto my shirt, soaking the fabric. But I cry with no sound. I don't dare make one, for fear that I'll miss a word of this.

"Do you have any questions?"

"Yeah," I say, sniffling and wiping at my tears. "I mean, that's a great story, but it makes it even harder to understand why she turned around and walked right out of my life fifteen years later."

Kris lets out an enormous sigh. I can tell she's trying to figure out what to say now.

"I wish I knew the answer to that," she says. "I'm sure your mom had her reasons, right or wrong. And even though I can't fathom it, I really do believe she thought she was doing the right thing. But I'll be honest, it doesn't make a whole lot of sense to me."

"Why did you even take in a foster kid to begin with? Weren't you, like, really young?"

She nods. "I was. But I'd just ended things with my fiancé, a guy I'd been with since college. I was on the cusp of doing the whole family thing when he left, and I just felt so ready. I didn't want to wait or start all over. And I was in a position where I felt like I had a lot to give. I was working on my dissertation, and I saw flyers up in my department at school. BE A FOSTER PARENT, they said in these big block letters. It felt like an order, or at least a good idea. They were offering the certification classes right on campus. So I signed up."

"Was I your only foster kid?"

She smiles and gives a little half shrug. "I didn't really anticipate having you for as long as I did, and I'd had no idea how hard it would be to give you back. It took me a long time to get over it, and by the time I felt ready, my life was different. I'd met Pete. I'd started teaching; I had research. But honestly, I think I used all that as an excuse because I worried I couldn't do it again.

"As for your nickname, you were, I don't know, maybe nine months old? You pulled yourself up on the coffee table and then tried to climb up on it. I stopped you, but you grinned at me with this toothy, mischievous baby smile that had me in stitches," she says, now beaming with the memory. "And I remember it just came out."

Me, a baby. That coffee table in the next room. A memory of us, of me, here. I want to hear more, but I'm also scared, like hearing it will somehow unravel my own memories of childhood. It'll be like that picture in *Back to the Future*. The more she tells me, the more my mother might fade from the image. I never had any memories of being that small. Nobody does. But you sort of construct them, either from photographs or stories or just ideas of what your babyhood was. And for me, my head and heart had always been filled with thoughts

212

of my mother rocking me to sleep or cheering me on as I took my first steps. But now I'm realizing that none of that was real. It didn't happen. Because my mother wasn't there. It was Kris. She was the one who fed me and sang songs to me and held my chubby little fists as I took my first steps. The reason I don't have pictures from that time isn't because my mother was too poor to afford a camera (as she told it), it was because she wasn't there to take the photos.

Kris replaces a tentative hand on my shoulder, and when I don't recoil, she squeezes. "I didn't think anyone called you that but me. Sometimes I'd call you Ritz Cracker, which always made you laugh."

And in spite of the tears and exhaustion and confusion, I laugh now, too.

"So you gave me my nickname," I say.

She smiles and shrugs. "I'm guessing your mom had the same impulse I did, to shorten Maritza to Ritzy. So we both gave you that nickname."

And with that, the image of my mom in the picture sharpens a little.

"I should have told you all this when you first got here. I just didn't know if you'd want to hear it. And when you didn't ask, I figured it was probably best to let you lead the way? I'm so sorry, I guess that was a mistake."

"It's okay. I really didn't know . . . I don't know. I didn't know what I didn't know, you know?"

"Unconscious incompetence, it's called," Kris says. I hear

her slip into what I imagine is her professor voice, the one she probably uses in lectures with her students. "It's from a learning model. You don't know that you don't know, so you can't ask for the information. That's why it was on me to tell you. And I promise, I won't make that mistake again."

The smell of something burning starts to drift over. I wrinkle my nose, and Kris leaps from her seat.

"Shit, the kettle!" she cries, yanking it off the burner. The bottom has a patina of soot. She sets it down in the sink and sighs. "Maritza, you need to be honest with me, okay? I know I'm not your mother, and I'd never try to be. But I do care about you. Can you understand that?"

I nod.

"I think maybe we haven't been doing a very good job at this," she says.

"At what?"

"At being, well, whatever it is we are." She gestures at an invisible bond between us.

"And what are we?"

She pauses, thinking for a moment. "I think the fact that neither of us has any idea is a pretty good sign that we're falling down on the job."

I quirk a crooked smile. She's right.

"So what now?"

"Well, now we try again. Better this time," she says. "You need to talk to me. Tell me what's going on with you. Don't be afraid to ask for things."

"Okay," I say. Then knowing it'll be a struggle, I add, "I'll try."

"I'm going to treat you like family, because that's what you are to me."

Family.

"I'm sorry. For making you worry," I say.

"I know you are," she says. "And in the spirit of family, you're grounded."

CHAPTER SIXTEEN

LIBBY LEADS ME DOWN THE FAMILIAR, beautifully landscaped path to the clubhouse, where she swings open the door. Inside is the barely contained chaos I heard yesterday on the phone, the energy practically pulsing at the four walls of the building. There's music playing at top volume, one of those kiddie remakes of a pop song that sounds like the singers have been sucking down sugar and helium. There are a few kids executing wild attempts at break dancing that mostly look like they're having fits on the floor. At a table nearby, a small group in smocks are painting, though it looks like they've long since abandoned the paper in front of them and are instead opting to create their masterpieces on the wooden tabletop (and, in the case of one little girl, up and down her pale, freckled arms). In the back of the room, I spot Ryan starting to scale a bookshelf, a backpack on his back.

"Ryan, I *told* you, we do not play Arctic explorer inside," Annie says, her attempt at patience starting to fray around the edges. As soon as she's sure Ryan is on his way *down* the bookcase instead of *up*, she hurries over to the table, where she plucks the paintbrush from the little girl perfecting her body art and takes her by the hand. "To the bathroom, please. Wash this off."

"But I did *butterflies!*" The little girl stomps off toward a door at the back of the room, huffing with each step.

"Painting on paper only, please!" Annie says to the rest of the group, though that ship has long since sailed.

"Annie, your reinforcements have arrived, background checked and ready to go. Or reinforcement. Singular," Libby says, gazing around the room like she's observing hyenas on safari. "You good?"

Annie reaches up and brushes a lock of blond hair from her brow, leaving a streak of blue paint across her forehead. "I will be," she says, turning to me. "Thank *god* you're here. Two eyes are definitely not enough on this wild bunch."

As if on cue, a cup of red paint tips over on the table, running in a river straight to the edge and gushing over onto the floor.

"Oh *crud*," Annie says, but I rush forward, grabbing a roll of paper towels from the counter by the door.

"I got it," I say. It's one thing I at least know how to do. I have the paint mostly cleaned from the floor when I hear a loud whistle. I look up to see Annie standing in the middle of the chaos, her hands on her hips, leveling a stern gaze around the room. And I'm shocked to find that the kids, upon hearing the whistle, stop. The painters look up, paintbrushes paused over their art. The dancers freeze in place, save for one who rushes over to the bookcase to turn off the music streaming from an iPad on a stand.

"Okay, everyone, we've got a new counselor here to help us out. Everyone say hi to Maritza."

"Hi, Maritza," comes the singsong reply.

I stand up from the floor, paint-covered paper towels still wadded in my hand. "Hi, everyone!"

"Quickly, let's go around and introduce ourselves, okay?"

And then, rapid-fire, I meet Abel, Everly, Hadley, Otis, Cal, Theo, a pair of identical twins named Violet and Iris, Charlie, Sarah, and Celia. Ryan waves at me from the back.

And that's all the orientation I get, or maybe all the orientation these kids can handle, before the chaos resumes. The music blares, the dancing continues, and at the table, new sheets of paper are laid across the rapidly drying layer of paint to begin creation anew.

"I tried to get them to wear name tags, but that was like getting cats to wear shoes. It was just not happening," Annie says, coming over to stand next to me and survey the madness.

"Are there any, um, activities?" I've never been to camp, but the notion always conjured up images of structured crafts, campfire songs, maybe some kind of sports situation. A *schedule* at the very least.

Annie sighs. "Not really. Mostly we just keep them entertained and alive while their parents play golf or tennis or take a steam. Less camp, more babysitting, you know? We do have swimming at eleven, followed by lunch, before their parents pick them up at twelve thirty. Oh, and at some point, we've got to work on the Fourth of July show, but I can't even begin to think about that right now."

A little boy with curly red hair who introduced himself as Abel—he of the grape gum in the ponytail incident—runs over, practically skidding to a stop at our feet. "Is it lunchtime yet?"

"Abel, you just got here. Lunch isn't until the end."

He pauses, turning the information over in his mind. "How much longer?"

Annie points at the clock on the wall behind him. "Lunch is at noon. You tell me how much longer."

Abel just rolls his eyes in response before turning and bolting back to the amateur dance crew.

"Oh, by the way, can you sing?" Annie asks me.

"Um, what?"

"Can you sing?" When she sees my horrified face, she rolls her eyes. "I'm not asking if you're gonna audition for a reality singing competition. I'm asking if you can passably carry a tune."

"Why, exactly?"

"We're supposed to put on a Fourth of July musical

extravaganza"—she gives sarcastic jazz hands—"and I can't sing to save my life. Aubrey was supposed to take the lead on that one, but you know how *that* went."

Most of my singing experience is relegated to performances with Lainey in Barney. I don't know if I'm any good, but Lainey never complained. "As long as I don't have to sing in front of anyone, I think I can maybe handle that."

"Great. Just teach them some patriotic songs or whatever. I'll deal with making a backdrop. You've got two weeks."

I give her a two-fingered salute. "Aye, aye, captain," I reply.

"Save it for the production," she says.

The rest of the morning is basically spent playing elementary school traffic cop, trying to stave off tears and injury every few minutes. At ten thirty, Annie gives another one of her loud camp whistles, and the action stops long enough for me to tell everyone that they need to start thinking of which famous American they want to dress up as for the show. It's an idea that comes to me while watching our little break-dance troupe in the back choreograph their own routine to a song from *Hamilton*. It would be like one of the elementary school plays I did as a kid, where we'd dress up as something and stand on risers and sing a bunch of songs on a theme. We were little, so basically anything we did was adorable, and the parents were only half listening anyway, most of them buried behind their phones snapping pictures or recording video. Well, everyone except my mom, who usually either missed the show for some class she was taking or forgot to attend altogether.

By the time twelve thirty rolls around and parents start showing up to retrieve their kids, I feel like I'm barely alive on my feet. When Annie proposes going to the Pen that night, I'm almost glad I'm grounded so I have a reason to turn her down. All I can think about is falling face-first into my bed and not moving until morning.

At home, Kris is at the kitchen table, pecking away at her laptop. When she sees me, she quickly closes the lid.

"Welcome home," she says, and I try not to wince at the word. "I got you something." She reaches into a bag on the kitchen island and pulls out a small white box. She opens it to reveal a shiny new iPhone, all spotless glass and metal.

"I have a phone," I reply, wincing again, since I forgot to run that through my don't-be-an-asshole filter.

"I know, but I figured out why your phone hasn't been working," she says. "Turns out the bill didn't get paid, and since it's in your mother's name, I wasn't able to get access to do anything. I figured the fastest way to solve the problem was to just get you a new one. As we've discovered, you can't be running around without a phone. Besides, yours is cracked."

A new phone. Of course it would just be easier for her to buy a new phone. Of course she would drop a couple hundred bucks just to keep tabs on me. Of course she'd notice that my piece-of-shit phone has a strip of clear packing tape where a crack was starting to spiderweb across the bottom of the screen. I know she's just trying to be nice, to help, but it feels like an intrusion. My phone is . . . well, it's my *life*. It has my texts and pictures, and it's *mine*. And a new phone will mean a new number, one I'll have to learn and give out or lose contact with whoever in my old life doesn't have it. It's just a phone, but it feels like too much of *something*.

But when I look at Kris, I see the lines on her forehead spelling out some kind of worry, the corners of her mouth turned down. I realize she doesn't have any ulterior motive. She isn't trying to control me. She's just trying to solve the problem of my broken phone.

I reach for the new phone and lift it gently out of its plastic cradle. It has weight to it, and instantly I feel like I should be holding it with both hands.

"Thanks," I say. I press the power button and it glows to life. Hello, it says, just another stranger that has become part of my life.

She smiles, then reaches into her bag and pulls out a slip of paper. "It's all active, and here's the number. Since I had to get you a new phone, it's a new number and everything." I'll have to text Lainey and Ali, who, for all I know, have been trying to reach me just like Kris had. And of course, I hadn't even noticed their absence until Kris pointed out my phone problem last night. Because on top of being a terrible foster kid, I've also been a terrible friend.

"I got you a case, too." She produces a package containing

a black silicone sleeve. "It's plain, but it's just to tide you over until you see something you really want. Something that's really *you*."

It's perhaps the most absurd statement I've heard since this whole unreality began. I'm supposed to find *myself* in a *phone case*? Is this a thing people think about when they don't have more serious problems? If anything, a plain black, unassuming, easy-to-ignore, anonymous, free phone case is more *me* than anything I'd find in a store.

———

I don't see Spencer at the club on my first day, or that first week. Every day at pickup, I hold my breath waiting to see who will show up to retrieve Ryan, but it is always their mom who arrives in her chic workout wear. When I haven't seen him by Thursday, I even go so far as to peek at the schedule in the tennis pro's office, but his name is nowhere to be found.

I try to casually get the information out of Ryan, even though I feel sort of gross doing it.

"Hey, how's things at home?" I ask him one day while we are all walking in a line to the pool for swimming.

"Fine," he replies, but he is mostly focused on swinging his Merlin towel over his head like a lasso. I can't bring myself to try again. Pumping a seven-year-old for information just feels like ten kinds of wrong.

But then Friday morning, just as I'm making my way back

to the clubhouse, I catch a glimpse of Spencer's blond curly hair on the tennis court. He's standing next to a gangly, dark-haired boy practicing serves, and it looks like it's an uphill battle to get the ball over the net. I wait a moment to see if he'll glance over, maybe see me and wave, or better yet, smile. Anything so I know we're okay. But he keeps his focus on the kid, and I'm forced to leave before I'm late to camp.

When I see the big clock overhead in the clubhouse strike ten, I know his lesson has to be done, so I tell Annie I need to run to the bathroom. The kids are busy digging through the costume closet to find supplies for their Fourth of July show, which is only a week away. With them contained and not playing with glue or paint, I figure it's a safe time to duck out.

"No problem," Annie says, before telling Abel Marcus to please stop trying to stick the cotton balls intended to make Founding Fathers wigs into his ears.

I hustle out of the clubhouse, which is just down the path from the tennis courts. Spencer is there, wandering around the court scooping up stray balls while the boy he'd been working with wipes at a river of sweat pouring down his temple.

"Hey," I say as I wander onto the court, dodging the bright green tennis balls that litter the ground. He looks up, nearly dropping an armful of fuzzy green balls.

"Oh, hey," he says. "You out of jail?"

"Work release," I reply. "You?"

"Same. My dad's still pretty pissed about my 'disrespectful attitude,'" Spencer says, adopting the tone of the elder Ford. "For a minute, I thought he was going to make me quit teaching. Which would be just what he wants, since he's been pestering me to do an internship with one of his finance buddies since spring break."

"But he didn't?" I ask, and I suddenly realize I'm worried about not seeing him at the club every day. "Make you quit, I mean?"

"Nah. Teaching tennis lessons is great for my résumé." Spencer rolls his eyes, then a grin starts tugging at his lips. "I know you got in trouble, but is it weird to say that I had fun the other day?"

I shrug. "I won't take offense."

"Well, I did," he says. "And besides, my dad left for a business trip this morning. I doubt my mom is going to hold me to his grounding."

"Lucky," I say. "Kris appears to be sticking to her guns. It's work and home for me until next week."

"Bummer. You're gonna miss a Pen gathering or five."

I can hear a chorus of yelling coming from the direction of the clubhouse and realize I've been gone way too long. The kids are mostly good; they're just always operating on an energy level of eleven. If I don't get back soon, they may wind themselves up enough to achieve liftoff.

"I better get back," I say. "Camp calls."

"Tell Ryan to simmer down," Spencer says.

"He's been good!"

"Yeah, but I'm sure he could be better."

I grin and start to walk off the court.

"Later, Taffy," I hear him say as I exit the gate. I can't stop the wide grin that spreads across my face, but I manage to dial it down a smidge before I turn back to him.

"Later, Joe."

CHAPTER SEVENTEEN

"GOT ANY BIG PLANS FOR THE WEEKEND?" Spencer asks.

It's the end of a long week of camp, where I swear the moms decided to give their children IVs of high fructose corn syrup before sending them to see us. My ears are ringing from the constant yelling, and I'm not talking fighting. I'm talking simple requests for a cup of water or a new box of crayons being made at max volume. I didn't know having a tiny human shout "MORE STRAWBERRIES, PLEASE!" at you could be so physically painful, but I feel like I'll be hearing that one echo in my nightmares all weekend.

What got me through the week more than anything else was knowing that come Friday, I'll finally, *finally* get to go out with Ali. I'd texted him from my new phone so he'd have the number, which had started a flirtatious text chain that continued all week.

But for some reason, I don't want to tell Spencer about my date, so instead I just shrug. "Not really."

"You want to hang out or something? I mean, we don't have to run off to a fair or anything. We could just hang around the island."

I glance at my phone. It's only one o'clock. Ali won't be coming to pick me up for a few hours. My grounding is up today, which means I'm free to leave the house again. *Why not?* "Uh, sure."

"Cool. I'll give you a ride."

"I rode my bike."

"I've got the Rover. We can throw it in the back."

I agree, partially because the sun is beating down on my bare shoulders and the thought of even a mile bike ride makes me want to curl up on a bench and go to sleep.

With the bike loaded in the back, we pull out of the parking lot. I shift in the seat of the car, peeling my bare thighs off the leather. Spencer glances over from the road, then reaches down and hits a button.

"Seat coolers," he says, and after a few seconds, yup, I notice my rear end start to cool considerably.

"You've got to be kidding me."

He glances at me over the top of his sunglasses, one eyebrow arched. "I am not. How else are you supposed to tolerate leather seats while living in the tropics?"

"Um, not have leather seats?"

"Then how would rich people show that they can afford to buy the most expensive thing there is?"

"Oh, I'm sure they'd think of something," I say. "I was watching one of those home renovation shows with Kris, and this woman had a two-story closet built. Two full stories just to house her clothes."

"And her shoes, I'm sure."

"Those had their own separate space!"

Spencer shakes his head in wonder. "Okay, now *that's* sick."

"You let the two-story closet slide, but the separate shoe closet is where you draw the line?"

"A guy's gotta have standards. I mean, at some point you have to say, *Nope, that's gauche.*"

"Gauche?"

"Yeah, it means—"

"I know what it means," I reply, maybe a little harsher than intended. "I'm just surprised to hear a teenage dude say it."

"A dude? That's what you think of me as? A *dude*?"

At his house, Spencer goes around to the back of the car and pulls out my bike. He leans it against the side of the garage and hangs the helmet carefully from the handlebar. We're halfway up the path when Mr. Ford appears on the front porch.

"I thought you had your own car," he says, his voice cool.

"I didn't know you were in town this weekend," Spencer

replies. If his dad notices the disdain dripping from Spencer's every word, he doesn't let on.

"Don't forget, you owe me two hours on the court today. I think you'll want to get those done before it gets any hotter."

I feel myself tense, even in my tired state. I've barely spent any time around Mr. Ford, but even in that short period, I know I don't want to spend any more.

"I'm going up to my office to get some work done. I expect to hear balls on that court. Two hours, Spencer."

"Yes, sir." I glance over at Spencer and see barely contained contempt. His brow is furrowed, and he is taking these long, slow, deep breaths, his shoulders rising and falling with the rhythm. He closes his eyes tight for a few seconds, but when he opens them, all his tension is gone, disappeared as if by magic trick. A smile is on his face, though I can't help but notice it doesn't reach his eyes.

"I can head home," I say, pointing over my shoulder as if he doesn't know I stay *right there*. "We can hang out when you're done."

"Oh, you're going home," Spencer says, "but you're coming back in tennis clothes."

I can't keep from grimacing. "*Tennis* clothes?"

"Yep. Something you can run around in." He points down at my flip-flops. "And tennis shoes, please."

"Are tennis shoes the same as sneakers? Because that's all I've got."

"Gym shoes," he says with a laugh.

"But I'm *tired*," I reply, miming a dramatic yawn. And I was when camp let out, but for some reason, standing here with Spencer, I feel a rush of new energy.

He squares his shoulders and affects a stern tone that sounds shockingly like his father's. "Buck up, young lady. It's tennis time."

"Ugh, *fine*," I reply with a smirk. "But I don't know how to play tennis."

"Which is why I'm going to teach you. I don't know if you've heard, but I've been known to teach a lesson or two." He turns and starts trotting toward the court in his backyard. "Meet me on the court in fifteen minutes," he calls over his shoulder, his racket bag slung across his back like a guitar.

I head down the hill and into the house. Kris is in her office, and I buzz past, hoping to avoid a conversation. But her ears must be tuned to my frequency, because I hear her rise from her desk chair almost immediately.

"How was camp?"

"Good!" I call as I start tearing through my drawers for gym clothes. I find a pair of black yoga pants, but the thought of running around on a tennis court at the hottest part of the day in long pants makes me want to die. "Only two kids cried today."

"That's great," she says, her voice nearer, and I turn to see her leaning in my doorway. "What are you looking for?"

"Tennis clothes," I reply. I think I've got a pair of cotton shorts I wore in gym at Southwest last year, if I could just find them.

"I'm sorry, you're looking for *tennis* clothes?"

"Yes."

"Do you actually have tennis clothes, or are you just hoping that they'll magically appear if you rummage hard enough?"

I shoot her a look, and she straightens, chastened.

"Come with me." She cocks her head, then turns on her bare heel and pads down the hallway. She steps into her (one-story) closet, then comes out with a fistful of spandex and what appears to be something with a ruffle. She lays the pink-and-white tank top flat on her bed, then adds the pink tennis skirt beneath it. The bottom looks to be about six inches long, making the term *skirt* generous. It's just about the girliest thing I've ever seen, much less worn. Kris tosses a roll of white ankle socks down on the bed next to the ensemble.

"Why do you own this?" I finger the skirt.

"I play tennis," she says, sounding indignant.

"You do?"

"I mean, I know how to swing a racket. I'm not any good, but around here, tennis is ninety percent social. It's like going for coffee."

"I don't like coffee."

"But if someone asked you to go get coffee, you'd still go, right?"

"Yeah."

"That's tennis around here." She affects a prissy southern accent. "*We should play tennis!* they say, and the next thing you know you're volleying a few before sitting under an umbrella drinking white wine and gossiping."

"Is there some kind of handbook I could get for life around here?"

"I'll talk to someone in the Anthropology Department at the college," she says. "So you and Spencer seem to be getting to be good friends." She cocks her head at the window, which looks out toward the Ford family tennis court. I can hear the thwack, thwack of balls already. Spencer is waiting. Which means I can make a hasty exit without having to get into any of the specifics about my friendship with Spencer.

I snatch the clothes off the bed. "I'll save my thanks until after I've seen myself wearing this."

"You're going to look great, which is really all you need to play tennis on Helena."

Five minutes later, I'm trudging across the lawn in Kris's pristine tennis clothes and my ratty, scuffed Nikes that I own only because Southwest required gym every semester. With each step, I feel myself reaching for the hem of the skirt and tugging it southward. The skirt comes fitted with a pair of bloomers that keep me from any kind of I-see-London situation, but it doesn't make me feel any less exposed.

Spencer is serving balls from a stand next to him on the court, one after the other with a powerful thwack and a grunt.

They scream across the court in a streak of neon green at a blink-and-you'll-miss-it speed. This is the first time I've watched him play up close since that first night, when I didn't notice how good he was. Practically lethal with his serve (seriously, I make a mental note to avoid it). I pause at the entrance to the court and watch him, in a deep rhythm: ball, toss, serve. Ball, toss, serve. It takes him a moment to notice I'm there, but the bright pink must catch his eye, because mid-rhythm, he misses, his racket audibly whiffing as he stumbles forward.

"I thought you said you didn't have tennis clothes." His eyes start to drift down to my tanned legs, but he quickly sucks in a breath and forces his eyes back to my face.

"Kris helped me out." I step onto the court holding her racket. "But don't mistake my attire for any kind of skill. I've literally never swung a tennis racket in my life."

His eyebrows shoot up. "Seriously?"

"This is probably the first time I've ever held one," I reply. We didn't even play tennis in gym class. Southwest PE class was mostly basketball, walking the track when it was nice outside, and playing dodgeball on Fridays. If it rained, I kid you not, our gym coach would put on a *Sweatin' to the Oldies* tape and make us bounce along.

"Well, then we've got a lot to learn," he says, a sparkle in his eye. He holds up one of the fuzzy green balls from the basket. "This is a tennis ball," he says, tossing it to me. I hit it directly back at him. Or I mean to, but the ball goes a little wild and arcs high over his head, nearly clearing the fence surrounding the court.

"Okay, killer. It's tennis, not baseball," he says between chuckles, then trots around the net to me. "First things first, we need to get that under control."

We spend the next hour working on holding the racket and hitting the ball straight (as opposed to over the fence or clanging off to the right or left into the fence, which appears to be my specialty). By the end of our impromptu lesson, I'm covered in sweat, but I can *mostly* hit it over the net and into one of the little boxes that mark the boundary lines. Granted, my tennis balls appear to be moving at a speed that could be described as elderly compared to Spencer's rapid-fire serves. But he's an encouraging teacher, all smiles and confidence, so I almost start to feel like, if not a Williams sister, then maybe a distant cousin. I can see why his students at the club seem to like him so much. We start volleying back and forth, and though I know he's going as easy as humanly possible on me, I'm proud of being able to return it each time.

I send the ball across to him after a particularly long volley, and he lunges dramatically, his racket clanging onto the court as the ball sails past him. He collapses in a heap onto the court.

"Damn, dude, you're losing your edge," I call. "Maybe I need to give *you* a lesson."

He looks up, his blond hair falling over his eyes in sweaty strands. And then in a flash, he's up and racing around the net and running toward me, lifting me over his shoulder in one effortless move.

"Someone's getting a little too big for her tennis skirt!" he shouts, the words disappearing into the breeze, because suddenly he's running—still holding me—off the court and down the grassy hill toward the house. I can't see where we're going until I hear his shoes hit concrete, and then we're in the air, flying for a split second, until *splash*. Into the deep end of the pool we go.

I come up gasping with laughter, the hair that escaped my ponytail plastered to my face. The water is cool and feels amazing on my skin, which is warm and pink from the midday sun. I brush the hair from my face and lean back, floating as I stare at the blue sky overhead. Next to me, Spencer dives to the bottom of the pool, then swims across the floor, emerging over by the steps in the shallow end.

"Who lives on the beach and also has a pool?" I ask.

"The pool is heated. We can use it almost all year except for the really cold snaps in January," he replies, his explanation sounding as obvious as why a house would have more than one bathroom. "Hey, don't look at me like that. This isn't a two-story closet."

"No, it's a pool when you live next to the world's *largest* pool."

"This is different!" he cries.

"They're both salt water!"

He rolls his eyes, giving me a playful splash. "Fine. You got me. We're decadent rich people. Just awful and terrible. But aren't you having *fun*?"

I groan and sink beneath the surface, because he has me there. I have no response for that. This *is* fun, and as much as I like to snark on rich people with Lainey or tease Spencer, I'd be the worst liar in the world if I said I didn't thoroughly enjoy all of this.

When I come back up for air, Spencer is treading water in front of me.

"You still have another hour, don't you?" I ask him, giving him a little splash to that smug face.

"Nah, he won't notice." Spencer splashes me back. "Besides, he'll be gone soon. Who cares?"

"It's too bad you hate tennis so much, because you're really good."

"Who says I hate it?"

"You don't?"

"No," he says with an intensity that practically causes ripples in the water. "I love it. The power, the quickness. I love feeling my body twitch and react to the ball, and that feeling of really slamming the hell out of it. When I'm on the court during a game, it's like there's nothing else. No noise, no drama, no nothing. Just me and the racket and the ball. I love it."

"I just thought since your dad was, you know, so . . ." I fumble for the words.

"So much of a dick?"

I splash him again. "I was going to say *overbearing.*"

"An overbearing *dick*," he replies.

My eyes dart around the pool deck to make sure Mr. Ford isn't lurking in the shadows somewhere overhearing this.

"Why do you think he's like that?" I ask.

"How should I know?"

"Because he's your dad and he lives in your house?"

"Barely. My dad spends most of his time in New York. He even has a New York driver's license. We moved down here before middle school, but I don't think my dad ever really did."

Turns out I'm not the only one with a distant parent. Guess money has very little to do with it.

"Anyway, don't worry about it; he's in his office, which is on the other side of the house, and even if he was right next to the pool, he's probably got his cell phone glued to his ear. He hears nothing when he's yelling at people from his office."

I let out a breath realizing we're in the clear. "So what's the deal with that?"

"With what?"

"Your dad working in New York and you guys living here? Are your parents, um, separated or something?"

He scoffs. "Emotionally? Probably. But legally? Nope. This has always been our vacation house, but we moved down here when Ryan was about a year old. Dad wasn't about to leave his job, so he decided to commute."

"So your dad has a *two thousand–mile* commute?"

"Actually, Google Maps has it at just under a thousand. He comes home most weekends and holidays. I have this suspicion that once we go off to college they'll finally pull the trigger on a divorce, but who can say? Grown-ups are weird."

"So why did you move at all?"

"I don't think my mom was ever very happy in the city, and after Ryan was born, I think she wanted to get us away from that life."

"What life?"

"Oh, just a lot of competitive shit. Elite private schools and all the pressure."

As if summoned by magic, Ryan comes sprinting out of the house, the French doors slamming behind him.

"Cannonball!" he screams like a war cry as he hurtles his little body into the pool. He makes a decent-sized splash for such a little guy and surfaces sputtering and grinning, a new and sizable gap in his smile.

"What happened to you?" I ask him. "Did you get in a fight?"

"No way," he says, suddenly all serious. He flings himself onto a blue inner tube that's been floating lazily across the surface of the water, letting his butt sink into the middle, his arms and legs draped over the sides. "You get kicked out of camp if you get in a fight."

"She knows that, Ry," Spencer says, splashing him. "She was teasing you about your tooth."

"Oh yeah. I lost it."

"Cool," I say.

"No, really, I lost it. I *swallowed* it last night while I was sleeping!" His triumphant grin stretches across his face as he shares what must be a truly morbid fact for a seven-year-old.

"That's gonna make it awfully hard for the tooth fairy to come," I say.

"We already told him not to take any heroic measures to get it back," Spencer cuts in, then looks pointedly at Ryan. "The tooth fairy will be happy with a note explaining the situation."

"Yup, I already wrote it. It's under my pillow now!" He flips over on his stomach and kicks to propel himself toward the shallow end. "Hey, ya think if I go take a nap, the tooth fairy will come now?"

"Doubtful," Spencer replies.

"Oh yeah, I forgot. Mom's at yoga," he says, the whole tooth fairy illusion shattering.

"My mom always said the tooth fairy doesn't come once you stop believing in her," I tell him. I don't tell him that my mom used this as cover for the time in first grade when she didn't have cash, ignoring the fact that I really and truly *did* still believe in the tooth fairy, though not anymore after that.

"Well, *that's* not true. I haven't believed in her in forever, and I got five dollars last month for my other front tooth."

"Five bucks, eh? Nice haul for a tooth."

"I invested it," Ryan replies matter-of-factly, then slips off the inner tube quick as a fish and disappears below the surface of the water.

"He means he put it in his piggy bank," Spencer explains.

He rolls his eyes. "He's been listening to Dad's phone calls too much."

Ryan gathers a handful of rubber rings in his hand, then flings them toward the deep end. In a blink, he's under again, swimming for his bounty. For having only one full arm, he swims better than I do, slicing through the water like a human missile. I'm mostly a doggy paddler with a touch more finesse.

"What happened to his arm?" I ask, my voice low as if he'll be able to hear me beneath the surface.

"Why don't you ask him?" Spencer replies. Ryan surfaces for a big gulp of air, then disappears again.

"Is that rude?"

"You mean more rude than talking behind his back?"

I'm thankful that my cheeks are already red from exertion and the sun so he can't see the embarrassed blush I feel creeping up into my face.

Ryan bursts up from the bottom of the pool, a fistful of rings in his hand.

"Hey, buddy!" Spencer calls. Ryan drops the rings at the edge of the pool and whips around so fast he sprays water from his floppy hair. "Maritza wants to know what happened to your arm."

"Gestational amputation." The words sound far too grown-up in his tiny, gap-toothed mouth. "Just a genetic hiccup," he explains with a shrug, like he's describing getting a splinter. "I was born with it. This is how I was 'apposed to be."

"Supposed to be," Spencer corrects.

"Yeah, supposed to be," Ryan replies. He sticks his tongue out at his big brother. "I know the word, I was just talking too fast." Then he disappears beneath the water again. It seems like Ryan does most things fast.

Spencer shakes his head at the spot where Ryan was in the water, a glowing pride sweeping across his face. "Never slowed him down. Because he never had a full arm, he just learned to do everything the first time without it."

"That's great," I say.

"He's awesome," Spencer says. His face transforms as he says it, his eyes glancing over at the little boy swimming through the water, a smile quirking up at the corner of his mouth. "But not because of or in spite of the arm, but just because he's a cool little guy, ya know?"

I flop over a noodle, resting my chin over my crossed arms, enjoying the lazy bob of the pool water.

Mr. Ford strides out of the house, tucking his phone into his back pocket. He spots us in the pool, and something like a smile appears on his face, though it looks alien to me, and from the lines on his forehead, it seems like it might be a little alien to him, too.

"You up for a game?" he asks Spencer, swinging an invisible racket.

"Sorry, Dad," Spencer says, shrugging. "All wet."

"Come on, it's hot. You'll dry."

"No thanks," Spencer says, his voice firm and dismissive.

"I'll play!" Ryan says, furiously treading water in the deep end. He kicks hard toward the side and starts to pull himself out of the pool.

"Nah, that's okay, kid," Mr. Ford says, glancing back down at his phone, furiously tapping at the screen. Then he shakes his head and ruffles Ryan's hair with his hand before turning back toward the house. "I've gotta deal with this. Another time."

Ryan's shoulders droop for about fifteen seconds, then he shakes like a dog drying off and resets his smile. It's almost like the move I'd seen Spencer pull earlier after his dad demanded tennis time.

"Cannonball!" he cries again, this time producing a splash nearly as big as his voice.

The tension around us squeezes me right in the heart.

"My dad treats Ryan like he can't do anything," Spencer says, the venom in his voice unmistakable. He glances over to make sure Ryan isn't listening, but he's busy climbing out of the pool and executing consecutively larger cannonballs at top speed. "All the time he's pestering me to get on the court, when Ryan would die to play with him. And that thing about investing his money? Ryan would probably love to be pressured into going into Dad's line of work, but does he ever get the full weight of parental expectations? Nope."

Spencer slips beneath the surface and kicks off, swimming silently like a predator toward the ladder. When he emerges, he stalks out of the water and peels off his shirt. He turns to wring it out over the surface of the pool, and the sight of his clouded face is only overshadowed by the tanned, taut skin of his chest, water rolling down in fat drips. He shakes his head hard, water flying off him. His hair fluffs and falls in his face. Swimming is over, I guess, even though Ryan is still splashing around like a madman.

"Gotta get out, dude," Spencer calls to his brother. "You know the rules. No swimming without adult supervision."

"You're not an adult," he replies, but Spencer gives him a look that has Ryan making his way reluctantly out of the water. The two of them head toward the pool house and return with a stack of fluffy white towels. Ryan takes his and bolts for the back door, barely drying a drip. Spencer and I towel off in silence.

"I should go get out of these wet clothes," I say, tugging at the fabric of the skirt, which is now soaked and bunched up around my left hip.

"Yeah, same," he says. Whatever ease he had earlier, either on the court or in the pool, is gone.

"Thanks for the tennis lesson."

"Anytime."

I hand the towel back to him and turn to start back toward Kris's house.

"Hey," he calls, and I spin around at the sound of his voice. He's got an armful of towels clutched to his chest, bright white contrasting against his tan. He's practically glowing in a sunbeam, and when he smiles, I swear there's a twinkle and an attendant *ding*.

"Yeah?" I ask, though I'm not sure he hears me, since my voice is practically breathless at the sight of him.

"You wanna go do something?"

"You mean something other than a tennis lesson and a reverse skinny-dip?"

He laughs at that, and my stomach does a somersault. But then it stops with a splat when I remember my plans for the evening. In fact, I probably need to hustle if I'm going to get showered and ready before Ali arrives at five. He didn't tell me what the plan is for tonight, so I'm aiming to go casual, but I at least want dry hair and some lip gloss. I'm not an animal.

"I can't," I say, fumbling for an explanation. I decide to leave it vague. "I've got plans in a few hours."

He gives a short nod. "Oh, okay. Well, maybe another time."

"Definitely," I say, answering a little too quickly. "Thanks for the lesson."

"It was nothin'," he replies. He tosses the towel into a wicker bin by the door. "Later."

The door shuts behind him, and I'm left standing there, dripping on the concrete, wondering if he's upset that we aren't hanging out tonight, and wondering why I care so much.

CHAPTER EIGHTEEN

I'M JUST APPLYING A SWIPE OF MY FAVOR-
ite cherry lip gloss when I hear the doorbell chime in the house.
In my haste to make it to the door first, I catch my foot on the
fringed edge of the Oriental rug in my bedroom, which sends
me flying arms-first into the hall and crashing into the opposite
wall like some manic cartoon character. I land with an emphatic "*oof*" before righting myself.

"Hot date?"

I turn to see Pete standing at his bedroom door in running
gear. I must make an eyes-widened face of horror that makes
him realize how spot-on he was, because he immediately starts
trying to walk it back. "Oh, uh, well, you look nice. Do you
want me to get the door or . . . something?"

Before I can answer, I hear Kris beat us both to it.

"Hi there," she says. I run to the top of the stairs in time
to see her step aside and invite Ali in. *Crap.* I was hoping to
meet him at the door and then bolt, avoiding any weird

meet-the-foster-parents situation. But apparently that is happening whether I want it to or not. At least this gives me a moment to take him in and remind myself of the evening ahead. Ali is wearing a pair of dark jeans, a soft emerald-green shirt that my fingers are itching to touch, and flip-flops on his feet. I breathe out a sigh of relief, because I'd opted for a pair of jeans I cuffed at the ankles and a simple white tank top, my hair braided loosely down one shoulder. The aforementioned lip gloss was the only makeup I'd decided to wear. I chose correctly.

"You must be Ali. Can I get you something to drink before you guys head out?" Kris cocks her head, and he nervously steps in, his eyes sweeping around the entryway. It reminds me of my first night here, when everything was new to me. I wonder what he's seeing, what he thinks of the house. But if I want to try and extract us as quickly as possible, I need to get down there before any kind of beverage is poured, or—god forbid—Kris tries to make tea.

"Hey, I'm ready!" I call from the top of the stairs, then take them down two at a time. I prepped Kris for my date by telling her just enough about Ali (soccer player, parents own a restaurant, super-nice guy) to keep her from asking a million questions, in hopes that it would keep her from asking *him* a million questions. Now it's time to see if that gamble paid off. "We're going to head on out."

Pete must have been behind me on the stairs, because Kris trades a questioning look over my shoulder. Apparently, I have

Pete on my side, because Kris smiles and nods. "Well, remember your curfew, okay? And text to let me know where you are."

It takes everything I have not to visibly bristle at this new rule. Why doesn't she just put one of Pete's GPS trackers in my purse and cut out the middleman? But I don't want to argue about it, so I just say okay. Then at the bottom of the stairs, I grab Ali's hand and pull him out the door, letting it swing shut behind us.

"They're nice," Ali says. "Are they relatives?"

"Family friends," I reply. I haven't yet told him the truth, and I'm not about to have that conversation standing here on the porch. I hear a car engine start from somewhere nearby, and my heart nearly stops when I see the black Range Rover pull down the Fords' driveway, but a quick glance shows only Mr. Ford in the driver's seat. I step off the porch and toward Ali's Jeep. I glance at the Taste of India decal on the side, and suddenly I want to get as far away from Helena as possible. "You ready?"

"Yeah," Ali replies, then ambles over to the passenger door and opens it for me. He grins that same dopey grin I'd been staring at for years, and whatever sour feelings I had are gone.

"I was thinking Jim Shaw's," Ali says as he kicks the Jeep into gear, and we go bouncing down the gravel drive.

"On a Friday night?" It's already five fifteen, and by the

time we get all the way back there, it'll be close to six, with traffic. Jim Shaw's is a popular spot, and notoriously does not take reservations. On a Friday night, you can sit for hours on the hard benches outside the restaurant waiting for your table to be called. I've only been twice for Lainey's birthday, and both times we showed up right at 5:00 P.M., when the place opens, so we were the first in the door.

Ali flashes me a grin and navigates off the island with the help of the GPS on his phone. "I'm sure it'll be fine," he says, and he's so confident, I figure he must have some kind of plan or secret trick or in with the hostess.

He doesn't.

We arrive to find the parking lot completely full, and we have to park at the strip mall across the road. I can already see the line of people waiting, couples chatting or staring at their phones, kids running around while their parents try desperately to keep them entertained during the wait. I hold out one last shred of hope as Ali, who says nothing about the crowd, directs us past the line and to the hostess stand.

"Two, please," he says. He gives his name, and the hostess picks up her wax pencil, adding us to the end of what looks like a very long list.

"Probably an hour and a half," she says, reaching up to tighten her ponytail.

I turn to Ali, ready to strategize another plan. There's an Italian place nearby that I've heard good things about, an old meatball-and-red-sauce place that's supposed to be cheap but yummy. I have no interest in waiting an hour and a half to eat Jim Shaw's menu of fried miscellany.

But Ali just nods and heads back out the door, holding it for me as I follow him wordlessly to an empty spot on a bench at the far end of the restaurant, practically in the parking lot.

"Are you sure you don't want to go somewhere else?" I ask. My stomach grumbles, and I realize that I haven't eaten a thing since lunch, and in between I took a tennis lesson *and* a swim. I need food *now*, not an hour and a half from now.

"That's not a bad wait for a Friday night," Ali replies, leaning his head back against the pink stucco of the restaurant's exterior.

I can barely suppress a huff of frustration, but then I remind myself that at least I'm here with Ali. I mean, a few weeks ago I would have done backflips at the prospect of sitting on a bench with him, an open stretch of time to talk and connect and, I don't know, fall madly in love.

But the conversation doesn't come. We sit there, both of us people watching, neither saying a word. It's *brutal*. And I realize that I've never spent time alone with Ali before, not outside of the four walls of Southwest High. Every time we've been together, we've always been in a big, rowdy crowd, with lots of voices and jokes to fill any space there might be.

"How's your summer going?" Ali asks after what feels like an eternity, but a quick glance at my phone tells me it has only been four minutes. *Four minutes.* Crap, I'm going to have to eat my own arm before we get in there.

"It's good," I reply, almost as a reflex. I comb through the past couple of weeks, trying to find something safe to tell Ali about, something that doesn't reveal my tragic new foster kid situation, but all I can think of is Spencer on the tennis court, that first night and today, and the sound of his racket on a tennis ball and the sharp exhale of air that came with the connection. It sends a chill up my spine before I'm brought back to the restaurant by the hostess calling out a name—not ours. "Oh, uh, I'm working at a day camp on Helena. As a counselor."

"That's cool," Ali says. "I'm working at the restaurant."

"Cool." This I knew. And then that line of conversation ends. "What else are you up to this summer?"

"Studying for the SAT. I'm in that prep class at the library. It's *so* boring, but Lainey is in there with me, so it's not too bad. We have a good time. I'm helping her with the vocab, and she's schooling me on the math. I'd be lost without her."

I bite my lip, feeling that same prickle of annoyance I felt at the beach when Ali mentioned spending time with Lainey. And I'm comforted by it, because it's the first tug of my crush I've felt since he picked me up.

"That's cool," I say, painfully aware of the fact that we're skirting close to rendering the word *cool* completely meaningless.

"Yeah."

And then the silence descends between us *again*. The hostess calls out four more tables, none of them ours. A time check shows another six minutes ticked off the clock, and my stomach growls.

"So what do you usually order?" I ask. We've been sitting outside long enough that I'm starting to sweat, and I need to distract myself from the creeping trickle rolling down into my bra.

"Fried shrimp. Always the fried shrimp. So good," he replies. *Seriously?* It's Florida. Fried shrimp is fried shrimp, and it's on nearly every menu in town. What cosmic thing could they possibly be doing to their fried shrimp in there to warrant an hour-and-a-half wait outside in the heat?

But we wait. And wait and wait and wait. I swear I feel every single minute of that wait, and when the hostess *finally* pops her head out the door and calls, "Ali, party of two," I leap up from the bench as if electrocuted. Maybe once we're inside at a table, sitting across from each other like a proper date, we can get over this conversational hump. Maybe it's the heat and starvation causing our brains to atrophy.

But it doesn't happen. Oh, we talk, sure, about the menu first, until we order. And then we trade stories about Southwest, anecdotes about the more ridiculous teachers or students. Even that feels like we're standing in a dark room, both reaching out, hoping eventually we'll grab hands. When the food comes, we dive in, and I wonder if he feels as thankful as I do to have a reason not to talk (or even try to). By the end of the date, it feels like I'm having dinner with someone I've never even met before, and someone I probably won't ever call again. Ali places his credit card down on the check and waves away my offer to split it. It's the only indication that what we're doing is an actual *date*.

By the time we get out to the parking lot, I'm ready to get back to Helena and also text Lainey and debrief about this date that's felt like a low-speed car accident: not enough to ding your insurance, but still not very fun. This has been the romantic equivalent of a fender bender.

Ali stops at the passenger door, unlocking it and opening it for me, the move of a gentleman, but it doesn't spark anything for me. I place my Styrofoam leftover box on the floorboard and turn to climb in when I notice that Ali is still standing there. We're beneath a streetlight, and for a moment I see him as I did back in the parking lot of Southwest High, when he shyly asked me to go out with him. *Just us.* My stomach flips for the first time all night, and though small, the movement feels like full-on fireworks.

Ali leans in, like he's going in for a kiss, and my first thought is *why?* What about this evening said that we'd be ending in a kiss? Still, I'm willing to go along with it, because I've spent way too much time these last few years wondering what it would be like to kiss Ali. I lean in, carefully lowering my eyes so that I appear what I think might be bashful or sexy. I tilt my head, but I miscalculate, and suddenly my forehead catches his chin with a heavy thud.

I jerk back and see his arms out and realize right away what's gone wrong. Ali wasn't leaning in for a kiss, he was going for a friendly *hug*. He was probably going to give me one of those backslaps dudes do when they want to make abundantly clear to themselves and anyone else in a six-mile radius that they're *just friends*. Because of course that's what we are, after this lukewarm approximation of a date. Turns out years of fantasy can give you a hell of a lot more stomach flips than the real thing. Because while in my head Ali and I were on fire, in real life, there are no sparks at all.

"I'm so sorry," I say, and I'm not sure if it's for the head bonk or the fact that this evening was such a big *womp womp*.

"It's okay," he replies. He rubs his chin, where there's a small red mark, which must match the sore spot on my forehead, and also the embarrassment I can feel rapidly creeping up my neck and over my ears before trailing into my cheeks.

I glance at my watch, all showy, since I know exactly what time it is. "We should probably get going. There might be traffic, and I don't want to miss curfew."

"Yeah, of course," he replies, and there's no resistance in his voice, no sense that he's going to try to save this. We both know what's here. Or what's not.

Ali lowers the windows and cranks the stereo for the drive home, and I find myself actually bopping along to his '80s stadium-rock playlist. I would have thought crashing and burning so spectacularly with Ali would send me crawling under the covers, or worse, hiding under the bed, coaxed out only by Lainey and several pints of the expensive ice cream. But for some reason I feel okay. And when we pull onto the gravel drive of Kris's house, well ahead of my curfew, I turn to Ali and give him a genuine smile, perhaps the first one since this ill-fated night began.

"Thanks," I tell him, and I mean it, because now I know. Now I don't have to wonder. Now I have one less thing to miss.

"Yeah, sorry about, well—" he starts, sputtering, grasping for words.

"I know. But hey, we'll hang out sometime, okay?"

And there's his big dopey grin again, the one that used to feel like a match to a bonfire in my insides. Only now it just feels nice. "Totally. See you around, Ritzy."

"Bye, Ali," I say, and jump out of the car. I take the porch steps in one leap and am in the door with enough momentum to hopefully get me all the way to my room with minimal conversation.

"You're home early," Kris says. She's curled up in one of the big leather chairs in the living room, maybe waiting for me. "Bad night?"

I turn and shrug. "Eh. Not a bad night, just not a particularly good one."

And before she can ask any more questions, I take the stairs two at a time up to my room. As soon as the door is closed behind me, I pull out my phone and text Lainey.

Ritzy: Swing and a miss. But it's all good. We're
   friends.

Then I fall back on my bed, the smell of deep-fat fryer
wafting off every part of me. I reach for the end of my braid
and sniff it. Ugh, I smell like a carnival. Thanks, Jim Shaw's.
My phone buzzes with a text.

Lainey: Sorry, dude. Sucks. But hey, gimme a call
   when you can, k?

Lainey and I have texted, but we haven't actually *talked*
since the beach. And I *really* want to call her and have a true
WTF moment over this date. But right now, all I can think
about is showering the last stench of the evening off me. So
instead I type back, will do, then stuff my phone under my
pillow and head for the shower.

CHAPTER NINETEEN

AFTER MY DATE WITH ALI, IT BECOMES shockingly easy to forget about my old life back in Jacksonville. It helps that the next two weeks are nonstop madness at work, getting ready for the Fourth of July events at the club. Apparently, the Island Club takes the Fourth of July *seriously*, with an all-day cookout and party, culminating in a private fireworks show from a barge parked out in the ocean.

And so, on the afternoon of the holiday, I find myself standing in the clubhouse while a miniature Abraham Lincoln attempts to break-dance with a tiny Mark Twain while Eleanor Roosevelt beatboxes.

"Guys, don't mess up your costumes, okay?" I say, glancing at my watch. I need this show to be over, because for a person who has produced a show comprised of a group of elementary schoolers singing a collection of American standards, I'm a bundle of nerves. From the detail on some of these costumes,

I have a feeling the parents are expecting a level of harmony I just can't promise.

Ryan comes tearing into the clubhouse with just minutes to spare. He's in a wet suit, a Styrofoam boogie board tucked under his arm, a comically large bite taken out of one end.

"Who are you supposed to be?" Abel asks. He's dressed in a shockingly detailed and expensive-looking miniaturized George Washington costume. The only hat tip to this being a kids' camp show and not, you know, Broadway, is the wig made of cotton balls.

"I'm Bethany Hamilton!" Ryan replies, his voice dripping with *duh!*

Abel wrinkles his nose. "Who?"

Ryan alternately waves his arm and his boogie board. "She's the surfer who got her arm bit off by the *shark*."

"You're a *girl*?" Abel starts guffawing, swiping at Otis, who's either dressed as a Supreme Court justice or a priest. His black robes could go either way.

"Oh, like George Washington's so tough. Did he fight off a *shark*?" Ryan shoots back, and the boys somehow look chastened.

"I like your costume, Ryan," Violet says as she sweeps by in white pantsuit and pearls, a teeny-tiny Hillary Clinton. Ryan smiles at her, and as soon as she's passed, he sticks his tongue out at Abel and Otis.

"I wanted to be the greatest one-armed American I could think of," Ryan says. "Until me, of course. I'm gonna be *awesome*."

I ruffle his hair. "You already are, bud. Now go get in line. We're headed down to the stage any minute now."

Ryan dashes off to the end of the line, where he proceeds to grin at Violet. Ah, young love.

A whistle turns all the heads to the front, where Annie is standing, clipboard in hand. "All righty, guys, it's time. Just remember to smile, okay?" She presses her fingers into the corner of her mouth, showing them how to do it like a proper stage mom. And then we file out, me bringing up the rear to make sure we don't lose any great Americans on the way to our performance.

The stage, which is basically just a platform about six inches off the ground, has been positioned near the first hole of the golf course. The kids stomp up, taking their places in two lines, just like we practiced. The audience is made up mostly of parents and the white-haired contingent of club members who find tiny children singing "America the Beautiful" endlessly cute. Though it's hard to make out too many faces amid the endless flapping of American flag fans. Whoever decided to put on an outdoor play at 5:00 P.M. in July was cracked. I'm headed toward the front, where I'll cue them for each of their songs, when I see Spencer standing at the back of the rows of chairs.

"So is this thing gonna be worth the price of admission?" he asks.

"Well, that depends. How much was your ticket?"

"It was free."

"Then buckle up for a fantastic show," I reply.

"Oh, and you can thank me later," Spencer says.

"For?"

"I talked Ryan into being Bethany Hamilton post-healing, a costume that includes a whole hell of a lot less fake blood."

I have a moment of envisioning red paint splattering his fellow great Americans and the first couple rows of parents, then give Spencer a whispered "Bless you."

I take my place near the corner of the stage, sitting cross-legged in the grass. I give the crowd one last glance before I kick off the show, and that's when I see them. Kris and Pete are sitting among the eager parents, grinning like I'm the one who's about to perform. When Kris sees me, she gives me a wave and mouths, "Break a leg." I can't believe they came. I mentioned the show a couple of times in the course of answering the *How was work today?* question, but I never expected them to show up.

I turn back to my charges and signal Celia, who kicks off the festivities. All kids will get a chance to step up to the microphone and introduce themselves to the crowd as their character. Celia, dressed as a turn-of-the-century suffragette, complete with VOTES FOR WOMEN sash, tells the crowd about Alice Paul, complete with lisp. Then she steps back, and I raise my hands like a conductor. Their eyes are glued on me, so I take the moment to mime a great big smile, and then they launch into "America the Beautiful." And so it goes, from Amelia Earhart to Buzz Aldrin to John F. Kennedy, from "God Bless America" to "You're a Grand Old Flag," the show buzzes along at a breakneck pace. Ryan scores a round of applause with his enthusiastic endorsement of one-armed surfing. Charlie's beard slips during his lines about Abraham Lincoln, prompting muffled laughter from the audience. And the crowd only winces slightly when the kids screech through the national anthem, hitting the high notes in only the way a bunch of tone-deaf elementary school students can. By the time it's over, my legs have fallen asleep from sitting in the grass, and I'm drenched in sweat.

"Two thumbs way up," Spencer says, offering a hand to pull me up from the ground.

"Oh my god, thank god that's done," Annie says, having made her way through the crowd from the back, where she'd been working the sound system. "I'm going to sit in the sauna until my eyeballs fall out of my head."

And before I can say anything, she's gone. Our job is done, after all, with the parents gathering their kids to move them along to the next part of the day, which likely involves the pool and a metric ton of sugar.

"That was great!" Kris says after making her way to the front of the stage. "The kids were adorable!"

"An excellent directorial debut," Pete adds, passing me a

small, cellophane-wrapped bouquet of pink roses. "I wanted to get the carnations that were dyed red, white, and blue, but Kris nixed that."

"Those Franken-flowers were gross," she says with a laugh. I take the bouquet and cradle it in my arms. All around me the kids are holding similar bouquets, a tradition I didn't even know existed until just now. I can't help but smile.

"Thank you," I say. "And thanks for coming."

"We wouldn't have missed it," Kris says, pulling me into a hug. I'm becoming used to her kamikaze embraces, and this one I don't even try to resist. I throw my arms around her neck and use the bouquet in my hand to pat her gently on the back. When we pull apart, I notice her eyes are wet, but she looks away quickly, and when she meets my eyes again, any trace of tears is gone. "Okay, well, we're off to get food. We'll let you guys have fun sans grown-ups."

I glance at Spencer. It hadn't occurred to me that we'd be spending the evening together, but he smiles at them and gives them a wave as they head back through the crowd.

"So, food?"

"Lead the way," I reply.

CHAPTER TWENTY

THE BUFFET IS SET UP RIGHT ON THE SANDY strip of beach, the tide pulling farther and farther from the line of tables as the sun gets closer to the horizon. The usual smell of salt has been overtaken by charcoal and smoke and barbecue. There are a number of stations set up, but Spencer seems to key in on one table in particular. I follow him and hop to the end of the line, which moves quickly.

At the front, there's an enormous silver dish piled high with cooked crabs. Spencer takes one of those paper boat things and piles three into it. Then he takes another and puts three more in, handing that one to me. I inhale the salty, briny scent of them, my mouth starting to water. Spencer grabs for a fat stack of napkins and what looks like a surgical kit from another tray, then cocks his head for me to follow him.

"Where are we going?"

"Secret place. C'mon."

I follow him back through the crowd and up the stairs, into the club, and around to the back.

"If you're taking me to the staff lounge, think again," I say, the smell of the steaming crab still drifting up and making my mouth water. "That place smells like a locker room."

Spencer pauses at a door at the end of a long hall. It has one of those bright red push bars across it that warn of an alarm sounding if you so much as look wrong at it. Spencer turns to me and leans his back into it, and I brace myself for the siren that doesn't come.

"It's broken," he says with a wink. The door swings open to reveal a dim stairwell. "Up."

And so we climb, around and up two, maybe three stories; it's hard to tell without floor markers. The only stop is the metal door at the top, which also opens with only a rusty protest. I emerge onto the roof of the club just as the sun is making its initial arc of descent. The sky is an incredible display of orange and pink and purple.

There's nothing up here, save for big metal contraptions that must be air conditioners or water tanks or something. Spencer plops down right in the middle, where we can see past the railing to the vast expanse of the ocean, already dark out on the horizon.

"You know how to break down a crab?" He reaches for one and shakes it, the juices running onto the ground beside him.

"I have to do this myself?" I say, my voice squeaking. The closest I've ever come to crabs is watching them in a Red

Lobster commercial, and those always look like someone has at least started the dirty work for you.

Spencer sets to work methodically cracking the shells like it's nothing. "You've just got to imagine it's a piece of fruit or a vegetable you've got to open up. Like a pomegranate or an artichoke."

Sure, because those are daily parts of my diet.

"Try it once, and if it freaks you out, I'll open them for you."

Something about his tone picks at me. Maybe it's the boy savior thing of him having to help me, a damsel in distress, eat her dinner, or maybe it's a bit of rich boy snobbery he doesn't even realize he has. Whatever it is, it sends my hand straight into my plate, pulling out a medium-sized crab. I take one of the silver cracker things from him and mimic his movements, placing it on the joint of one of the legs and squeezing. My first two attempts splinter the shell into enough pieces that I practically have to do surgery to get the meat out. But by my third crab, I'm starting to get the hang of it. When a claw slides easily from the shell, leaving a perfect lollipop of meat behind, I practically squeal in delight. And once I don't have to work so hard, I'm able to enjoy the flavor, which is salty and buttery and sort of sweet.

We spend the next fifteen minutes eating like savages, tearing at the poor little creatures and slurping out bits of meat from the shell. By the time we're done, my hands are salty and covered in the red seasoning from the crabs. I'm pretty sure my face hasn't escaped the wrath either. One look at Spencer, who has a streak of red dripping down his chin, and I know it doesn't matter. We're in this thing together.

We attack the stack of napkins and tear into the little packets of wet wipes, basically giving ourselves a mini sponge bath.

"All good?" Spencer asks, wadding up a napkin and tossing it into his paper plate, now littered with bits of shells and claws.

"It looks like a massacre," I say, nodding at the carnage.

"All the best food does," he says.

"Yeah, I'm going to test your premise on that one," I say, wiping my hands on a last Wet-Nap. "Reese's Cups? German chocolate cake? Almond Joy?"

"Ugh, you eat those? They taste like chocolate-coated sunscreen."

I wrinkle my nose at him. "Look, I'm very sorry that someone performed some terrible coconut-related tragedy on you at some point, but that's not an excuse to take it out on the best candy bar there ever was. Anyway, don't distract from my point, which is that very few of the best foods look like a massacre."

"You listen to me when I talk?" He laughs. "Usually I'm just saying stuff to see what sticks."

He sets his plate down on the ground next to him and wanders over to the railing that faces the ocean. I follow. We can see flits of sparklers weaving through crowds, the flickering of tiki torches stuck in the sand giving a warm glow to the festivities down below.

"Do you ever wish you still lived in New York?" I ask.

He shrugs, shaking his curls. "Nah. I mean, it would be cool to go to Knicks games and concerts and stuff, but this is way better. Winter sucks, and I need more space than we had there." He pulls himself off and ambles toward the stone ledge that surrounds the roof. "Hey, look," he says, pointing. "Dolphins!"

I jump up and hustle over, scanning the water, but I don't see them until Spencer steps behind me, takes my hand in his, and then lifts it until he's using my hand as a guide, pointing until I spot the fin. First one, then a second, bobbing up and down in the water. And then a third appears.

"I see them!" I giggle. I've never seen a dolphin that wasn't in an aquarium, and something about their playful jumping in that big blue ocean makes me giddy. Or maybe it's that, even after spotting the fins, Spencer is still behind me, his arm out, his hand wrapped gently around my wrist, pointing. And then he rests his chin on my shoulder, just for a split second, and sighs. I start to tilt my head into his just out of sheer instinct, because it feels like the right thing to do, like when you spot two puzzle pieces in a thousand-piece box and realize they go together. An inevitability. But then he steps back and drops my arm, moving next to me, and the moment passes.

I allow myself a sneaking sideways glance and see a blush creeping into his cheeks that I suspect has nothing to do with the sun beating down. I wish I could see his eyes, but they're hidden behind the mirrored lenses of his sunglasses. All I have to go on in that moment is his chin heavy on my shoulder, his breath in my ear, and the delicate feeling of his fingers on my skin.

"Do you get seasick?" he asks.

"Why?"

"Just answer the question."

"No," I reply, though I'm not sure if it's the truth. The *truth* is that I've never actually been on a boat before, which is insane to say when you've grown up on the coast of Florida. But my Florida childhood wasn't Spencer's Florida childhood. I didn't grow up on the water, I grew up surrounded by concrete and pavement, apartment buildings and strip malls, cars and buses and streetlights.

"Good, because I just stuffed you full of crab, and I *really* don't want to see that in reverse." He stands up, takes my plate, and stacks it atop his, then grabs my hand and pulls me back through the door. We weave back down the stairs and through the club. He dumps our plates in a trash can, then keeps going. I follow him all the way out to the parking lot, where his little blue car is parked. He opens the passenger door of the MG, and I climb in. He doesn't say a word, just flashes me a mysterious grin as we pull out of the parking lot.

I remember the bouquet of flowers I stupidly left up on the roof. "Hey, I don't want to spoil your surprise, but I should probably let Kris know where I'm going," I say.

"Tell her we're headed back to my house, and that my parents are home, so no worries," he says. I tap the message into my phone, and within seconds I see the little dots indicating a reply.

Kris: Thanks for the heads-up. Be safe. See you at home!

When we arrive, Spencer puts the car in park and leads me down to the beach behind his house. I haven't been on his side of the beach yet, and when we get down to the sand, I'm surprised to find boats pulled ashore, anchored to big pylons driven into the sand. There's a rowboat and a pair of kayaks, something small and sporty with a rolled-up sail, and at the end, a long, narrow metal boat with a motor on one end. He tromps through the sand to this one and untethers it from its chain.

"You go around back and push; I'll pull," he says, and for a moment I'm sure he must be joking. There's no way the two of us will be able to move this thing, but within seconds it's sliding across the sand nearly silent and with little effort, much lighter than it looks. Spencer kicks his flip-flops into the boat and tromps into the water up to his knees, the hem of his shorts getting damp, before he turns around to the back.

"Okay, you first." He steadies the front of the boat as I climb in. He gives it a running push until it's fully in the water, then takes a flying leap into the back. It bobs heavily, then settles. Spencer lowers the motor, fidgets with it for a second, then gives the string a hard tug until it sputters to life. It sounds only slightly better than his car, but that hasn't let us down yet, so I let go of any worry I have about sinking or throwing up. Instead, I turn my face out to the open blackness of the ocean, then gaze up at the moon, which is full and crystal clear.

"People always say there's a man in the moon, but I can't not see a rabbit riding a bicycle," I call over the roar of the engine.

"I'm sorry, did you just say a rabbit? Riding a bicycle?" he shouts back.

"Yeah!" I point, my finger arcing the bike's path up the side of the moon. "You don't see it?"

I look back at him and watch him squint up at it, his nose scrunching as the smile widens on his face.

"A rabbit riding a bicycle," he says with a laugh. "I think I do."

We stare at it for another beat, and then he tells me to hang on. Not knowing what I'm supposed to hang on *to*, I hunker down onto the seat and grab the sides of the boat. And then we're off. And if I thought the MG had some pickup, this boat, this little nothing of a metal bin, is suddenly flying across the water. No, *on top* of the water, the nose rising up high with the speed. We bounce over waves, sometimes banging down hard. I allow myself a glance over my shoulder to see Spencer piloting the boat with utter confidence, his hair blown back in the wind, a smile on his face. He looks *so happy*. So at ease. So in his element. I want to be that sure about anything.

We bounce across the water for a few minutes, then the engine cuts out. I'm nervous at first, thinking something has gone wrong, but then I see Spencer drop an anchor.

"We have arrived," he says as the anchor splashes and disappears below.

"To the place where you're going to drop my body?" I ask, but he doesn't laugh. Instead, he reaches for my shoulders and points me toward the shore. And then as if he commanded it, the sky explodes in a shower of rainbow sparks. I feel the attendant booms deep in my bones.

"This is the best view of them, I think," he says as the fireworks light up the sky over and over again. He climbs over and settles next to me on the seat. It isn't until that moment that I realize it's a bit cold out on the water, what with the ocean breeze, and so I lean into him until his arm goes around my waist. I tuck my shoulder under his and settle into him. We sit there, bobbing up and down in the water, for what feels like an hour, but is probably only a few minutes. And during that time, I feel acutely aware of every fiber of my body, every place that mine is touching his. Every place where we're connected feels warm and tingly, a sensation I'm not eager to lose. I tilt my head to the side and rest it on his shoulder, and he tilts his head to meet it. I take a deep breath and sigh out all the happiness this night has filled me with, blowing it out onto the breeze like I'm releasing it back into the world, just hoping it will come back to me.

"Good night?" Spencer asks.

"The best," I reply. "And what about you?"

"It was pretty good," he says. "I mean, I think it could be better."

"Oh?"

I feel him shift, turn slightly, and when I look up, I see his eyes gazing down at mine. A shudder starts deep in my chest and rushes up through my neck and shoulders, and I shiver, but I'm not cold. He ducks, and I close my eyes, and then his lips are on mine, salty from the ocean spray and warm. He gives me the slightest nudge with his tongue, and I part my lips for him. His arms snake around my waist, and I let mine wander around his neck until we're pulling each other tight, core to core. We sink into the rhythm of the water that is sending the boat bobbing up and down, and I let myself get carried away by it.

He leans back slightly and bumps my nose with his.

"Now it's the best," he says, planting the softest kiss on my forehead, and I'm so happy I can't even find the words to agree.

CHAPTER TWENTY-ONE

WHEN I WAKE TO THE SUN STREAMING through my open windows, I can still taste the lingering salt on my lips. Though the flavor is light, the memory is vivid, and I want to wrap myself in my blankets and roll over and fall back into a dream so I can experience it again.

"Breakfast!" Kris trills from downstairs, so I fling off the covers and leap out of bed. Because it occurs to me, maybe I don't have to dream about the kiss. Maybe this is my reality now.

I rummage through my drawers for a pair of shorts and a tank top, slip my feet into my flip-flops, and slap down the stairs to the kitchen where Kris is making some kind of egg situation. I take a seat at the table and sip my orange juice, freshly squeezed, and let myself wonder how in the living hell I got this damn lucky. First a kiss with a hot guy, then a home-cooked breakfast? It definitely doesn't suck.

Kris comes over with the hot pan and slides a piece of toast onto my plate, a perfectly round circle in the middle filled with fried egg.

"What's this?" I ask, leaning in to smell the butter and salt and yeasty goodness.

"Eggs in a basket. Or egg in a hole. Or, like, a million other names, but my mom always called it egg in a basket. She used to make it for me every Sunday morning, so I figured I'd make it for you since you seemed to have had quite a night."

My eyes widen with my grin. "What are you talking about?"

"Oh, please, you practically floated through that door as if carried in on angel's wings with some heavenly glow about you." She puts a piece of egg toast on her own plate, places the pan in the sink, then takes a seat across from me at the table. She arches an eyebrow. "I was young once, you know."

I laugh, but it isn't hard to imagine her young. She's barely forty, but I can see the teenager still in her face. Maybe it's the light in her eyes or the way she's so quick with a smile and a laugh, but she feels so much more like a friend than a mom.

"What was it like back then?" I ask, though what I want to ask was what was *she* like back then.

"Helena? Well, there were fewer full-timers on the island then, so it was kind of lonely in the winter. None of the other houses you see around were here. We were basically alone out on the point."

"It sounds peaceful."

"It's peaceful *now*, but when I was seventeen it was boring as all get-out. That's why I couldn't wait to get the hell off the island."

"Seriously? You wanted to leave?"

"Absolutely. I wanted out like a captive. I ran all the way to New York trying to escape Helena, not just geographically, but culturally. I swore I'd never come back."

"So how did you end up here?"

"Believe it or not, it was a broken heart."

Now *that* is not what I was expecting.

"I finished my undergrad at Columbia, was dating this great guy, thought I had it all figured out. I was going to apply to grad school in New York, we were going to get married, start a family. And then one day not long after graduation, that was all gone. He just up and decided he wasn't ready, and wouldn't *be* ready for a long time. At least not with me."

"And so you left New York?"

"Looking back, it was probably overly impulsive, but I had wrapped my whole life up in this guy. And then he was gone, and I felt like I didn't know who I was anymore. Or at least I didn't know who I was going to *be*."

It sounds awfully familiar.

"Anyway, my dad had always said he was going to move to Paris when he finally retired. I always figured it was a joke, but it turned out that he'd literally saved every penny and invested and prepared. So while my life was falling apart, my parents were like, 'Au revoir, honey!'"

I laugh. "Harsh!"

"Well, they didn't know. I didn't exactly confide in them, or anyone really." She smiles into her mug of tea. "And besides, they gave me the house, so it was hard to be too mad."

So *that's* how Kris wound up living on Helena, and that's why she doesn't quite seem like the spandex-wearing, tennis-playing mothers who brunch at the club, who bought their way onto the island. Kris inherited it. It's in her blood.

"Anyway, I had sort of an identity crisis, decided that I was going to go with the plan I originally had, and applied to grad school here while also becoming a foster parent. Figured if the guy wasn't going to stick around, I'd do it on my own."

"And that's when I happened."

"And now we're all caught up with our story."

We stab at our eggs, munching away in silence. I marvel, as I always do, at how amazing Kris's food is. I can't believe how she can take things she finds at a grocery store and turn them into this. If you handed me eggs and bread, well, I could make toast. The eggs—I'd have no idea what to do with them. My best guess would be to launch them at the homes of my enemies. But that seems to be how Kris moves through life: taking the ordinary and turning it into something extraordinary. That's what she did with her heartbreak. That's what she did with mine, too.

"Enough with the sappy talk," she says, tapping her fork on my plate. "Are you going to share your adventures with

Young Master Ford? No pressure, of course. Don't worry, Pete's out for a training run. He won't be back for at least an hour."

Her elbows are on the table, her coffee mug clutched between her hands as she leans forward, and I instantly flash to Lainey. Because this should be a conversation I am having with her. She's my best friend. Who I haven't seen in weeks, or talked to that much at all. I feel a pang, realizing what a shit friend I've been. I didn't mean to ghost her, it just sort of happened. She had work, and I had work, and there's a forty-five-minute drive between us. We kept trading short updates over text, but I always forgot to call. Dammit, she *asked* me to call, and I forgot.

I make a mental note to text her, and then I spill the details of last night's adventure. I tell Kris about learning to crack crabs. And I tell her that Spencer and I kissed out on the boat while watching the fireworks, but I leave it at that.

"Was it a good kiss?" she asks.

"The best," I reply. "Not that I have any basis for comparison."

She smiles warmly. "Oh, with things like that, you don't need a basis for comparison. You just know what you feel, and if it felt like the best, it was the best."

As if she can sense that that is as far as I want to go with the conversation, she sets her mug down on the table and cuts into her other piece of toast, the yellow yolk running across the plate. I mirror her movements, cutting a little triangle of bread and running it through my own river of egg yolk. The bite is warm and gooey and delicious.

"So, big plans for today?" I see her eyebrow arch, and I know she's asking if I have big plans *with Spencer*, but the truth is, I have no idea. When he left me on the lawn, his fingers lingering in my hand just a bit longer as he pulled away, he flashed me a dazzling smile and said, "See you tomorrow?"

I don't remember if I nodded or said yes or maybe even turned a backflip, but I'm pretty sure there was an affirmative. But when I reach into my pocket to check my phone, the screen is blank. *Ugh, boys.*

"Not sure," I reply, "but I think I'm just going to head down to the water and read for a bit before it gets too hot."

"Excellent plan. I may join you, if you don't mind. I'm making my billionth attempt at *Anna Karenina*, and maybe safety in numbers will help me plow on."

"I don't know how much fortitude you'll get from me," I say. I reach for the chubby romance novel I left on the counter yesterday, the one I pulled from her shelves. "I don't think Fabio has ever graced the cover of a Russian novel."

"Screw Tolstoy, I need some bodice-ripping action," she says, and laughs.

"Meet me down by the water?"

Down at the water, I settle into an Adirondack chair and crack the spine on my book. I'm happy to find that I left off just before a juicy sexy-times scene, and I like the way the warmth that spreads through me brings back memories of the boat last night.

Heath is just about to bust the seams of Lady Aria's emerald gown when I hear the sound of sandy footfalls. I look up to see Spencer running down the beach toward me from his house. He comes right up to my chair and starts jogging in place. It must have been the start of his run, because he's barely broken a sweat, and I can still smell the sporty detergent his mom (or his cleaning lady) uses on his gym shorts.

"Join me?" he asks, barely breathing hard as he prances in the sand next to me.

"You're kidding," I reply, a statement of fact, not a question.

"Come on, join me!" He tosses his head down the beach, as if the route of the run is going to rouse me from this chair.

"I'm wearing flip-flops."

He shrugs. "I'll wait."

I arch an eyebrow at him. "Jogging in place the whole time?"

Guess I'm going to have to lay the hammer to his dreams that he made out with a sporty girl, because *no*.

"Look, tennis was one thing, but I only run if—"

"Bears are chasing you, yeah, yeah," he says.

"Actually, no, if a bear is chasing me, I'm curling up on the ground, playing dead, and hoping for the best. Don't you watch the Discovery Channel?"

"So under what circumstances do you run?"

I pause, tapping my finger on my chin like I'm really thinking about it. "Now that I'm pressed to think about it, none. Under no circumstances do I run."

This is enough to pause Spencer in place, and to my delight he doesn't look horrified or disappointed. Instead, he bends over, hands on his knees and laughs, shaking his wild hair.

"How's about this," I say. "You take off and enjoy your run, and I will remain here enjoying my book and exercising my *mind*."

"That exercises your mind?" he asks, eyeing the scrolling, metallic font and the shirtless man on my water-spotted, warped paperback.

"Do not dare judge a book by its cover, Spencer Ford," I say, swatting him with my book, but he dances away, jogging in a little circle around my chair.

"You'll be here when I get back?"

I flip the remaining one hundred or so pages at him. "If you hustle, you just might beat me. But I'm a fast reader."

"Good thing I'm a really fast runner!" he says, and then he's off like a shot down the beach, the sound of his laughter echoing behind him, carried by the wind.

Spencer's fast, but I'm faster. I finish the final pages of my book (Heath and Lady Aria live happily ever after, sans bodice, of course) and head back to the house to get ready for whatever Spencer could possibly have planned. After yesterday, really, anything is possible, though I'll honestly be happy if we take the boat out into the water again and kiss until the sun goes down.

When I see him rounding the bend back to his house, I head back up to Kris's house to deposit my finished book and grab my phone. Kris never did join me on the beach. I swing by her office, but it's empty. I'm just about to knock on her bedroom door when I hear what sounds like sniffles, the kind that come after a good cry. It's so unusual for Kris to appear as anything other than put together that I can't imagine she wants an audience for this. So I back away and head to Spencer's. I start for the front door, but decide I don't want to risk running into his dad. Instead, I circle around the back and go to settle into one of the lounge chairs by the pool, figuring I'll text Spencer and let him know I'm waiting out here for him. But before I can pull out my phone, I hear a familiar voice drifting out of a nearby window.

"Spencer, you don't understand. I only want what's best for you."

Mr. Ford sounds exasperated; that's nothing new, but there's something else in his voice that makes me pause. I know I shouldn't, but I rise from the chair and cross the patio toward the open window, where I hear Spencer next.

"No, you want what's best for *you*, and that's having a kid created in your image. Well, I'm not interested. Why don't you try Ryan, who might actually want that? Oh, I forgot, because he's not the perfect son you wanted." Spencer sounds defiant. And so, *so* very sure.

"What are you even talking about?"

"I see the way you treat him. Like he's a broken toy."

"That's not true!"

"It is! He wants to play golf. He wants to play tennis with you. But you always blow him off. You leave him sitting there on the benches at the club, wondering why his dad, who clearly loves all that stuff, doesn't want to be seen with him."

"That's because I'm trying to protect him! I don't want people to stare at him. I don't want him to feel like he's different."

"*You* make him feel different."

There's a long sigh.

"Spencer, that's not what I—"

"Forget it. You've never cared what I have to say before. Why start now?" And then I hear a door slam.

I hurry back to the lounge chair so Spencer won't realize I was eavesdropping, but it doesn't matter. It takes only a minute for my phone to buzz with a text from him.

Rain check? Something came up.

Of course I know he's lying. I imagine he's somewhere in his house, maybe up in his room, pacing like a caged animal, wishing he had a tennis racket to throw. But I let him have his lie, because I know what it's like to want to keep it to yourself. I know what it's like to need to melt down without other people watching, even people who want to help.

CHAPTER
TWENTY-TWO

I'M IN KRIS'S OFFICE, SCANNING HER bookshelves for something new to read, when I hear the doorbell. My heart picks up an extra beat thinking maybe it's Spencer, having cooled down from his fight with his dad.

I take the steps downstairs two at a time, jumping down the last three with a loud *thud* on the wood floors. I swing the door open, so full of excitement that I could leap into Spencer's arms.

Only it's not Spencer at the door.

Tess is standing on the porch in her professional social worker outfit, her ubiquitous overstuffed tote bag on her shoulder.

"Oh, hi," I say, trying not to look too disappointed to see her. "Was there an appointment I forgot about?"

"No," she says, a tight smile on her face. "Can I come in?"

"Sure." I move aside, and she steps through the door. We

head for the living room, where she takes a seat on the couch, but I stay standing by the entry. "Do you want me to get Kris?"

"Actually, I spoke with Kris on the phone earlier. I'm here to see you. I have some news." She pulls her leather legal pad holder thing out of her tote bag and opens it on her lap and gestures to the chair across from her, so I sit. "Your mom is back."

It was only a few weeks ago that I was at the DCF office, but it feels like a lifetime ago. It *was* another life. But now that life is waiting for me in a conference room.

"You'll have half an hour," Tess says. "Unfortunately, it's a busy day, so we have a lot of people waiting. Space is at a premium around here."

She's not kidding. The hallway is lined with benches, and nearly every available space is occupied by kids. A few are sitting quietly, reading a book or tapping away at a phone. There are a handful of toddlers squirming impatiently while adults barely keep them contained. Two babies are crying at full volume while their adults bounce them in vain.

"I don't want to see him!" shouts a boy, probably middle-school aged.

"We've been through this. Every two weeks you have a visit. That's how it goes," says an elderly woman who is fanning herself furiously. The boy beside her fumes silently on the bench.

Tess leads Kris, Pete, and me through it all. She stops at a door that I recognize as her office. She opens it and gestures for Kris and Pete to go in.

"You guys can wait here. I'll come get you when we're done," she says.

Pete nods and heads in, but I can tell Kris is having a hard time following directions. She stands there, her hands clenched at her sides, looking at me.

"Are you sure you're okay? Do you need anything?" she asks me.

"I'm fine," I say. "I promise. It's fine."

She doesn't look like she believes me, and I'm not sure I believe me either. It's been just over a month since I last saw my mother. We were halfway to the state statute on abandonment before she showed back up. Part of me is relieved that she made it, part of me is still so mad at her for leaving, and part of me is filled with dread over what might happen now. All that anxiety and uncertainly from those first few days has come rolling back and settled in right in the pit of my stomach.

"This way, Maritza," Tess says. She pulls her office door shut and directs me to the door at the end of the hall.

"Is she in there?" I ask, my heart pounding.

"She's waiting for you," she replies. "You ready?"

Yes. No. I don't know.

I nod.

She's sitting in the chair at the head of the table, her hair pulled up, a bright yellow scarf tied around her head to hold back all the curls attempting to escape. She's wearing a long skirt in the same yellow, and a white shirt with delicate eyelet embroidery. Her skin is a little more tan, the freckles on her nose a bit more pronounced, but otherwise she looks the same, which seems wrong. She should look different, and I should look different. I *am* different.

When she sees me, she sucks in a breath, jumping out of her chair so quickly it screeches across the scuffed linoleum tile. I wince at the sound.

"Ritzy! It's so good to see you!" she says, wrapping me up in a hug. She steps back, like she's assessing me. What does she see? Do *I* look different?

"I spoke with that social worker," she says, her nose wrinkling on the title as if it were "prison guard" or "booger picker." She steps back and returns to her chair, gesturing for me to take the one next to her. "She said that I abandoned you and that I could lose my parental rights. Can you believe that? Not that I'd ever claim to have *rights* over you. I mean, you're an independent person, after all. You chart your *own* destiny."

I bark out a laugh. Yup, definitely still the same mom. "You *did* abandon me."

She recoils like she's been slapped. "I did not! I told you exactly where I was going."

"Yeah, but I'm seventeen. And you *left*."

"Well, you seem fine. It wasn't some kind of disaster, right?"

I can only blink at her. I hear another baby cry out in the hall, followed by the start of an epic toddler tantrum. Yeah, I'm fine. I ended up with Kris and Pete, living in their beautiful home on Helena, welcomed into the family unquestioningly. But that was literally the best-case scenario. It could have gone in any other direction. It could have ended up anywhere. I could have ended up someplace terrible, with terrible people. Yeah, I'm fine, but it was only thanks to a metric ton of luck that things turned out that way.

I want to tell her all of this. I want to scare her, to make her feel bad, but she's sitting there staring at me, just so *clueless*.

"You didn't call or write," I say finally.

She sighs. "We were on a very strict regimen of silent meditation, Ritzy."

Like that's a good excuse for cutting me off completely. I cannot suppress the eye roll. I swear you could see it from space. "You can't spare a moment for your own daughter?"

"But it *was* for you . . . for us," she says, and now I'm more confused than ever.

"What are you even talking about?"

She sighs. "I know you think the Bodhi Foundation is silly. I realize that. But I really do think it's a path forward for me."

"Here we go," I mutter, ready to hear another New Age sales pitch.

"Ritzy, stop," she says, her voice suddenly firm. All that

airy-fairy, breathless tone she usually uses to talk about her spiritual journeys is gone. It's just Mom. "I did this because it's the start of an opportunity. A *business* opportunity. I can start to actually build something here. And with you getting ready for college, I really need that. I know there's financial aid, but there will still be expenses to cover, and my collection of part-time jobs won't cover it. I could really make a go at being a life coach with Bodhi. I could be *good* at this, Ritzy. And it could make a difference for us."

Whoa. Setting aside the ridiculousness that the Bodhi Foundation sounds like, with its New Age pyramid scheme, I can't believe what I'm hearing. Words like *financial aid* and *expenses* sound like she's speaking a foreign language. I didn't realize she'd been paying any attention to the brochures and letters coming home from school, to the bulletins from the guidance office and the bulk mailing from half the admissions offices in the southeast. She actually *was* trying to do something good. Something sort of unselfish, even if it was in her own flaky way.

She sighs. "I'm sorry, Ritzy, that you got pulled into all of *this*." She gestures around the spare conference room. "If I had known you'd wind up here, I never would have left. I didn't expect you to be ripped from your life. Has it been just *awful*?"

Seeing her take in this life as if I've been in some kind of hovel pricks at me. Sure, Kris is sort of overbearing and pathologically chipper. And no, I haven't always felt like I fit in there. But Kris and Pete have been nothing but kind and generous. They took me in when my mother walked out on me, and even if she can dress it up as trust and freedom, it still feels like abandonment.

Mom must take my silence for agreement, because she doesn't wait for an answer. "Well, that social worker said that you're not allowed to just come home with me."

"Mom, there is no home. Our apartment is gone."

"Oh, you know that's not what I meant by *home*," she says, brushing off the place we shared for three years like it's nothing. "I'm staying with Rose at her place. The whole upstairs is finished, you know. There's a place for you, of course, but that *social worker*—"

"Tess," I say, because I can't take her snotty tone about the first person to reach out and help me after she left.

"Right, *Tess*, she gave me a list of things I need to do before you can come home, all of which seem excessive. I mean, *parenting classes*? You're seventeen. I'll do it to get this all cleared up, of course." And then she pauses, looking at me for real, for perhaps the first time since she sat down. Her eyes narrow ever so slightly, not angrily, just studying me. She must see it, that this hasn't been *just awful*, as she described it.

"I have a job. I have friends . . ." I start to tell her, only to trail off, because I had those things before she left. I had those things, and I left them behind. Would I have to do that again?

"Well, of course, Ritzy. I'm not going to force you to come with me. It's entirely up to you."

"What?"

"I was serious when I said you were old enough to follow your own path. You are. And you're certainly old enough to decide if you want to stay with them," she says, and I know she means Kris and Pete. "It's up to you, Ritzy."

And there it is. Suddenly the mysterious path I've supposedly been set upon appears before me, the proverbial fork. It's finally up to me to actually choose. I can choose to go back with my mom, to my old life, finish school at Southwest with Lainey. Or I can stay with Kris and Pete. And Spencer.

The conference room door opens, and Tess pops in.

"Everything going okay in here?" she asks.

"We're fine, thank you," Mom says, and I nod, still trying to take in what she said.

"Well, time's up for now, unfortunately," Tess says. I glance over at Mom and see her gritting her teeth, practically pulling a muscle not to roll her eyes.

"Yes, I should probably go," Mom says, rising from her chair, as if this was all part of *her* plan. "I'm so sorry, Ritzy. You have to know I didn't mean for all this to happen. I really and truly thought you'd be waiting for me back at the apartment when I got back."

"Oh," I say, the word escaping on a huff of breath. Everything I thought I knew about this summer has just been turned upside down, and I feel like the choice she's given me keeps it spinning. I have no idea which way is up anymore. I have no idea which way is *home*.

"I love you, Ritzy," she says. I stand up from my chair, and she comes over, throwing her arms around me. I breathe in the smell of patchouli or whatever the herbal scent is that seems to trail her from place to place. My breath catches in my throat as I feel tears well up. I'm still mad at her—*so* mad—but that smell, and the feel of her arms around my neck. It's home.

She pulls back and places her forehead against mine, her hands cradling my face.

"I'll see you soon," she whispers. "No matter what you decide."

I nod against her forehead, trying desperately to hold in the tears that spill over onto my cheeks.

"I love you, too, Mom," I reply, words finally coming to me just before she's gone.

CHAPTER TWENTY-THREE

I HAVEN'T SEEN SPENCER FOR THREE days. He's been at a tennis tournament with his dad, some big regional country club thing where the players can only wear white and the prizes are silver platters.

When he left, I thought his absence would feel like an eternity. But then Tess showed up. And my mom. And I forgot all about how badly I wanted to kiss him.

But when my phone buzzes with a text letting me know he's back, I bolt out onto the lawn, full of excitement and anticipation. I settle down into the grass to wait for him and begin combing through it for four-leaf clovers, as is my habit, though I've never actually found one.

"Lose something?"

I look up to see Spencer striding across the lawn from his house. I stand, and when he gets to me, he winds an arm around my waist, pulling me toward him for a kiss. I rise up on my toes to meet his lips, and for a moment I let myself sink into him.

He releases me when we hear a throat clearing from behind us. Pete is on the porch holding a bottle of water, back from his run.

"I see you're back from the western front," he says to Spencer, arching an eyebrow.

"Yes, sir, hope not to be shipped off again till fall," he replies with a two-fingered salute and that crooked grin I love.

"You two are too much," he says. "Save some oxygen for the rest of us mere mortals?" He turns his attention to me. "Kris still isn't feeling well. You okay to be on your own for dinner? Or I could order a pizza."

"You can come to my house," Spencer says.

It's quiet, and I realize it's because they're waiting for me to tell them what I want. I could almost laugh at the idea that I'm supposed to make a decision about *pizza* when I've got choices to make about the rest of my *life*.

"I'm not hungry," I reply finally. Pete's studying me, but he doesn't say anything about what must be my dour attitude. Then he turns and heads back into the house.

I'm alone with Spencer now, and beside me I can feel him practically vibrating with energy. On any other day, I'd be excited to see what kind of adventures we'd get up to, but right now I feel like I need to sit down and spill everything that's happened. But I don't know how to start this crazy conversation, so I go for something else first.

"Did you win?" I ask Spencer.

"Nah, second."

"So no platter?"

"No, I got one. But it's probably only big enough for a side salad. Definitely not a whole Thanksgiving turkey."

I nod, because I don't know what else to say. My brain has only been focused on one singular thought since yesterday: *Stay here? Or go back?*

"You okay? You seem sort of . . . absent," Spencer says.

"Yeah," I reply, then grab a fistful of grass and pull. The feeling of it breaking free in my hand is only temporarily gratifying. "No. Actually, no I'm not."

"What's going on?"

"My mom is back."

"I thought your mom was in Mexico."

"Apparently not anymore. She's all trained up to be a life coach or something, and she wants me to come live with her. Or her and her friend Rose, the palm reader who has space in her house."

"But she can't just do that, right? I mean, there are courts involved?"

"Yeah, but there's a way for her to do some things, classes and counseling and stuff, and then I can go back to live with her." I pause, letting the grass fall out of my hand into a little pile on the ground. "If I want to."

"Well, obviously you don't."

My head snaps up to meet his gaze. He sounds *so sure*. How can he be so sure?

"Why is it obvious?" I ask.

"Um, because she abandoned you? And instead of going to live with a palm reader or whatever, you can stay *here*." He gestures to Kris's house and around to the ocean, like he's showing me the grand prize on a game show. "I mean, this is an upgrade, right?"

I don't know why, but that stings. "This isn't like getting bumped to first class or something, Spencer. We're talking about my *mom*."

"Yeah, who left you alone to get scooped up by a social worker. What kind of person does that?"

"It's more complicated than that," I tell him, but of course he'd have no idea why my mom did what she did, even if I explained it to him. Money is something he's never had to worry about, something he's probably never even had to *think* about. Which can tend to make life a little more cut-and-dried. But when you don't have it, suddenly things get murky. Like, *leave your daughter to go pursue a job opportunity in Mexico* murky.

"Why are you making excuses for her?" he asks.

I shake my head. "Stop it, Spencer."

"No, seriously. Why are you ignoring the fact that she totally abandoned you? Why would you want to go back to that when you have the opportunity for something so much better?"

"Just because you have a shitty relationship with your dad doesn't mean you have any idea of what my life is like," I snap.

He scoffs. "Oh, please, like you have any perspective on what a family is really all about."

The words land between us like a grenade. "That was . . . ," I start, but I can't figure out a way to convey what I'm feeling. Is that really what he thinks of me?

He realizes right away that he's gone a step too far.

"Come on, Maritza. You said a shitty thing." Okay, so not an apology. Just an excuse.

"Yeah, and then you went and said a nuclear shitty thing."

My voice cracks, the tears starting to spill. He flinches but seems to get himself back quickly. He's not done being mad at me. He's holding on to it, just like he holds on to his anger with his dad. I want to say something final, maybe something devastating, but no words come. So instead I stand up and brush the grass clippings off my butt. Then I turn and stride across the lawn toward Kris's house. I want to turn and look to see if he's watching, and also I don't.

In the end, I don't glance back. Neither option would make me feel better anyway.

⌣

The house is silent when I go in. I figure Pete must be in his post-run shower, while Kris is upstairs recovering from whatever is ailing her. I tiptoe up the stairs, not wanting to run into anyone to have to talk about what just happened with Spencer.

When I get to the top of the stairs, I hear voices coming from the study. I pause just before I pass. It's Pete and Kris, who seems to have recovered.

"You don't need to pretend this didn't happen," Pete says. "You're allowed to be sad."

Is he talking about me? About my mom coming back? Kris has been strangely quiet since our visit to DCF. I didn't tell her about my mom's offer. I figure Tess probably told them my mom wants me to come back with her, but I don't really want to talk about it with Kris. I don't know what I'm going to do yet, and I'm worried that talking it over with her might make Kris feel worse. She said the first time I left it nearly broke her. It sounds like it's happening again.

"I'm not pretending it didn't happen," Kris says. "I spent the last day crying about it. I'm done now. I'm ready to do something else."

"I don't think a day is enough. I think built-up stress is part of the problem here, but okay. Let's go with your plan. Why don't we talk about what we're going to do next?"

"What do you mean?" Her tone says she's trying very hard to stay distant. It's a practiced disengagement. I recognize it from all the times I've been trying to avoid a conversation.

"I think it's clear that the fertility treatments aren't going to work. But we still have the number of the adoption lawyer," Pete says. "And you're obviously still in the foster system."

I have to cover my mouth to suppress the gasp.

"We couldn't start all that. We have Ritzy." She tosses it off like he's an idiot for not considering me, whatever that means.

"So you're saying we put this on hold for eighteen months? We put our *family* on hold?"

And then I realize what's going on. This wasn't a surprise. The prescriptions and the tension. Kris going from happy to miserable so quickly. They want a baby. Because of course they do. And they were trying to have one before I came back. And now they're having to talk about other options. Because my arrival and the subsequent stress caused a hiccup in that plan.

I turn and slowly creep back down the stairs, realizing they think I'm with Spencer. They didn't count on me coming home. They didn't count on me showing up here in the first place, but that's another story, one that caused enough stress on Kris to make whatever planning they had going fail. *I* did that. *I* ruined their plan. *I* ruined their family.

I'm not thinking about what to do next or where to go. I just walk out the front door and start down the road toward town. I want to put as much distance between me and the house as I can. I should have known the notion of that being my home was an illusion. It's felt real, but like all good Hollywood special effects, it's completely fake. I'm not part of that family. I'm the thing *keeping* those two people from having their own family—their own kid. I'm just a tourist here.

I walk until I find myself in downtown Helena, which is enjoying its usual Saturday bustle. People are walking dogs, eating lunch, toting shopping bags. All of them belong here, but I don't.

CHAPTER
TWENTY-FOUR

I DON'T KNOW WHERE TO GO. I WANT OFF this island, but I'm too scared to just walk over the bridge. I don't have my phone. It's back in my room at the house. I was supposed to be hanging out with Spencer. I wasn't supposed to overhear that. It wasn't supposed to all fall apart.

I sit down on the curb in front of Heather's shop. I have no phone, no wallet, and nowhere to go.

"You look sad."

A skinny little shadow falls over me, just barely shielding me from the sun. I look up and see Ryan standing over me.

"I am," I say.

He wrinkles his nose.

"Want me to tell you a joke?"

I can't tell a seven-year-old that my problems are too big to be fixed by a joke, so instead I say sure.

He plops down on the curb next to me, thinking for a

minute, clearly searching for the perfect joke that he thinks will turn my frown upside down.

"Okay, I got one," he says finally. "Why did the scarecrow win an award?"

"Why?"

"For being outstanding in his field!" And then, like all kids telling jokes, he dissolves into fits of laughter at his own hilarity. And maybe it's the total badness of the joke or the sight of him laughing, but I laugh, too.

"Are you still sad?" Ryan asks when he's caught his breath.

"Yeah, but that helped," I say. "Thanks, Ryan."

"Did Spencer make you sad?"

I look up at him sharply. "What makes you think that?"

"Because he's been a major butt-face today."

"Oh? How come?"

"He keeps fighting with my dad. It's so dumb."

"What do they fight about?"

"Ugh, *everything*," he says, rolling his eyes. "Mom says it's because they're so much alike."

I find that hard to believe. Granted, I've only known them a short time, but I've never seen any shades of similarity between Spencer and Mr. Ford, at least not in personality. Until today, that is.

"How so?" I ask.

"Stubborn," Ryan says. "They're both really stubborn. And Mom says they don't deal with it very well. They both get really grumpy and mean. It sucks."

"You shouldn't say *sucks*."

"Okay, it *stinks*," he says, rolling his eyes. "Anyway, if Spencer said something mean, he didn't mean it. Sometimes he does that. Mom says it's because he forgets to get out of his own head. He'll say he's sorry. He always does to me."

I think back to the night on the tennis court. He was definitely in his own head that night. And the time he nearly left me at the Pen. Believe it or not, this seven-year-old's psychological assessment of his older brother is pretty spot-on.

"Ryan, you ready?" I glance up and see Mrs. Ford coming out of Heather's shop, a lavender bag on her arm. "Oh, hi, Maritza. Are you okay?"

I try to give her a smile to reassure her, but from the look on her face, I think it only makes it worse. "I'm fine," I tell her, but she's clearly not buying it.

"Do you need a ride?"

I shake my head.

"Are you sure? Because I can take you anywhere."

There's only one place that I can think of that I want to go right now. One person I want to see.

"Actually, there is someplace you could take me," I say. "It's kind of far, though."

She hits the button on her keys, and the Suburban two spaces down beeps. "Get in."

⌒

"You know I'm going to tell Kris about this," Mrs. Ford says when we're nearly there.

"I know." Leaving wasn't about trying to punish her or freak her out. In fact, leaving felt like a thing I could do for her, a thing she might need. But I still don't want her to worry, so I'm glad Mrs. Ford will be there to fill her in.

I give her directions, finally sending her onto Vineville Road. It's dotted with a motley collection of shotgun homes and bungalows, many in various stages of disrepair. There are bent chain-link fences, overgrown lawns, and cars that haven't run since sometime in the last decade. More than one house is completely boarded up, with official and angry-looking NO TRESPASSING signs nailed to the front door.

"Do you live here?" Ryan sounds incredulous, and a glance in the rearview mirror shows him with his nose pressed to the window, taking in every passing bit of scenery.

"Ryan," Mrs. Ford says, a subtle admonishment in her tone.

"What? It's really far away," Ryan says. "I like you living next door. I bet Spencer would be sad if you lived here."

"Now *him* I don't have to tell, if you don't want me to," she says, her eyes on the road, but she keeps glancing back at my reddened, tearstained face in the rearview mirror.

"Yeah, I won't tell either," Ryan chimes in from the back.

I give her a grateful smile. "I'll talk to him soon. We just need . . ." I trail off, not actually sure what we need. "Some time" is what I finally settle on.

Mrs. Ford nods. "My son is a wonderful boy, but even I have to admit that he can be a tremendous idiot sometimes."

"I already told her, Mom," Ryan says.

"Whatever it was, give him a chance to explain, okay? It doesn't have to be today, or even anytime soon. Just leave the door cracked."

"I will," I tell her. "Thanks."

The pink house is coming up on the right, and I point Mrs. Ford toward the open spot in front of the house. She whips the car into it.

"You sure you're okay?"

"Yeah, this is my best friend's house," I say, hoping the first part is still true. I haven't talked to her in so long, not since our text the night of my date with Ali. I was supposed to call her, and it just got away from me.

"Okay. Well, I'll wait to make sure she's here," Mrs. Ford says. I can tell she's trying not to be judgmental about the neighborhood, but she's nervous to leave me here nonetheless.

"Thank you again for the ride," I say. "I know it probably wasn't how you were planning on spending your Saturday."

She smiles. "I'm happy to help."

I give her a final, tight smile, tell Ryan good-bye, and climb out of the car. I try not to wonder if this is the last time I'm going to see them. If what I heard back at Kris's house is true, then my decision just got a lot easier.

I ring the bell and then step back. I hear her footsteps right away. When she opens the door, I can tell I'm the last person she expected to find here. I turn and give Mrs. Ford a wave so she won't wait, because if Lainey is going to yell at me, maybe even send me away, I don't want her to see that. She waves back, and then the car slowly pulls away from the curb.

"Who was that?" Lainey asks.

"Spencer's mom," I say, then realize she probably doesn't even remember who Spencer is. "The guy who lives next door?"

She arches an eyebrow at me.

"It's a long story," I tell her.

"When it's been this many weeks, they're *all* long stories."

"I'm sorry," I say, testing the waters. "I really didn't mean to go that long without seeing you."

"Or talking to me?" She cocks her head at me, ready to lay all my crimes at my feet. As well she should. I feel like crap. Like *I* should.

"Yeah," I say. My mouth goes dry as I try to calculate how long it's been.

"Three weeks," she says. She always could read what was going on in my head. "I haven't heard from you in almost three weeks. Which is pretty damn crappy. And it's not like before that we were super chatty. I finally stopped texting because I felt like a pathetic stalker. I'm not going to beg you to be my friend, Ritzy."

"Lainey? Everything okay?" Ali comes up behind Lainey in the doorway, and my eyes drift down to where his hand has snaked around her waist and is resting on her hip.

Holy. Crap.

As soon as he sees me standing on the stoop, his face drops first, then his hand. Then he takes a step away from Lainey, like he can erase what just happened. I glance at Lainey, expecting to see her freaking out or looking nervous or *something* that indicates that she's apparently hooked up with my former crush, but she just arches her eyebrow at me.

"Ali, can you give us a second?" she says to him, and he looks all too happy to disappear back into the house.

I know I shouldn't say it, that I have no right, but I can't stop the words from tumbling out of my mouth. "What the hell, Lainey? You and Ali?"

She offers nothing but a defiant look.

"For how long? And how did this happen?"

"It's new. Not even two weeks," she says. "We had that SAT prep class, and then we've been spending a lot of time together. Which is more than I can say about you and me."

The statement feels like a slap, and now I'm even madder. Lainey, who listened to me talk about Ali for *years*, who helped orchestrate our first date attempt, is now *dating him*? This feels so wrong.

"Why didn't you tell me?"

She rolls her eyes. "I *tried*. I texted you. I told you I needed to talk to you. But you were never available. You were always busy with work or your new friends." She crosses her arms over her chest, her gaze leveled at me hard. "You completely disappeared on me because you were too busy having a fantastic time in your fabulous new life with your amazing new friends.

And so forgive me for not sitting around on the hook trying to smooth things over with someone who didn't even care enough to *call me back*."

I want to look at her, but now I can't bring myself to pull my eyes away from the ground. My cheeks are hot and red, I'm sure, and I can feel the telltale pinprick in the corner of my eyes that tells me tears could be imminent. I hadn't meant to be such a bad friend. I really hadn't.

"I'm sorry, Lainey," I say, the shame forcing my voice out at barely above a whisper. "I'm really sorry."

"I know you are," Lainey says. "You should be. I *needed* you."

I don't say a word.

"Your life may have moved somewhere else, but I didn't. And I would have thought you'd know better than that. I would have thought our friendship meant more than that."

We stand there on the porch, her in the doorway, me staring at my shoes, for a long time, neither of us saying anything. I came here to talk to her about my mom coming back. To get her advice. I knew she'd listen and not judge me, not like Spencer did. But now I feel like a shit friend just showing up to have her sift through my own personal drama again. She's always been there for me, but I clearly haven't been there for her.

Just when I'm starting to feel desperate, Lainey sighs.

"Do you need to come in?"

The smell of Lainey's house envelops me like a security blanket, a mix of her peachy body lotion and the apple-cinnamon candles her mother loves to burn.

"Well, Ritzy, isn't this a surprise! How you doing?" Jana walks into the room in jeans and a T-shirt, her apron over her shoulder. She's reaching for her purse.

"I'm all right," I tell her, thankful my voice is able to hold steady at this moment. "You headed to work?"

"Sure am," she says. She holds up her fingers, showing me the narrowest space between them. "I'm *this* close to being done with job number two. Maybe only another week or so I can quit the diner. And not a moment too soon. I think my feet are about to pack up and find another owner."

"That's great news," I say, trying to muster the enthusiasm it deserves. Because it *is* great. Jana's been working her ass off for months, and I know she wants nothing more than to be home at night with Lainey. I know Lainey wants that, too.

"Yes, it is," Jana says. "Now I've got to head out. But you make yourself at home, Ritzy. And next time, don't go so long without coming to see us, okay?" She gives me a look that says she knows what a terrible friend I've been.

I settle onto the couch, ready to fall apart, when Ali appears from the kitchen. He looks so uncomfortable he's practically vibrating.

"Hey, so, um, I'm gonna go," he says, pointing at the front door like we need the visual.

"Yeah. I'll call you later?" Lainey says. For the first time, the temperature in her voice rises above frosty, because she's talking to Ali and not to me.

Ali gives his trademark crooked grin, the one that used to make my heart explode. And from the smile on Lainey's face, I can see she knows that feeling. She really likes him. "Later," he says, then his eyes cut to me. "Uh, good to see you, Ritzy."

I pull together my best smile, trying to let them know that I'm not going to freak out. Because I'm not (I don't think). "You too, Ali," I say, and then he's gone, the door slamming behind him.

Now that we're alone, Lainey takes a seat next to me on the couch. She looks like she can't decide between yelling at me or hugging me. Finally, she says, "You look like hell."

"I feel like hell," I say, and I wait for her to tell me, *Good, you should*, but when she doesn't, I let the truth escape. "I don't know where I belong anymore."

And that's when it all falls apart. I dissolve into tears, the whole thing pouring out. I tell Lainey all about seeing my mom and what I learned. I tell her about my fight with Spencer, and about what I overheard between Kris and Pete.

"I didn't know where to go. I know I don't deserve to be here. But I just, I didn't—" I break off, sounding as hopeless as I feel. But then Lainey reaches out and pulls me into a hug.

"I'm still pissed," she says as she squeezes me tight. "But I'm also still your best friend. Which means I'll always be giving you hell, but I'll also always be here for you."

I let out a long, slow breath like I've been holding it for

days. The only thing that breaks us apart is the ringing of Lainey's phone. She reaches for it, then cocks an eyebrow.

"Who is it?" I ask.

She flips her phone around so I can see the screen, showing a picture of me with my head thrown back, singing along to the radio in Barney.

"It's you."

———

An hour later, Kris is sitting on the sofa in Lainey's living room. True to her word, Mrs. Ford had gone straight back to Helena and directly to Kris's house, where she told Kris about where she'd taken me and the state I'd been in on the drive. Kris tried to call me, but found my cell phone ringing on my bedside table where I'd left it to charge. And so she'd used it to find Lainey's number, and then she did what I didn't. She called my best friend.

I think as far as she knew I'd had a fight with Spencer, and that was all. Though I wondered if she suspected, or if she could imagine, that maybe I'd overheard. Because all she said was, "Give me the address. I'm coming over."

And forty-five minutes later, here she is, an already-sweating glass of ice water clutched in her hand. Lainey lingers in the doorway for a moment before telling us she's going to check on some laundry in the basement. As soon as she's gone, Kris turns to me.

"We said we were going to be honest with each other. So let's start now."

"Okay," I say, though I still don't know *where* to start.

"Why did you leave? Without saying anything?" she asks.

I sigh. So I guess we're starting there. "Spencer and I had a fight, and so I came back to the house. I don't think you guys were expecting me, and I heard . . ." I trail off. She bites her lip and sighs. "I heard Pete say that you guys want to have a baby, and that I'm slowing that down."

Her mouth drops open, her eyes wide. There's a beat of silence, where all I hear is her sharp intake of breath.

"Oh, Ritzy, that's not what he meant. It's not what he meant at all," she says finally. She places the glass of water down on the floor by her feet and turns to me, pulling a knee up onto the couch. "Pete and I have been trying to start a family for a while. For a few years, actually. And it's been . . . difficult. I'm not exactly twenty-five, you know." She laughs, but I can tell it's forced. Nothing about this is funny to her.

"And then I showed up," I say, filling in the rest of the story.

"Yes, and then you showed up! And it was wonderful!" she exclaims. When I don't return her smile, she sighs. "We'd been trying fertility treatments, but they weren't going well. Just failure after failure, and it was really starting to wear me down. But you showing up again reminded me about all the ways there are to make a family. You reminded me that there isn't just one way."

"But what if I don't stay?"

"No matter where you go, you'll always be part of my family, Ritzy. You can have your mother, and you can have us, too. It doesn't have to be one or the other."

I think I hoped that at some point the decision would be made for me. Maybe part of me was even relieved when I thought overhearing their conversation did that. But now I'm right back where I started.

"I just don't know what to do, Kris," I tell her. "I don't know where I belong."

CHAPTER TWENTY-FIVE

THE COURTHOUSE IS EXACTLY THE SAME as I remember it, which is to say, it's still thoroughly unimpressive. This time is a little different, though. This time my mom is with us.

We're sitting on the bench outside the courtroom, waiting for my case to be called. Pete is a little bit down the hall, on his phone. Something about an orientation disaster on campus. Tess is leafing through papers in her file folders, double- and triple-checking that everything is in order.

And Kris and my mom are chatting, which is weird. They're having some discussion about various yoga practices, both pretending like they don't think the other is an alien creature. My mom is actually dressed up for today in a pair of black pants and a flowing yellow tunic top, a black cardigan over the top. She almost looks like someone you might hire to be your life coach, which is good, because she's gone all in on that venture. Lainey helped her set up a website, uploading the headshot I took of her on my phone.

"All parties in the matter of Maritza Reed please report to courtroom four," the voice crackles over the loudspeaker.

We all jump up like we've been electrocuted. I see Kris gesture to Pete down the hall, who quickly hangs up and strides over.

"Okay, guys, are we ready?" he asks, clapping his hands like we're about to take the field.

"Hey, that's my line," Tess says with a smile. She hikes her tote bag over her shoulder, and we follow her into the courtroom. Justin Fellows, my appointed lawyer, is already waiting. I take the seat next to him, and Pete, Kris, and Mom file into the row of seats behind him. I'm just about to turn to face the judge when the door to the courtroom opens, and Lainey and her mom slip in. They drop into the row of seats behind Kris, Pete, and Mom, Lainey giving me a big smile and a double thumbs-up.

"Thanks," I whisper, and then hear the slam of the gavel.

The judge does his legalese introduction, all parties in the matter of and blah, blah, blah. I can barely sit still in my chair and have to wedge my hands under my thighs just to keep from tapping them on the table in front of me.

"Okay, so it appears we've reached an arrangement in the guardianship of Maritza Reed?" the judge says when he's settled in.

"Yes, Your Honor," Justin says. "You should have copies of the guardianship agreement signed by all parties."

"Yes, yes," he says, flipping through the pages in the folder in front of him. "So Marybelle Reed, the minor's mother, will retain parental rights, but has agreed to grant guardianship of the minor to Kristin Stokes and Peter Carmichael." He glances up over the top of his glasses. "Do I have that correct?"

I nod, and turn to see the adults behind me nodding as well.

"Don't be shy, folks," he says. "Let's hear it. Marybelle Reed, you agree to this arrangement?"

"Yes, Your Honor," Mom says.

"And Mr. Carmichael and Ms. Stokes, you agree to serve as guardians for Maritza Reed?"

"Yes!" Kris says, only barely containing her enthusiasm.

"Yes, Your Honor," Pete says, and though his response is slightly more controlled, I can hear the smile in his voice.

"Okay, then. And most importantly, how do you feel about this, Maritza? Does this arrangement sound good to you?"

"Yes," I say. "It sounds good to me."

It took me a long time to figure out what to do, and even now I wish I could say that I'm sure it's the right choice. But the judge didn't ask me if it was right. He just asked me if it sounds good. And that, at least, is true.

Living in the attic studio of Rose Renee's roadside palm-reading emporium wasn't the place for me. There wasn't space, and it wasn't even in Southwest's district, so I'd have to change schools anyway. But the thought of my mom not being my *mom* anymore, of the state severing her parental rights, was too much. And so Tess had proposed a compromise, which allowed me to stay with Kris and Pete, to call their house *home*, and instead make my family bigger.

I turn around to take in my entourage, my family. They're all smiling, and in that instant, I realize that I *am* sure it's the right choice.

"Okay, then, we'll be back here in six months to revisit the agreement, at which point the minor will no longer be a minor, so we'll have less to talk about. But if the Department of Children and Families is in agreement with all parties—" He pauses and looks at Tess, who stands.

"Yes, Your Honor," she says.

"Okay, then, we'll see you in six months, and congratulations to all parties." He smiles, then bangs his gavel, already handing off my file to a clerk and opening up the next in his stack.

EPILOGUE

KRIS PULLS A HANDFUL OF PLAID OUT OF the brown paper bag and begins spreading items out on the kitchen table. I step closer and see that they're skirts. Three of them, all identical navy blue and gray with lines of gold. Then come three long-sleeved button-up shirts with stitching over the breast pocket, and last but definitely not least, a navy-blue blazer with an enormous gold-stitched crest that looks like it's been stolen off a member of the Lonely Hearts Club Band.

"Please tell me this isn't—" I say.

"Your uniform!"

I examine the shirts closer and see that the navy stitching reads THE HARBOR SCHOOL over the breast pocket, and the big gold emblem on the blazer has a curly, yet still stately, *H* in the middle.

I gulp. "When I agreed to this, I wasn't factoring in the uniform," I tell her. A few of the charter schools in my old district made their students wear khaki pants and polo shirts like they're all at vacation bible school, but as far as I know, none of them have uniforms *this* extensive. I did *not* consider the blazer in my decision to enroll in Harbor. Who wears a blazer when it's over 70 degrees for most of the school year?

I do, apparently.

In the end, I'd decided that I wasn't going to decide. I was lucky enough to have two families. I had two women who were willing to sacrifice to make my life better, even if they had two very different ideas of how to do it. My mom started working through the judge's permanency plan so that she'd maintain her parental rights. She'd stay my mother, legally. But since the permanency plan takes time, and school is set to start in just under a month, I'll be staying with Kris for senior year. I'll be enrolling at the Harbor School, Helena's private prep school, along with Spencer and Annie. My mom moved in with Rose, who is letting her use the shop as her home base for Awakening by Marybelle Reed, Mom's life-coaching venture. It turns out the Bodhi Foundation is a little less of a scam than I'd initially thought. She really had learned stuff and gotten some certificates that allow her to start her own business. I was still skeptical that my mom was really qualified to be a life coach, certificates or not, but she seemed to be making a decent go of it. She even scored her first client, an essential oils dealer in the midst of a messy divorce.

As soon as I'd made the decision, a weight had lifted. It felt good to have a home *and* still have my mom. I felt tethered.

I won't lie, though. Looking at this uniform is giving me second thoughts. But I guess what's done is done.

"Please tell me there aren't shoes to go with," I say to Kris, fingering the hem of the skirt, which is surprisingly short.

"Funny you should mention that," she replies, pulling a shoe box out of another bag. Inside are the ugliest brown loafer things I've ever seen. Kris must see the look on my face. "What? They're what all the kids wear!"

I pull out my phone and snap a photo, sending it to Annie with an SOS. "I'm definitely going to check into that claim," I tell Kris.

"Just think of how much time you'll save getting dressed in the morning," Kris says, folding all the uniform pieces and replacing them in the bag.

I gesture down to my usual uniform of cutoff shorts and a tank top. "Does it look like I spend that much time getting dressed in the morning?"

"Touché," she replies, then hands me the bag. "Big plans for today?"

I wave a water-spotted paperback at her, a page marked midway through. "Just following the adventures of a seductive rake," I tell her. "Care to join?"

"Sadly, we're closing in on the school year, so I've got to work on my syllabi," she replies. "I'll be up in my office if you need me."

Down on the beach, I instantly lose myself in the pages of the romance novel. I'm close to working my way through

Kris's collection, and she's promised to drive me to a used bookstore just off the island to restock. I can probably squeeze in another five or ten before school orientation in two weeks. After that, something tells me that the Harbor School isn't going to afford me as much free reading time as Southwest did.

I'm lost in a particularly juicy sex scene when I hear the familiar sound of feet pounding the sand. It can't be Pete, who's on doctor-ordered rest from marathon training after some knee pain. Which can only mean—

I'd managed to avoid Spencer for the last few weeks since our fight, which was sort of hard. His schedule was posted at the club, so I steered clear of the courts while he was teaching and made myself busy during camp pickup so we didn't have to talk when he was retrieving Ryan. And otherwise, he'd done the work for me. With all his tennis tournaments, he'd been thankfully absent from most group get-togethers, and Annie had been happy to let me know when I should stay home from the Pen to avoid an awkward encounter. I'd feel bad about ditching, except for the fact that he seemed perfectly happy to avoid me, too.

But the best-laid plans often go awry, as they say, and now here he is, jogging down the beach toward me. I take a quick glance over my book, wondering if he's going to simply jog right past me, but I see him start to slow immediately. He looks just as I remember him, all tan and trim, his hair a wild mess of cowlicks and curls.

He slows his pace until he's come to a stop in front of me, but he doesn't smile.

"Hey," he says, panting and out of breath.

"Hi," I reply.

And then we're at a conversational stalemate, staring at each other across the sand. Finally, he strides over and drops into the empty chair next to me.

"Sorry for being a dick," he says.

I bark out a laugh. "Seriously?"

He turns. "What?"

"After all this time, that's all you've got?"

He deflates, his shoulders rolling in, his head dropping down into his hands. "I'm really not good at this," he says. "Just ask my dad."

I roll my eyes at him. "You're still doing that?"

"What?"

"That thing where you blame your dad for everything?"

He shakes his head, sand and sweat flying off him. "No, actually. You can ask my dad because I sucked at apologizing to him, too."

Now that I was not expecting.

"You were right, Maritza."

"You made up with your dad?" I couldn't be more shocked than if he told me he grew wings and flew back to New York.

"I did. I mean, it's a work in progress, I guess. But we've been traveling for these tournaments the last month, and we sort of couldn't help but talk to each other. And you were right. He didn't realize the way he was treating Ryan. And when I told him that I didn't want to do the finance and law thing, he didn't totally lose his mind. Especially when I told him what I *do* want to do."

"Spencer, that's great."

"It is," he says. "He's actually taking me to look at a few schools that have biomedical undergrad programs. You were right."

"So I have to ask . . . why did it take you nearly a month to come and tell me this?"

"Because I didn't know how to face you after what I said," he confesses. "I was such a complete and total asshole. I didn't think you'd forgive me. I wasn't sure if you *should*. And so I just stayed away."

"Well, that was the wrong choice," I tell him.

He glances up through sweaty curls, his cheeks red from running, and maybe from something else.

"Yeah?"

I nod. "Yeah." I close my book, carefully marking my place before dropping it into the sand. "I missed you."

He stands from the chair and comes in front of me, reaching down for my hands. I take his, and he pulls me up to him. His skin is warm and sticky from the salt and sweat, and he smells a little bit like a locker room, but also like detergent and the woody, piney smell that's just so *Spencer*.

He looks me straight in the eye, his blue eyes practically

glowing neon in the late summer sun. "I'm sorry, Maritza. Truly sorry, for what I said, and for avoiding you."

I think back to what Mrs. Ford said in the car on the way to Lainey's, about leaving the door cracked for him. And now here he is, flinging it wide open, letting in everything I've been missing.

"Apology accepted," I tell him, but the words are barely out of my mouth before he bends down, his lips on mine. The kiss tastes salty, and sand is swirling around us in a heavy ocean breeze that's kicking up, but I don't care.

All I care about is that now, finally, I feel like I'm home.

ACKNOWLEDGMENTS

Thank you first and foremost to my agent, Stephen Barbara, a genius matchmaker and strategist who found this book a home and a champion with Joy Peskin.

Joy, I owe you an enormous debt of gratitude for making this book so much better. It was a long road to get to the final draft, but I loved every conversation we had. This book would not be this book without you.

Thank you to the team at Farrar Straus Giroux, including Nancy Elgin, Elizabeth Lee, Nicholas Henderson, and Trisha de Guzman. And thank you to Aimee Fleck for this glorious cover.

Thank you to Jackson Pearce for being the person I can say things to and for eating all that Jeni's ice cream with me while we talked about books and writing.

Thank you to my family for being my biggest cheer-leaders. Special thanks to my sister, Claire Prisock, a former social worker and current awesome children's librarian. Thank you for answering all my many questions. Any mistakes are solely my fault.

But my biggest thank-you is reserved for my husband, Adam. You never let me feel sorry for myself, even when publishing was hard and scary. I had to write this book through pregnancy and birth and newborn days and a toddler in a body cast *twice*. But you always made sure I had time to write. Freddie, Leo, and I are so, *so* lucky to have you. And thank you for making me buy those *Hamilton* tickets. This book probably wouldn't exist without that trip. I love you more than Picard loves Earl Grey.